LOVE CAN'T FEED YOU

LOVE CAN'T FEED YOU

a novel

CHERRY LOU SY

DUTTON

DUTTON
An imprint of Penguin Random House LLC
penguinrandomhouse.com

LIBRARY OF CONGRESS CATALOGING-IN-PUBLICATION DATA

Names: Sy, Cherry Lou, author.
Title: Love can't feed you: a novel / Cherry Lou Sy. Other titles: Love cannot feed you
Description: [New York]: Dutton, 2024.
Identifiers: LCCN 2024006059 (print) | LCCN 2024006060 (ebook) |
ISBN 9780593474549 (hardcover) | ISBN 9780593474563 (ebook)
Subjects: LCGFT: Bildungsromans. | Novels.
Classification: LCC PS3619.Y25 L68 2024 (print) | LCC PS3619.Y25 (ebook) |
DDC 813/.6—dc23/eng/20240223
LC record available at https://lccn.loc.gov/2024006059
LC ebook record available at https://lccn.loc.gov/2024006060

Printed in the United States of America
1st Printing

BOOK DESIGN BY KRISTIN DEL ROSARIO

For my father

There will be time, there will be time
To prepare a face to meet the faces that you meet;
. . .
And indeed there will be time
To wonder, "Do I dare?" and, "Do I dare?"

—T. S. ELIOT,
"THE LOVE SONG OF J. ALFRED PRUFROCK"

LOVE CAN'T FEED YOU

PART ONE

I am going to die. My body contracts the second the plane descends from thirty thousand feet. I feel bile in my throat and grab another vomit bag. I think of the stories others will tell about me—gone too soon, what a shame that she didn't get to live out her potential. This is not how anyone imagines arriving to America.

Papa tells me to pray. My mouth forms Hail Marys, but the monster in my stomach shoves its way to my throat again. The queasiness possesses me with violence and pins me to my seat as I lurch like the women from back home—the ones who thrash on the ground filled with the Holy Spirit.

"I should have given you the Dramamine," Papa says for the tenth time since we left Ninoy Aquino International Airport in Manila.

Papa didn't let me eat anything he could save for later: the crumbly granola bars, foil-wrapped biscuits, and even the hard dinner rolls. He pocketed the silverware too.

He complains to the flight attendant and asks for more vomit bags since I have used mine, his, and even Junior's vomit bags. Junior sleeps soundly on the other side of Papa, his legs akimbo. A white woman next to me turns to her young companion and shakes her head. Her disgust pierces through my nausea.

"Never have children," she says.

My ears pop and the rest of her words blur. The plane rocks from the turbulence of November winds. My eyes roll to the back of my head.

"Can't you do something about your grandchild?" the woman asks Papa.

Papa apologizes to her, ashamed to say that I am not his grandchild but his teenage daughter. How could he explain his silver hair to her? How could he explain that he fathered his first child—who has done nothing but stir trouble—at the age of fifty? He says that I've been throwing up nonstop because he didn't give me Dramamine. How this is our first plane ride. How he should have known that this was like taking a long bus ride, only worse. He even tells this stranger that he would give me Dramamine as a two-year-old to control the motion sickness, a sickness that made me a terrible travel companion when what he needed was a good girl who never made a fuss.

The white woman softens a little and tells him how she learned from a Chinese herbalist that ginger is good for motion sickness, and that he should be giving me ginger instead. She mentions that the herbalist helped her with her many health issues, explaining the concept of hot and cold air in the body, the yin and yang.

"Aren't you Chinese?" she asks him. Papa's tongue loosens and says yes, but not exactly Chinese. The woman's mouth makes an O.

He tells her that his parents moved from China to the Philippines and that he was born and left in the hospital for two years because his parents couldn't afford to have another mouth to feed.

"What a shame," the woman says, then asks him if we are going to the US for a visit. Papa pauses. It feels like the same question the man from the embassy asked us a few months before. Papa tells her the story we all rehearsed before the interview to get our visas. That we're tourists visiting Ma, who's been in New York working as a nurse for the last five years. That we're going to see snow for the first time. That five years is long enough for a mother to go without seeing her family.

"What do you do?" the woman asks.

"Business," Papa says.

The little lies and the big lies all meld. He doesn't tell her about all the money he lost—how he bought wholesale rice the year when three Category 3 typhoons flooded the rice fields, along with the stockrooms that housed the harvested rice, or that his partner ran away with the money that was supposed to be used to pay off their creditors. He doesn't tell her about getting into the export business with an Australian man who fled after the big earthquake and left him with a storage house filled with giant rotting wood carvings. He doesn't tell her that he wants to start fresh in America. He doesn't tell her about his plans for his son and daughter to go to American schools and have American lives, or that we bought round-trip tickets for a one-way journey. This is inside talk that she doesn't need to hear.

"How long are you going to stay?" she asks.

We are on alert. Junior, whose eyes were closed a moment earlier, turns and looks at Papa. Even in my state, where every movement causes me discomfort, I sense danger and turn my head a little with my eyes closed. Papa slows down, careful not to give away too much, though he has given away so much already.

"Until the end of winter," he says, repeating the rehearsed words we said to the man in the gray suit at the embassy as he looked us over, one by one, trying to gauge what was true and what was not. Junior asked Papa then, before the interview, if it's all right to lie, and Papa said yes—when you have to.

The woman hails one of the flight attendants and clears her throat. "Do you have Dramamine by any chance?" she asks, pointing to me.

The flight attendant, a thin young woman with long hair, looks at me and says in a low voice, "We're not supposed to have it. Regulations, you know."

Someone from across the aisle overhears her and fishes something out of her bag, a tube of Dramamine. She offers it to our neighbor. "I forgot I had this."

At this moment, I vomit again and some of the bile gets on my T-shirt, jeans, and jacket—clothes from the last balikbayan box Ma sent in preparation for the trip. The strong, distinct scent of puke emanates from my mouth, all traces of food I've eaten on the plane from Manila to Japan combined into a fermented, sour mess.

"She may not be able to hold this down if she keeps throwing up like that," the woman who talked about yin and yang says, wrinkling her nose.

None of these humiliations are enough, of course. My sanitary pad needed changing over two hours ago, but I don't dare get up to go to the bathroom. I can't anyway. My body defies me and here I am, an animal sitting in her own bloody filth. Another jolt in the air. Another wave of nausea. I reach for the vomit bag. I moan.

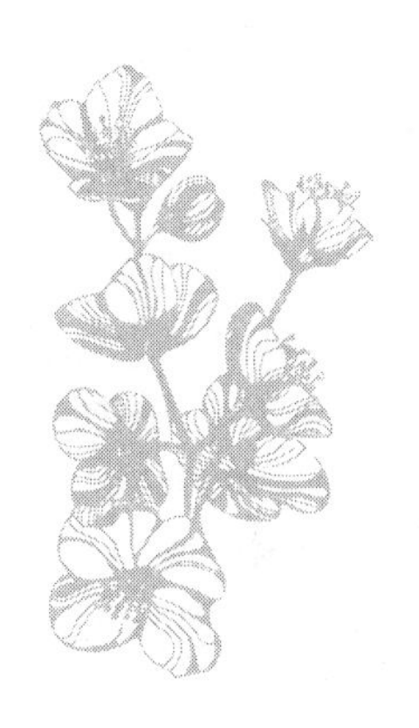

JFK, NEW YORK

When the plane lands, in the confusion, Papa loses an entire bag of handmade salakot, native headgear and hats he purchased from roadside sellers. They are supposed to be souvenir gifts for Ma's friends.

They put me in a blue wheelchair. I cling tightly to the handles and fight back exhaustion. A Black woman with long brown braids pushes my wheelchair, her hands covered in blue latex gloves.

"She's been throwing up. Nonstop," she says to the man in uniform behind the counter. He nods, then looks through our passports and asks Papa about the purpose of our trip.

"A vacation," Papa says.

We go through customs and passport control a bit too easily. They take pity on the sick girl; the tired, confused elderly man with her; and the boy who looks just as tired and confused as the old man.

We see Ma at the arrival gate. She looks like someone we know and don't know. Her made-up face smoothened by concealer, foundation, and powder—but we can see the edges where her skin begins and the makeup ends. Eyes brightened by mascara, eye shadow, and eyeliner. Lips painted with bright red lipstick. She chats with a short, plump woman holding a small dog tucked into her arm like a baby. We recognize her and her dog from pictures Ma has sent. Tita Cynthia, an older Filipina widow who befriended her at the hospital, where they both worked on a medical-surgical floor.

I am too weak to get up, but I notice how Papa looks at Ma. The way his irises go up and down, as if looking at her directly would hurt his eyes, so he focuses on points of her. Her shoulders arched back with her chest lifted. Her hair done up with highlights. Her shaped eyebrows. She looks sleek and expensive. Like a woman we see on television.

A woman I remember seeing once.

When I was twelve, a few months before Ma left for New York, we went to the local Jollibee and ordered a round of cheeseburgers, Chickenjoys, sweet spaghetti, and plastic cups of pineapple juice. For the first time, I hardly recognized Ma at all. Her expression was blank, faraway, like she was watching for something that was about to happen. This moment stands out to me as a portent—I had just learned that word, *portent*, from the thick dictionary I often skimmed to look up English words, like *octet*, *officious*, and *fallacious*. Perhaps this was the moment when we lost Ma.

She seemed both girl and woman, familiar and unfamiliar, beautiful and ethereal. When she got up to go to the bathroom, Ate Tessie sat down in her place. My mind froze. How quickly a person can be replaced. All she needs to do is to disappear from the space she once occupied. I cried out in alarm, and everyone looked at me.

When Ma came back, her face was normal again. But with that glimpse of her, that woman who was my mother and not my mother, something changed in me.

—

Here she is now. A woman, once again, transformed.

Ma hugs Junior first and comments on how big he's gotten. She last saw him at five years old, and Junior has shot to ten in a blink. He barely remembers her, but he still puts his arms out to embrace our mother.

"Hug me harder," Ma says, and he does.

When she turns to me, her eyes widen as she takes in my frozen hands, matted hair, and pale face. She asks Papa what happened. He repeats what he's been telling everyone this whole trip. He forgot to give me Dramamine. Ma rolls her eyes. With this small action, I knew her again. Until this moment, I didn't know whether I would.

She's about to say something to me when I lean in and whisper, "Do you have a pad? I need one."

SUNSET PARK, BROOKLYN

"Your mother's changed," Papa says to Junior and me in between bites of lo mein, sesame chicken, and pork fried rice. We nod in agreement. She is as foreign as this new place we are in.

Everything in this city seems new, old, and strange. That balmy November, the first thing we noticed driving on the highway from JFK was the expanse of New York. In Manila, the cars, tricycles, jeepneys, and trucks choked each other's space like weeds. The traffic was so unbelievable that men, women, and children could walk by and steal purses and belongings if you cracked your window open for some of the tepid air. But driving into Brooklyn was strange. Everything was grimy. Our fears shot up looking at our neighborhood in Sunset Park. Graffiti and dilapidated buildings everywhere. No white people in sight. This was not what we expected. We expected to see the Big Apple from the movies right away. The Empire State Building. The skyscrapers. Men in suits. Wall Street. White people everywhere doing American things like in TV shows. Papa even asks Ma, "Where are all the Americans?"

We want to be here and not back home, where everyone is trying to leave. I'd seen in movies how people, upon arrival, would kiss the ground and scream. But we don't belong in the movies, so we don't act big, screaming our joy.

It takes five full days before the nausea subsides. I barely notice the apartment, which is smaller than the basement we lived in previously, which had three small bedrooms in addition to the kitchen and living room. Here, there is only one bedroom. Papa seemed disappointed when he looked around and noticed the single queen-sized bed and a small futon on the floor. "Bakit ganoon?" he asked. Ma shrugged and said that he could sleep on the couch in the living room if he wanted. He hasn't been in a good mood since.

"Everyone changes here," Ma says. She's coming out from the shower wrapped in a baby-pink terry cloth robe, drying her hair with a towel. She walks to the bedroom, and we all watch her, mesmerized. The way she carries herself, head held high, her steps so sure of where they're going, and even how she smells—pungent from liberal sprays of what I discovered is Victoria's Secret body spray. This is not the Ma we knew.

"Everyone's got to start working," Ma says. "I owe a lot of money for bringing you all here." None of us respond, shocked that she would bring this up.

"Even me?" Junior asks, his eyes wide.

"No, you're ten. So you go to school since it's free."

"How about me?" I ask.

"We can get work for you—"

"But I want to go to college!"

"Yes, you can do that and still work, but right now, it's better to go to work."

This was not what she said months ago on the phone. When I mentioned that it'd be cheaper if I stayed in the Philippines and went to one of the universities, she claimed I'd be able to go to college in the US. We both knew that attending school in the Philippines is not what I wanted. There was prestige in going to school abroad. Ma said I could be an American college student. My high school classmates, when they found out I was migrating, were jealous and compared their lives to mine. "Buti ka pa, pa-abroad abroad ka pa," they said. Ma instructed me to tell the embassy interviewer that I *might* go get my degree in America, *if* we liked it, and I would pay for my degree out of pocket. "They like to hear that we'll spend money here," she said.

"Now, wait a minute," Papa finally says, "this is not what we talked about."

Ma rolls her eyes, of course.

"That's not what we told the guy in the interview," I say, reminding her.

"You lie, big deal. Everyone does it. How do you think anyone gets by?" Ma is irritated. "A new life costs money," she says, and she starts listing her hardships. She arrived in New York with the clothes on her back, one small piece of luggage, and six hundred dollars to her name. She tells us how she worked nights and took extra shifts while trying to pass her licensing exam, which she took not once but three times. It was a feat, and did we not know it?

"You want a new life, you earn it."

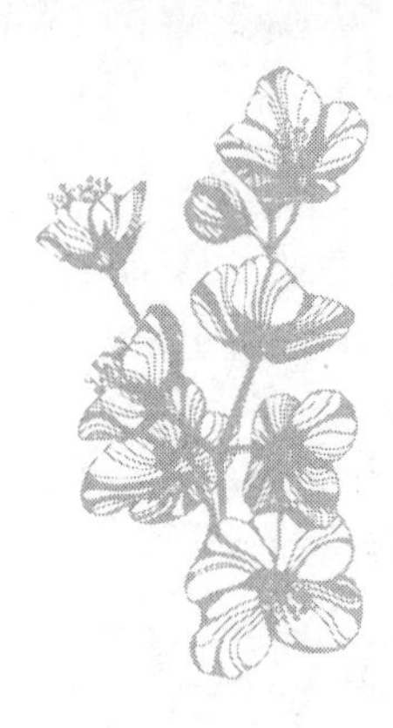

"You stink," Ma says, curling her nose up when Papa enters the apartment, the sides of his shoes coated with unidentifiable gunk.

"What do you expect?" Papa retorts.

Ma had gotten him a job as a part-time janitor for a residential building from someone she knows at the hospital. A twenty-minute walk from where we lived. A job good enough for someone who has overstayed his tourist visa. The money isn't great, but money is money, as Ma says.

"That's what janitors do. They clean up other people's shit," he says, then reminds Ma that he was once in charge of exporting wood carvings for an Australian, that he had owned his own business.

"That work is better than being a garbageman," he says.

"What do you think I do in the hospital?" Ma asks him.

Papa grumbles, saying that at least she gets paid money, and she reminds him that she's legal with her work papers.

"Can't you swallow your pride for once?" she asks.

Instead of screaming at her, he goes to the kitchen and opens the refrigerator. He takes out a can of PBR he picked up from the corner deli. Ma eyes the can and clucks her tongue.

"I thought you didn't like alcohol," she says.

"I don't," he says as he pops off the aluminum tab and takes a sip.

The creaking of floors. The weight of someone sitting down. In my mind's eye, Ma rubs her own feet, swollen to the size of her forearms with corns and calluses from wearing her tight old shoes while working the night shift.

Papa's high-pitched voice from the other room tells me it's seven thirty on the dot. The sunlight streams through the window and metal bars cast shadows that make the bedroom look like prison. The walls are so thin that his voice carries and takes flight, the sound expanding to fill the room.

Junior, the favorite child, snores next to me ignoring everything. Ma, just back from the hospital, keeps up with Papa's voice in sound, intensity, and depth.

"What's easy?"

She yells. "You think I asked for this?" The key phrase. No one asks for anything. Unless you're owed something.

Never a thank-you.

Never a hello.

Good-mornings, good-nights, and words of endearment fester in our throats and render us incapable of saying anything.

Our silences. Deep pools of petrifying words. The agony of longing for wholeness. Only exploding in moments when the hate, shame, and anger have nowhere else to go and so they catapult from our mouths sharp like knives.

My parents are two prized cocks pecking each other to the death in a game of sabong. In that small apartment. In that room. Each day, their fights escalate, and each argument is a continuation of the previous one.

—

Papa's voice rises from the kitchen. "You know what your problem is? You're acting like you're the man in this house!"

"Someone's got to act like one," Ma spits back.

The clang of dishes pierces my eardrums and the smell of burned meat hits my nose. My body lurches toward the door and leans in, heavy. I stay there, sluggish, hoping I will vanish. My hand touches the knob and I open the door slowly.

"Why don't you learn how to do this?" Papa asks, handing me a charred skillet with burned white rice and burned sausages.

Ma snorts, looks at me, and says that when she was seventeen, she didn't eat if she didn't work. "You're not born a princess, Queenie."

But then Ma turns to Papa, her rage baring teeth. "You're lazy and I can't believe I married you."

They bring up their ledgers of past sins and future woes. Nothing new to my ears.

—I thought you had money.

—I thought you were a virgin.

—I thought I didn't have to work after I married you.

—You let that man look at you.

—You're a poor Chinese guy.

—You're a whore.

—If I listened to you, I would have no future.

—If it weren't for me, you would be nothing.

They are miserable together and miserable separately.

The catalyst is me. Always me. The origin story of their love and hate.

"Twenty and alone, that was me," she screams.

"Yeah, tell your kids that so they don't turn out like you!" he screams back.

The first time she was pregnant, she was scared that she would have to tell my grandparents that she was not in Baguio City studying nursing, but in Olongapo working as a bar girl. People all know what bar girls do. They open their legs and have babies with strange men who love them and leave them. Maybe Papa was one of them. Except he didn't leave. Papa made promises. He felt sorry for her. What man in his right mind would marry a bar girl whose legs have opened for hordes of men? Ma believed him because that's the fairy tale everyone dreamed about. A knight in shining armor come to rescue the poor princess in rags. A planned accident (me). She thought he was a wealthy Chinese businessman. She had heard about the rich financiers who ran the country, and everyone knew they all had gold hidden in their houses. She thought, as had her friends who'd done the same thing, that having me would lift her out of poverty.

Over seventeen years later, and now, across the Pacific Ocean, they are still fighting over what to do with me.

Junior finally wakes up once Ma falls asleep, and Papa forces him to drink a glass of homogenized milk, a novelty since the only milk we had before was powdered. My brother complains that he won't drink unless there's Hershey's syrup in it.

"We didn't find it in the store, just use Nesquik."

In the small kitchen, I open the yellow canister and mix the chalky chocolate powder into the milk and hand it to Junior, who drinks it without any more protest. Ma thought another baby would push Papa to work harder. They all rejoiced when Junior came out a boy. Someone to carry Papa's name. A legacy. "A boy will never leave his mother behind," Ma would say, staring at Junior. This is what all the elders say.

Junior drags his feet, chocolate milk stains on his mouth, and Papa tells him to hurry up. I'm supposed to take Junior to school, but Papa needs to run errands for his work, so he decided to walk Junior to school instead.

As soon as the door closes, silence. Then, Ma's snores from the other side of the apartment. I open my library copy of *Anne of Green Gables* and lose myself in the Canadian land of Avonlea on Prince Edward Island. Instead of Anne with an *e*, I am Queenie with an *ie*, and I imagine myself as the orphan in the story, who was sent to live on a farm with an old brother and sister. They're expecting a white boy, but they get a Chinese Filipino girl instead.

Every day I read. Watch TV. Eat. Take Junior to school in between these activities. Read. Watch TV. Eat. To fill the time. To leave tragedies and old wounds behind. To discover how one transforms. To become someone else. Like Lot leaving Sodom and Gomorrah. Like Ma.

Thank God I have the library and my strange new friend, Yan.

—

I met Yan at the library on Fifty-Third Street the week after we arrived. I noticed a boy sitting across from me, staring. I met his eyes, then looked down. Maybe boys already wanted me in this country. My face turned hot and red at the thought. How unusual, because back in my hometown, the boys only looked at me to say something mean—like how they'd only like me because my skin was fair but my legs were too chunky for them. They even called me Igorota, those indigenous mountain women they perceived as not attractive because they thought Igorot bones were thick like trunks carved from climbing stone steps in the Cordilleras like mountain goats.

But this boy across from me was staring, and his gaze made my stomach complain not from hunger but from nervousness.

It was noon on a school day. I eyed him suspiciously. Maybe he was a delinquent. I didn't come to America to be around delinquents. I could hear some of my former classmates back in the Philippines, chiding me, like spectators who never stop heckling from the sidelines. *Pa-abroad-abroad ka, ganyan lang pala ang gagawin mo.*

Finally, he leaned over to me and said, "You have something on your face." He handed me a compact mirror and I saw that I had red sauce on the bottom of my lip and smeared on my left cheek. I was mortified. As if that wasn't enough, he engaged me in conversation.

"What are you?"

"Excuse me?"

My voice became shrill. The white, reed-thin librarian looked over and shushed us. The boy turned to him, smiled, and said, "All good, Mr. Higgins. Just making a friend." The librarian turned back to his book. In the Philippines, I was used to strangers commenting on each other's weight or physical appearance. But to ask the question "What are you"? What is wrong with people? Is this what they ask in America?

Yan continued to whisper. "Where are you from?"

"The Philippines. But I'm Chinese and Filipino."

He inspected me again and added, "You don't exactly look Chinese."

He said some words that I later find out were Cantonese and asked me if I understood him, and said that if I did, I should respond in kind. I didn't understand him at all. Not that I would know. I didn't even know what Mandarin or Hokkien sounded like. I only knew the occasional Beijing opera from a cassette tape that Papa played in the Philippines when he missed his father. When he played it loudly, the neighbors used to make fun and say that it sounded like cats screaming. It was all foreign to me, and Yan reminded me just how much I didn't understand.

"You're not Chinese."

"My dad is Chinese."

"You don't look it, though. You don't even talk any Chinese."

"My dad's family is Fukienese. Amoy? They speak Hokkien."

"Don't know what that is."

"Look, all I know is that my grandparents were from China, OK? They moved to the Philippines."

He shrugged. Since he was so forward, I decided I needed to be just as forward with him.

"Shouldn't you be in school?"

"I'm taking my GED. Tomorrow, as a matter of fact."

"What's that?"

Yan explained that it was a way for people like him to get their high school diploma without going to high school and encountering all the drama in classrooms and locker rooms where people expected you to either conform or rebel depending on what they deemed cool.

"People like you?"

"I'm considered trouble."

"Oh."

"I keep getting into fights in the schools."

He said that people didn't like how he looked or how he acted. Even the guidance counselors didn't spend time helping him, since they had their other problems with truants who gave them more trouble than he did with knife fights, theft, and vandalism on their records. Some had already ended up in juvie. He didn't want to deal with these so-called guidance counselors anyway. "They just want to get paid and not get in trouble," he said. He ended up going to this library and befriending one of the librarians, Mr. Higgins, who suggested that he take his GED and try to make something of himself.

"You're telling me a lot about yourself."

"I am."

"How come?"

"I like you."

Another day goes by in silence.

The usual when Ma and Papa aren't fighting.

Papa turns on the television. It's his day off and he likes to sit back and put his gnarly feet on the coffee table. We salvaged it from the street, like most of what we own in this converted three-room Sunset Park apartment, including the partitions we use to create the illusion of privacy.

He has his bowl of boiled peanuts, cracking them one by one with his fingers. He watches The Filipino Channel, TFC for short. A famous variety show is on.

One of the hosts, a woman with short brownish hair and skin the color of coffee lightened with cream, is talking. Her English sounds American, and her features are typical of mestizas we from the Philippines have seen—deep eyes, tall noses, fair skin—a portrait of a Europeanized face. Desirable and coveted. Her last name is Greene. Born in California to a Filipina mother and a white navy sailor, she found her way back to the Philippines and became a celebrity overnight. She worked the entertainment circuit as an actress in corny B movies and then became the host of this lunchtime variety show where all she has to do is look pretty. She also competed in a Miss Philippines pageant but didn't qualify to compete for Miss Universe because she lost to another mestiza whose father was from Lebanon.

Clad in a miniskirt, heels, and a neon-pink tube top, she looks every bit the starlet that she is. She reads something from a white index card and looks up, laughs, and continues with the show. But in that moment, Pa sees something that he fixates on. Her neck.

"Look at that. So ugly," he says, cracking boiled peanut shells. I look at her body closely and envy her waist, her face, the way confidence radiates from her.

"What's ugly about her neck?" I ask.

"Those lines in her neck mean she's going to age fast."

I look again and see the deep creases along her neck and feel a wash of repugnance. He's right, of course. My hands immediately travel to my neck and lift my chin to feel for the lines. What I feel instead are little tags of skin. I try to pull one off, but it hurts. I pull again and feel a stab of pain as I remove the small pouch of skin. I lift my thumb and forefinger and see blood. The actress laughs and I return my gaze to the TV. She throws her head back and I see her neck again. Doesn't she know?

I go to the bathroom and look in the mirror to see whether I have lines too. I do. Faintly nestled like crags between my head and body. Ugly. Seventeen with an old neck.

The exemplary neck is long and graceful. Like a swan's. I can't help but notice how my neck sits too close to my shoulders. Like a bulldog's. One time, I tried on one of Ma's necklaces that was on the dresser. On my mother's neck it looked elegant, but I looked like a dog wearing a too-tight collar.

When I come back into the living room, Papa is still watching, still eating his peanuts, and still judging the starlet.

"Her mother was a go-go dancer," he says.

"How do you know that?"

"Everyone knows that. And her father? A navy guy."

Papa talks about her—that before the navy father met that girl's mother, he was still working at Subic Bay. Then he took her to California when he retired before Mount Pinatubo exploded. But retirement was too expensive in California, so they went back to the Philippines.

I look at the mestiza girl again and imagine her mother as a young woman, dancing, with her clothes off. How everyone looked down on her. And how, maybe, she didn't care. And then G.I. Joe Greene became her Prince Charming. It didn't matter that he was old enough to be her father. It occurred to me, suddenly, that my father and this girl's father are probably about the same age now.

"Didn't you meet Ma near Olongapo?"

My father pretends not to hear me. I know better than to press. I leave the room and walk a few steps to the kitchen, where a mouse scurries past. I thought we left mice behind when we left our place in the Philippines, but there are mice everywhere, even in New York. Ma never mentioned the mice when we talked on the phone. I wondered about what other things she didn't mention.

The sink is filled with dirty dishes, including the charred skillet, the black pieces of burned rice and sausage stuck hard. No one's washed them yet. I pick up a sponge. Ma has trained me to do this. On her days off, she does the same, as if an inner alarm goes off and turns on a switch that propels her to do these chores. She gets upset if I don't follow her exactly, especially if my movements are clumsy. She wants me to move like her. She also wants me to sound like her. Even if the words are not there, she wants me to mouth them.

I'm a girl as she was, and girls are supposed to know these things from their deep, deep inside. It's supposed to run in the blood, this knowledge of what is expected. If I talk to the deep, deep girl inside me, where all the wisdom of womenfolk lives, and ask, *Who passes down all that know-how?* and look to Ma and all the other women like her, what will I find?

I take the skillet from the sink and look at all that's burned onto its surface. The day is filled with chores and questions of why me, why now, why this. Before I know it, it's time to pick Junior up from school. Papa leaves and I notice the trail of peanut shells behind him.

As I bend down to sweep, I hear movement from the other room. Ma is awake, and I brace myself. For something. For her to open her mouth. For the earth to shake, again.

She rubs the sleep crusts from her eyes as she moves toward the kitchen. Her long black hair sways below her hips. Even though she's thirty-seven, there are hardly any lines on her face, and her slim figure fools people into thinking that she is young and single. People often ask if we are sisters, which makes Ma giggle. Of course, when they see Junior, they know she is the mother. A young one.

In the kitchen, she pours herself a glass of water and squeezes some lemon juice in, a trick she learned from one of her coworkers who loved aerobics and health trends. Meanwhile, I am working on my second half glass of Tropicana orange juice.

"Too much sugar," Ma says, looking at my glass. "You're going to end up with diabetes like your lolo."

At the mention of my grandfather, I look at the juice with guilt. The last time we saw him in Pangasinan, he was going blind from his diabetes. Ma sends money to his sister's family to care for him. He might need surgery to amputate his leg soon. We don't know yet. When Ma calls him, all he ever wants is money. There's always a bill to pay, a sick relative who needs help, a calamity that needs money thrown at it.

If Lolo Manching were here, perhaps he would be experiencing America in the same way we are, spending time in this apartment, fattening himself on boxes of cereal and tubs of Breyers ice cream and Kozy Shack rice pudding, and his veins, like ours, would be running with Tropicana orange juice. He would know that food is always within reach.

I look at Ma's neck. She is so beautiful my breath stops in my throat. I wonder if Papa looked at her once and fell for her when she turned her head and revealed the young skin below her chin. Unscratched, smooth, and supple.

Old men like to put their dreams on young women. And young women, what dreams do they put on men?

If I could travel back in time and see them younger. To see what she saw in him. To see what he saw in her. The moment of friction where I end up being the point of no return.

I want to ask her: *Were there other men? Were there other women? Can I ask you about them? Who was the boy you liked? Why did you like him? Why did he break your heart? Why did you marry this Chinese man you don't like?*

Instead I ask, "How was work?"

"Terrible. You don't know what work is until you've worked in America," she says with conviction. "Your father doesn't know work, that's why he thinks what he's doing now is work. What's cleaning and taking out garbage? That's nothing."

I don't say anything more. I want to remind her that we paid a woman to live with us for sixteen years to help with cleaning, cooking, and caring for Junior and me. Ate Tessie hardly ever visited her own family because it would take her a week to get back to her village; she'd have to take a bus, then a ship all the way to the Visayas. The day we left, Ate Tessie bid us goodbye with tears streaming down her brown cheeks, even though I had been a terrible charge and stuck my tongue out at her when I was a rotten twelve-year-old kid. I feel a pang in my chest. Ate Tessie was more motherly than the woman in front of me. Because she was there. She paid attention to me even if she was paid to do it. What is a mother supposed to be? How is she supposed to act? How is she supposed to love?

My mouth shuts even though my insides rage. I pick up my book and try to get lost again in Avonlea. I should take Junior with me later and go to the library. That way, Ma and Papa can fight to their hearts' content.

Ma takes some frozen chicken drumsticks out of the freezer and puts the block of meat under running water, then prepares her breakfast of canned tomato sardines with garlic fried rice. She mixes instant coffee with creamer and puts hot water in a coffee mug that reads *Yes We Can*, a gift from one of her patients. As she's eating, she fumes.

"You think money grows on trees? This is life in America. You work or you don't eat. You understand, right?"

She's talking to me. My eyes glaze over. One time, I tried to butt in when they fought. But I got yelled at and was told that it was none of my business, which is probably true, since I am just a thing, an object they created from desire and need. They should have just gotten themselves a play doll.

Everyone in the Philippines thinks I am here to have a better life, to go to college. But I'm about to be a caregiver to an old lady for a few weeks to replace her aide who is going home to her country.

"Plans change," Ma says. Papa disagrees with her and tells her that no daughter of his will wipe anyone's shit. I am secretly thrilled he stands up for me, but Ma says that she owes money from bringing all of us here and that Lolo Manching's diabetes is getting worse. He never lived with us, because he and Papa never got along.

"It's karma," Papa says.

Ma doesn't respond. She is probably thinking about how Lolo Manching and Papa almost came to blows when Lolo Manching discovered that the most Chinese things about Papa are his face and surname. Every Chinese person Lolo Manching had ever heard about had money and property. Lolo Manching had thought his future son-in-law was going to lift the family out of poverty.

Ma changes the subject. "We're going to Ms. Flor's next week. All of us."

"So she can meet her new servant," I mutter.

"What's that?"

"Nothing."

At the edge of Sunset Park, people speak in Spanish and merengue blares from apartments and cars. It's so crowded and claustrophobic when everyone's out that I wonder how many people live inside each building. How much space does a person need? The rusted white gates too close to the doors so there's barely a front yard. Small and narrow row houses with Puerto Rican and American flags. Planters of half-dead trees, pots of drying yellow and orange marigolds, and garbage bins cram the concrete space in front of these structures that pass as houses and apartments. They almost remind me of the Tondo squatter houses I saw on TV when I was still in the Philippines. Almost. But this is America. No one lives under corrugated tin roofs and cardboard. There shouldn't be squatters here.

I call Yan's workplace at Chinatown Ice Cream Factory from a pay phone across the street using a quarter I found on the pavement earlier.

"Chinatown Ice Cream, can I help you?"

I recognize Yan's voice and ask him to come meet me at the subway station on Forty-Fifth.

"Are you OK?" he asks.

"No," I say.

"I get off in thirty minutes," he says.

"Don't worry. Take your time."

Yan is always a phone call away for the most part. In the months I've known him, we always meet outside. I've never been to his place, and he's never been to mine. It's an unspoken rule. We don't want each other's home problems to seep in, even though we often talk about them.

Yan passed his GED a few weeks back. When I asked him what his plan was after, he said, "Work," explaining that he did not know what else to do. He got himself a job in Chinatown scooping ice cream. We argued about school. He said, "I didn't get a GED so I can keep going to school. It's just something to get over with." Even Mr. Higgins, the librarian, was trying to talk sense into him and tell him that he must think about the future so he won't end up fifty and still working a minimum-wage job.

I sit down on the wooden bench on the Brooklyn side of the R train at the Forty-Fifth Street station and watch the clerk nap. It's quiet and warm, and I fan myself with my hand even though I know it won't help. It's a city summer and it's just as bad as Manila heat. The pavement feels as though the earth has a fever rising to my feet. The station is empty. This is not quite the New York City I imagined. I think about all the New York subways portrayed in Hollywood films I've seen from the VHS and Betamax tapes my father rented from a small shop off Session Road in our old city. The owner was an enterprising Filipino man who loved American movies so much he would go to movie theaters, secretly film the screen, and then rent his recordings out for a few pesos. It was hilarious to see dark figures get up and block the screen, presumably to go to the bathroom. The funniest ones were when they stood up during a tense scene, breaking the spell of the story.

As soon as I catch sight of Yan's face, I burst into tears. I barrel into him, and he hugs me. I cry so much I stain his shirt with my tears and snot. "I'm sorry, I'm sorry." He hands me some thin paper napkins. The train finally comes. We step inside and sit down and head nowhere in particular. He puts his arm around me, and I lean my head on his shoulder. I am crying openly, which makes people stare.

They must think I am running away. That I'm pregnant. And this is the father. Two teens on a train who don't know what to do or where to go.

Yan takes out a white paper bag from his JanSport and reveals a pint of ice cream.

"Oh shit, it's melted," he says as he licks the underside of the cover and scoops the sides with a plastic spoon. "We better eat this before it turns into a puddle."

"What flavor?"

"Almond cookie and black sesame on the bottom."

I grin despite my rage at Ma. Yan always chooses flavors I really like. I had never tasted almond cookies until I got to New York, or almonds for that matter.

I let the sweet coldness soothe me, but the ice cream melts faster than I can eat it. I get ice cream on my face. Yan looks at me and rolls his eyes. "Why are you always such a mess?"

Yan hands me another napkin. He watches me as I wipe my face and blow my nose.

"My dad used to throw toilet paper on the ground after he used it," I finally say.

"Eww."

"I mean, not toilet paper like toilet paper you use in the bathroom. He uses it to blow his nose. That's one of the things my parents fight about. Like, why can't he just throw it in the garbage can?"

I tell him about how we had a maid in the Philippines and how she would sweep the floors three times a day because my father threw his tissues and candy wrappers and other garbage on the floor of our apartment.

"A maid? What . . . you rich or something?"

"No, you don't have to be rich. I lived in a basement, you know." A pause. "It's complicated," I finally say.

"So you were a princess. No wonder you have a weird name. Who names their kid Queen Elizabeth?"

"My mom was into Princess Diana—"

"She could've named you Diana. It's more normal."

"My family doesn't roll like that. I got the Queen's name."

"OK, Princess."

"I did stuff too, you know. Chores."

"So that makes you not a princess? Did you cook or clean? Or did you even wash your clothes?"

"Cooking . . . yeah, sometimes I did. I can fry an egg and cook rice without a rice cooker. I took home economics and had to learn."

"It's like they were training you to be a housewife."

"Or somebody's maid," I say.

Yan shows me his rough hands. Years of work already in the lines of his palms. He takes my hands and looks at them. Mine are soft and plump.

"Who had to work so your hands could be this soft?" he asks.

Stunned, I look at him. I tell him about the mental anguish one goes through living in a society that requires hierarchies.

"That makes no sense," he says.

I open my mouth and close it again, feeling the weight of unexpressed feelings stuck in my chest. I don't know where to begin. How do I tell him that this psychological gymnastics routine is a result of over three hundred years of Spanish rule, the Japanese and American occupations, and how over the decades the country once known as "the Pearl of the Orient" became a cesspool of crime and poverty, falling apart from the corruption of the wealthy families that control all aspects of society, from the cheap TV and film entertainment to the monopoly of industries? I want to tell him about the children begging in the streets addicted to the smell of Rugby glue because they want to forget that they are hungry and have no future. About the gangs who deal in everything from child snatching to drugs and prostitution, and the parents who even sell their kids to pedophiles who come to the country to enjoy the merchandise. About the tides of bodies sweating and praying to the Immaculate Conception or the Sacred Heart of Jesus or Santo Niño to be taken out of hell. But all these words feel weak in my throat because what do I know? I left. I can forget. I let the explanation wither in my throat and say, "It doesn't matter anyway. It's not the Philippines. Here, we have a different life. A different set of problems."

Yan laughs. He knows it's true.

We step out of the subway and walk toward Wing Hua. Through the dirty Plexiglas window, we see Yan's distant relatives working inside—the billow of smoke and thick steam behind the counter, and the bustle of cooking and taking orders. The girl behind the counter packs white cartons; foam boxes; plasticware; packets of soy sauce, duck sauce, and hot sauce; and a fistful of fortune cookies into a brown paper bag. She yells something, and a man with a motorcycle helmet takes the bag and heads out the door. A delivery.

"What do you think is in that order?" I ask. "You know, since you're the expert." Yan gives me the middle finger with a smile. I laugh.

"Beef lo mein, pork fried rice, egg foo young, chicken with broccoli."

"You sure?"

"It doesn't matter. It's all the same."

"I can't believe you eat like that all the time."

Yan turns to me, his eyebrow cocked. "We do not eat that food, you know. We eat different food. Plainer things. Sautéed vegetables, plain white rice, and maybe a little meat."

Now my brows shoot up. Why wouldn't they eat what they sell? Is something wrong with the food? "No," he answers. "It's just, we're used to different food. You know, my parents told me that they had never even seen broccoli until they came here." I look at him in surprise.

"Did you have broccoli in the Philippines?"

"Yeah. It only grows in cooler climates, and where I grew up, the weather would get cold," I say, telling him that I'd even met people who said that it was like San Francisco weather, a place I'd never been to. They were balikbayan folks who vacationed in the Philippines, showing off their newfound wealth to friends and relatives, spending hundreds, sometimes thousands of US dollars taking them to restaurants, giving them money, and sometimes sending children they didn't know to school or restoring parts of their relatives' houses broken down from weather and wear.

"When my dad worked for someone else in another restaurant, I realized that people don't care about whoever is in the back making their food. People just want their food. Period. I never told you this because it's shit to talk about it, but he was hit with something on the back of his head, probably with a brick, when he was out delivering."

"No!" I gasp.

He runs his left hand through his greasy hair. I watch his fingers move through the blue tips of each strand, pulling gently, then circling his index finger, turning his hair into a noose at the end so that the tip of his finger swells from the lack of circulation. "You know, I wonder about that. What if we had the Chinese restaurant in the middle of a rich neighborhood with all the fancy high-rises? And then I went to a school right there. Like in Tribeca or something," he says. He puts his hand down. "Like, I don't want to go to a fancy building, then ring a bell and find out it's my asshole classmate who ordered takeout. You don't know who you're delivering to. Are they gonna pay? Are they gonna throw a brick at you?"

I cry again, but not for me this time. I cry for him and his father. Yan strokes my hair, and his hands and fingers find their way to my back, gently caressing my spine. He pulls me closer, and I let him. He kisses me close to the mouth. It feels like a breeze on my face. My heart jumps a little and I feel a twinge. I wish he would go further.

"So what are you going to do?"

"With what?" I ask, nervous.

"With life. I dunno. I mean, just think about it. What do you want to do?"

To be kissed, I almost say.

"Well?"

"I want to go to school," I say in such a low voice that Yan asks me to speak louder. I say the same thing, my voice more certain. He nods.

"Nobody's stopping you, you know. Mr. Higgins keeps bugging me about that. He's worse than my Chinese mom. I mean, he's nagging me so much I might as well just sign up for a class to shut him up. Hasn't he started bugging you too?"

I shake my head. "Why does he care so much?"

"He's just a nosy old man who's got no kids, that's why. He's as single as those jerky beef links you buy at the deli."

"At least he cares," I say, thinking about Ma, who cares only about money.

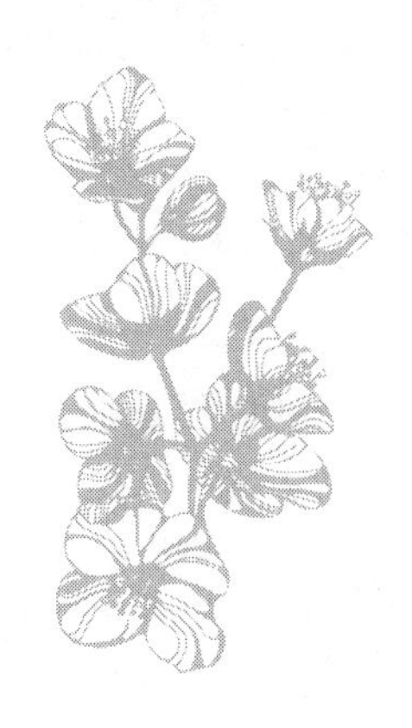

It takes me a few days to broach the subject of college with Mr. Higgins. He usually wears a light button-down shirt fastened all the way to his collar, his thick glasses punctuating the narrowness of his face, which is usually buried in a book. He is the thinnest white man I have ever seen. I always thought that white people were large. Compared to almost everyone in the Philippines, who looks emaciated from bouts of hunger and food rationing, especially in the poor villages or the slums, American men are bigger and taller since they are well fed. But Mr. Higgins is the exception. He looks like a Category 1 typhoon could blow him away. But nobody knows typhoons here in America. Mr. Higgins isn't that tall either. By many standards, he isn't a handsome man at all. He is pale, plain, and reminds me of a hairless newborn even though he has thin graying hair on his head. I could just hear old schoolmates, a gaggle of mean girls, gossiping and laughing, saying, *Sayang at hindi pogi itong 'kano na to.* They had no qualms calling anyone bakla, baboy, panget, and whatever other ugly word one could use to describe a person.

I clear my throat.

Mr. Higgins looks up at me and then approaches. "Can I help you?"

"I'm Yan's friend Queenie."

"Yes, I know. We met. You're here all the time."

I swallow whatever spit there is in my throat. I'm nervous, but I shouldn't be. This is a person who yells at Yan like he's known him all his life.

"Yan said I should ask you about college."

His demeanor changes a little, the corners of his mouth lifting into a slight smile, and he asks me what I'd like to know. I tell him my situation—that I've just come over from across the Pacific. I tell him Ma's plans of having me work before going to school. He nods and asks me about my grades. I tell him that my math and science grades are lackluster eighties, but history and English were in the nineties. I don't tell him that I was not great at grammar studies. My eyes glazed over when my teachers talked about subjects, predicates, dependent and independent clauses, and split infinitives. They lost me at the idea of the subjunctive.

"Those translate to Bs and As. That's not bad. Have you taken the SATs yet?"

"What's that?"

Mr. Higgins explains that it's the Scholastic Aptitude Test, a standardized exam that most high school students take to qualify for college admissions. He points to a section in the library with a sign that reads *Test Prep.* He says that the College Board recently changed the exam, and that instead of a total score of 1600 it's now 2400, which also includes an essay.

"It takes money to change an entire system, and even we had to buy new prep books," he says. "I couldn't bear to throw out the old ones, so I kept a lot of them." He points to a closed cabinet behind him. "You also have to take the TOEFL exam."

Mr. Higgins explains that it's an exam that tests foreigners on their ability to comprehend English. "I think you'll definitely do fine on that," he says.

He looks around and leans on the counter, his voice lowering. He beckons for me to lean in.

"I don't want to assume. And you don't have to answer this if you don't want to," he says, taking a pause. "It would just be easier for me to help if I know, you understand?"

I nod.

"Are you legal?"

I nod slowly. I am never sure how to answer this question. Looking over our paperwork, all I know is that we came legally. We don't exactly have tourist visas. We have H-4s. We're dependents. We were supposed to stay for a season, only to see the snow in New York and to see Ma. That's what we told the man in the suit at the embassy. But we're here to stay whether anyone likes it or not.

Mr. Higgins says it's good, but that I might be considered an international student, which would mean that I would pay an out-of-state tuition price. He walks to a section in the library and comes back with a thick book. He looks through a part and nods.

"Just as I thought. In CUNY schools, it's more than double if you're an international student. You pay by credit, actually."

"Would I be considered an international student?"

"I'm not sure. You'll have to ask someone who works for admissions."

He bites his lower lip, looks at the book again, and starts dialing a number on the library phone. "I'm calling BMCC," he says as he punches in the numbers, mentioning that the Borough of Manhattan Community College takes in a lot of foreign students. He explains my situation to someone at the other end of the line, but the person doesn't have the answer that he needs, and so he's told to contact the International Student Services Office. Mr. Higgins asks to be transferred, but the person he's speaking to says that he doesn't know how and that he's new, so he just gives him a number. Mr.

Higgins dials again. The person who answers, upon hearing my situation, asks him what kind of H-4 visa I have since there are H-4 visas for family members of those classified as H1-B and H1-C that are eligible for in-state tuition, and then there's H-4 visas from H-2 and H-3 visa holders that are not eligible for in-state tuition, and that if I fell into the latter, I would indeed be considered an international student and that scholarships are limited for international students. Mr. Higgins turns to me, his eyebrows raised. "Well?"

I think of Ma. Because she's a nurse, she was given a work visa. A coveted H1-B. I tell him that Ma has the good visa. Mr. Higgins nods, and the woman at the other end of the line tells him that I would just need to show residency for a year in New York State and then I would be eligible. He thanks her and hangs up.

My heart sinks a little. I've been in this country for eight months already. But I must wait longer. "That didn't sound good," I say.

"All is not lost. Still a better option for you once you can afford it."

He hands me a book. "I'm not supposed to do this since this is considered a reference book, but you can borrow this. It's old anyway and I'll have to get rid of it. I can't lend you the new SAT books, because kids are always looking at those."

I thank him and put the book in my book bag. I leave the library, depressed. All I can think about is the price tag. It's cheaper to pay for my mom's loan than to go to school right now. I wonder if Ma knows about any of this. Maybe she does. Maybe that's why she's adamant that I work and pay off a portion of our debt before I accumulate more. Maybe I should just do as she says.

Papa seethes. He has not stopped talking about how Ma has become an Amerikana. He says the word with such vitriol while his friend Mr. Park is folding clothes. It's become a Sunday routine, when Ma works the weekends.

Mr. Park from the laundromat is the only guy Pa gets along with. They bond over laundry because, in the old country, this was something men would never do.

Mr. Park and Pa began to talk after we got rid of the old mattress that we didn't know had bedbugs when we picked it up from the street. Pa complained about how it had seemed too good to be true, and Mr. Park said, "No such thing as free in America. There's always a catch." With those words from Mr. Park, Pa was convinced that he found a man of integrity. "He's a good man," Pa said of Mr. Park, whose backbone was as sturdy as construction beams. Mr. Park asked my father how we got bedbugs in the first place. Pa explained how my mother had told him to look through the streets in white neighborhoods on trash days. How most of the shelves, tables, and chairs in our apartment were from such pickings. How the offending blue quilted mattress was wrapped in thick industrial plastic so it almost looked brand-new, and we took it home and even called a car service and paid twenty dollars to avoid carrying it on the subway.

"This is why we came to America?" Papa sighs.

"The land shapes us," Mr. Park says. "Your wife is American now because she is in America."

I pick up an IKEA catalog from a chair and flip through the glossy pages. Mr. Park looks over at me and the magazine and says, "Still too expensive."

"People in this country waste too much. They even throw away brand-new TVs," Papa says, and then he tells Mr. Park that we just picked up a small coffee table from Park Slope.

"Did you ever pick up furniture off the street?" I ask Mr. Park.

He stops and wipes the sweat off his brow with a rough white towel. The working machines in the laundromat make it hot and humid. "It's bad luck to take other people's garbage. You don't know what they throw out—good luck or bad luck and you catch that like a disease," he says. "But sometimes you have to. If you have no money to buy, you take what's there."

Mr. Park tells us the story of how, when he was new to the country and his wife was still alive and pregnant with their daughter, he was forced to pick up a discarded stroller from the street in one of the nicer neighborhoods because he couldn't afford not to.

—

I remember a story I read from a children's book when I was in grade school about how Filipinos got their flat noses. In the olden days, all the races of men lived on one island where peace reigned. No one had noses as we know them now, just two holes on their faces. A goddess took interest in one of the men—a Filipino—maybe because she liked the way he sang songs. But the way gods and goddesses show affection can be brutal. Because she was a goddess, she decided to experiment. The poor Filipino, who was doing his chores and minding his own business, stumbled and fell into mud that stuck to his face. When he tried to wipe it off, it wouldn't come off. As he walked around the island, all the girls swooned, and all the other men grew jealous because of the swooning girls. But the Filipino man kept his cool, continued to be humble, and worked hard. The goddess observed the situation she had created and decided to make noses for these noseless men. She stayed up all day and all night creating noses. When she finally finished, she smiled and clapped her hands, and all the noses fell from the sky. With this rain of noses, all the men began to gather them and put them on their faces. The white men, especially. In fact, in their mad rush, they trampled on the noses. The Filipino men, who were short, could not get to the good noses fast enough. They took what was left: the noses trampled on by other men.

All the furniture felt like unwanted noses: tables, books, lamps, bags of worn clothes, hand-me-downs from strangers. We judged them for their wastefulness. In the Philippines, these discarded items would have ten thousand lives.

Filipinos always say "pwedeng remediohan iyan." "That can be remedied." There is a cure for everything. Even being used and broken. It's a way of life. The word *remedio* means "remedy" in English. A cure. A broken TV? No problem. Just find out which part is broken. Get that broken part from a chop shop. Still not fixed? No problem. Just bring the whole thing to the chop shop so it can be chopped up into usable parts to fix other broken things. People from the slums even picked through other people's trash. I saw a news clip one time about how people would scavenge and find bits of leftover meat from chewed-on bones from fast-food restaurants like Jollibee, McDonald's, or KFC. Sometimes they would scavenge expired food or frozen meat, fish, and vegetables discarded by supermarkets. They would take these bits, not even bothering to swat the flies hovering over them, and put whatever skin and meat they found into plastic basins. They would take their loot to their corrugated cardboard homes—joined together with pieces of plywood and sheet metal—and recook the meat and slather it with soy sauce, MSG, and fish sauce. Some would eat it, but the more enterprising ones would sell a portion of it with a cup of white rice. In the slums, this food is called pagpag. My face contorted in disgust. The newscaster, a woman in her twenties, tried to keep a straight face and asked the slum woman why she did this and wasn't she afraid of getting herself and other people sick? The slum woman shed her tears and said, "What else can we do?" The camera zoomed in on the crying woman's face. Then it cut to the newsroom, to the well-dressed and well-fed news anchors, shaking their heads and asking if our countrymen deserved this.

Nothing is wasted, even pain.

MALBA, QUEENS

The neighborhood has the grandest homes I've seen since coming to New York. The architecture of each house rivals the others. There is so much green I can almost imagine the streets paved with gold. This is the America I expected.

Ms. Flor, the woman who lent Ma money, opens the door when Ma and I arrive. I am carrying my backpack and pulling a small rolling suitcase borrowed from one of Ma's friends.

Ms. Flor smells so strongly of rotting flowers that I sneeze a few times when she passes by. She is wearing a lavender silk scarf wrapped around her neck and dark sunglasses; she could very well be a movie star straight out of the old black-and-white Sampaguita films I used to watch. I get another whiff of her perfume when she rushes out to go pick up her Maltese from the groomer. I wonder if her mother, the old lady I'm supposed to care for, is anything like her.

"I don't like to keep my fur baby, Daisy, waiting," she says, digging her heels into the ground. She turns around to face Ma and me, and says, referring to her housekeeper, "Lucia has my number should anything happen, and Michelle will instruct you on your daily schedule with Mama."

We watch Ms. Flor walk to the garage and drive out in a white BMW SUV. She unrolls the window, pulls her sunglasses down, and gives a few more orders to Lucia, whom I hadn't seen standing by the door. This scene reminds me eerily of when we visited Papa's brother's mansion in Manila. Whenever he or his wife would leave, his maids stood by the door, waiting to do their bidding. It was another kind of life, another kind of reality.

Lucia has been Ms. Flor's housekeeper for the last twenty years. She was hired when Ms. Flor's previous husband was still alive, and when her son was still a toddler. Once Ms. Beatriz's Alzheimer's worsened and she began needing twenty-four-hour care, Ms. Flor decided she needed more help because she didn't want her housekeeper to look after her mother at the expense of her house.

Lucia asks us to come in and we follow her inside to Ms. Beatriz's quarters. As we walk the length of the house to get there, I am reminded of the homes of the rich I've seen in TV. They have different places for different people and names for different rooms. The foyer, living room, primary bedroom, guest room, basement, kitchen, maids' quarters. In Tagalog, there is only *kwarto, banyo* or *inodoro, sala,* and *kusina*. Here, there are words like *pantry* and *kitchen counter.*

Lucia's footfall is so quiet that she reminds me of a rabbit. Ma tries to engage in conversation with Lucia, but Lucia just smiles without saying much.

When we look inside, a light-skinned Black woman named Michelle is about to put Ms. Beatriz onto the commode. Ma immediately springs into action. This is, after all, part of her routine. When Michelle and Ma expertly place the fragile Ms. Beatriz on the commode, Michelle expresses her surprise that Ms. Beatriz let Ma touch her.

"Your substitute is here while you're away. Her name is Queenie," Lucia says, pointing at me. "This is her mother, Mel."

Lucia excuses herself, saying that she needs to clean before Ms. Flor returns. Ma and I watch her leave. Michelle shrugs and nods at us and brings her attention back to her charge.

"She's usually so fussy about people," Michelle says. Ma beams when Michelle says something about Ms. Beatriz recognizing someone from her country.

"Don't watch while I do my business," Ms. Beatriz snaps.

"No one's watching, Ms. B," Michelle replies, before she and Ma exchange quips and make each other laugh. This is Ma's element. She is at home with caregiving. Michelle and Ma exchange gossip and talk easily to each other like they are old friends, like how she would with her friends over the phone.

Ma would complain about work at the hospital and, sometimes, the other staff: how a nurse was caught and fired for clocking out four hours after she was already done with her shift so she could claim overtime; how a ward clerk was caught on her knees in the morgue with another employee from Medical Supplies and was suspended and fired; how a nursing technician won a two-million-dollar sexual harassment lawsuit when the hospital did nothing to the respiratory technician supervisor with a history of touching and flirting with the light-skinned girls who worked on the floors.

Michelle and Ma laugh at some story Michelle shared. The stench of human waste makes me gag, and I watch in disbelief as these two women pay no attention. Both see my face and start grinning.

"You'll get used to it," Ma says.

Michelle laughs and talks about the first time she had to clean up an old man who refused the male attendant that the agency sent the first time around. He only liked women to clean him.

"He said he wanted to see if his willy still worked," Michelle says, shaking her head.

While Ma and Michelle reminisce about other patients, Ms. Beatriz takes me in from head to toe. "Nina," she says, half in English and half in Tagalog, "I told you, don't eat too much. How are you going to catch a man?" My face turns red. Even deep in her Alzheimer's, she cannot stop talking like an old Filipina woman with a lashing tongue, always criticizing.

"This is not Nina, Ms. B," Michelle says. She tells us that every time Ms. Beatriz sees a young Asian woman, she is one of three people: the housekeeper, Lucia; a woman named Isabel; or Nina, Ms. Beatriz's sister who died before the age of thirty.

"How does she recognize you?" Ma asks.

"She calls me Michelle when she remembers. Sometimes she'll ask me who I am, and I'll tell her. She won't argue with me like she does sometimes with Ms. Flor. She can be fresh with her."

They keep talking about Alzheimer's and the people they've known or taken care of, and I feel more and more distant from the conversation. Ma tries to get my attention, irritated that I am not participating more since I will be looking after Ms. Beatriz for the next few weeks.

"It's all right, I'll fill her in," Michelle says.

After a while, when it becomes clear that Lucia isn't coming back to offer any refreshments, Ma says that she has to go back to Brooklyn. She tells me she will be calling to check up on me.

"Don't worry 'bout her. She's in good hands," Michelle says.

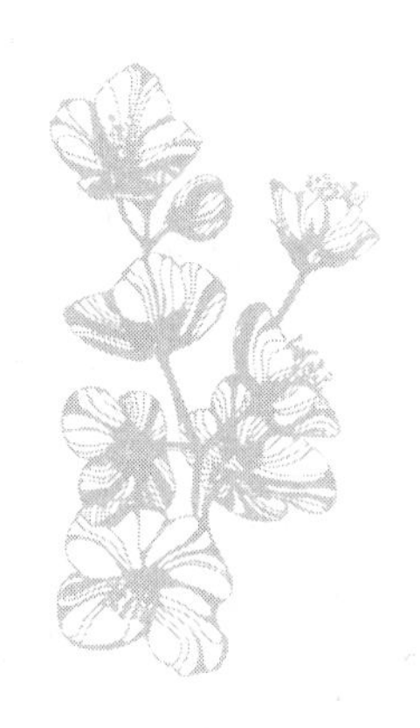

"You've never cared for anyone before, not even a baby?" Michelle asks me. I shake my head and wait for her to say something Ma would say—that I'm acting like a princess and why don't I know anything. But Michelle says something different.

"You got to start sometime, so it might as well be now."

She talks about the routine and what's expected. I'll have to wake up at six in the morning and make sure the guardrails are still up because Ms. B sometimes knocks them down while thrashing at night. I'll have to sleep on the cot next to her to make sure that when she starts screaming in the middle of the night, it's only a nightmare. I'll have to mash her food because she sometimes forgets to chew. Bananas are mashed and never cut. Oatmeal, which we called Quaker oats in the Philippines, must be made very watery so she doesn't choke. I'll have to put a diaper on her before she sleeps. I'll have to lift her when she needs to use the commode and let her take her time. I'll have to brush her hair and pin it back with barrettes, making sure that I use pink and lavender, her favorite colors. I'll have to remember to let Daisy come in for thirty minutes so Ms. Beatriz can pet her. To let her watch some TV programs from the cable channels she likes, and to read to her. To prepare her for dinner with the family and learn how to give her a shower using a special chair in the bathroom. I'll have to learn how to put her in the wheelchair and take her to the garden so she can enjoy the flowers and some sun.

"How do you know what to do?" I ask her.

"Trial and error. It just takes a little time, care, and observation," Michelle says.

"Don't you miss your privacy?" I'm already thinking that this is more than I bargained for.

She laughs loud, unexpectedly, and from her belly. "Oh, child," she says. "Sundays at church is my privacy. If I'd wanted my privacy, I would never have taken this job in the first place. You don't do this for the privacy. You do this because you need to."

"This might sound rude," I say, "but do you like doing this . . . ? As a job, I mean."

"Nobody chooses to do this. If I chose to do something like this, I might have wanted to be a nurse. Like your mother. Now, nurses . . . they make money." She looks at me. "The question is, why are you doing this?"

I explain that I'm doing it so I can partially pay off what Ma owes Ms. Flor. Michelle doesn't say anything at first. She continues packing for her trip back to her country, Trinidad. She talks about how she misses the cooking and the pace of life, but mostly she misses her daughters.

"In Trinidad, we have so many children who don't have their mothers. They're all over here or in England, working. Au pairs, nurses, caregivers. Sometimes children don't see their mothers for years. I haven't seen my daughters for a while. One's pregnant right now. I can hardly believe I'm going to be a grandmother!"

I find out her father is an Indian Hindu, and his people came from Madras and that they were called "coolies." I tell her that when I first heard her speak, I assumed that she was from England because of her nice accent.

"Your ears just aren't trained yet," she says, and explains how each Caribbean country has its own music and you can tell where people are from as soon as they open their mouths.

I ask her if anyone in the family bothers her. Philippine soap operas were rife with the help being abused by their employers. She looks me straight in the eye and, without batting an eyelash, says, "Don't mix pleasure and business, ya hear? Keep your nose clean."

She cooks her own curries in the small kitchen that night and shares with me the most flavorful meal I've eaten since coming to New York—curried chickpeas, rice, and roti. I ask her why she doesn't join the family for meals. "I sometimes do, but I miss my own food," she says.

When Ms. Flor comes home, she asks me if everything is all right and then retires to her room. I keep thinking there's so much more of the world that I don't know. There is so much to learn.

The days blend in a routine of tedium and endurance. I wake up next to Ms. Beatriz and smell her age. Talcum powder and the distinct smell of stale air that worsens when she accidentally pees or defecates on herself. I wonder if this is what everyone has to look forward to in their old age.

She confuses faces, places, and memories. She now forgets how to feel shame, sometimes letting her clothes slip because she feels a burning in her body, itching to be put out. If no one helps her, she takes off her clothes so that she's as naked as the day she was born. She screams at me and Lucia and sometimes even Ms. Flor. Then there are days when she screams at something, or someone, only she can see.

Ms. Beatriz is docile when the men are around. Dr. McDonnell, Ms. Flor's second husband, and Zeus, Ms. Flor's only child from her late husband, calm her down. One time, Ms. Beatriz didn't want me brushing her hair. She screamed at me to stop. A few minutes later, Zeus came by to say a quick hello to her.

He seemed to come out of nowhere, really.

I didn't even get a good look at him in the beginning, but there was already something in the air that I couldn't quite place. Something in the world shifted; it almost felt violent. Just a glimpse of his profile, the silhouette of his body, and how his dark hair framed his face. He was tall, towering two heads over his grandmother. These were enough incendiary properties for particles of my body to self-combust. My hands felt clammy, and my throat dried up.

My heart beat so fast I couldn't speak when he introduced himself to me, so he turned his complete attention to his grandmother. "Lola, you need to be nice to the girl," he said. She transformed as if he'd uttered a magical incantation. She giggled and acted all shy. Then he smiled at me. I couldn't take it and laughed a bit like how I imagined a donkey would, braying. I felt stupid. I thanked him and pretended to be busy brushing Ms. Beatriz's hair, and I breathed a sigh of relief when he finally left.

It's been a month since I started.

When Dr. McDonnell gets home from work, Ms. Flor insists that Ms. Beatriz and I join them in the formal dining room. She wants her mother to see her new son-in-law, whom she sometimes doesn't recognize.

I don't mind the breaks in my routine. Apart from reading whenever the old woman falls asleep, I am practically her shadow.

The occasional family dinner has provided me with a taste of how they live. It's a far cry from the life I know. Daisy, the beloved pet, has her own bowl next to Ms. Flor's feet, so she can fuss over her whenever she wants. The lucky dogs I knew in the Philippines were chained outdoors and served leftovers. It meant they belonged and had purpose. The unlucky ones were strays that scavenged for food.

I eat the same thing the family eats, including some food I have never seen before—corned beef that isn't canned, with mashed potatoes and fresh salads made by Lucia.

The dinners remind me of what I imagine dinners are like in the novels I read. I only know of three courses—appetizer, main dish, dessert—but Ms. Flor informs me that a meal can have up to twelve courses for formal occasions. "You should learn more about dining etiquette," Ms. Flor says more than once, adding that I'll never know when I'll need such knowledge. "After all, you're named after the

Queen of England," she likes to remind me, after Ma told her the story of my name. "Why not Diana?" Ms. Flor asked Ma. "The Queen is the Queen," Ma said.

Dr. McDonnell doesn't usually talk much, but Ms. Flor chatters away, asking me about how I lived in the Philippines.

"It wasn't easy—" I say, and before I can say anything else, she cuts me off.

"Nothing is easy," she says, and begins to tell me about her childhood in her hacienda and how the neighborhood feared her family and their wealth. There were always men with guns close to their house, lurking and waiting for an opportunity to use them. They even shot one of the houseboys in the leg for trying to run away. He had the misfortune of witnessing the men murder one of the hapless farmers in the hacienda.

"Life is not easy," she says, her eyes narrowing. She reminds me of the rich ladies in the telenovelas, wanting to know how the poor live but not actually caring about that life at all.

I discover, during one of these dinners, that there are forks and spoons and knives for each course. Strange words from the French. Amuse-bouche. A big word to talk about a small piece of food.

Ms. Flor doesn't like eating with her hands. She prefers eating her food with a knife and fork—not even a spoon and fork like most Filipinos do if they're not using their hands.

"It's not as barbaric," she says.

One afternoon, I fall asleep on the couch next to Ms. Beatriz while she is watching a popular soap opera on TFC. When I wake up, Lucia is hovering over me. She turns the TV off.

"Don't fall asleep," she says.

I rub my eyes and tell her that I'm exhausted because Ms. Beatriz had nightmares, moaning and screaming in a dialect I didn't understand. Lucia begins cleaning up around me. I yawn, stretch my limbs, and finally stand up and ask Lucia if she needs help. She stops what she's doing—bending and wiping the floor with a damp cloth—and looks at me, surprised. She is so stunned that I think that I must have said something wrong. Before I can say anything else, Ms. B wakes up and sees Lucia. She speaks to her in the same dialect I heard last night. Lucia responds, her words timid and measured. Then she takes the remote control, turns on the TV, and sits next to Ms. B. They watch the Filipino soap opera.

"What dialect is that?" I ask Lucia.

"Kapampangan po," she says, adding the honorific at the end, and I feel my back stiffening at the sound and its implications.

"You don't need to talk to me that way, since I'm younger than you," I tell her. She doesn't say anything and continues watching with Ms. B. I look at the television blankly, thinking about Kapampangans and Pampanga, a place I have never been but have heard about. I knew that the region was hard-hit when the volcano Mount Pinatubo exploded in 1991 after over five hundred years of being dormant, and this was one of the reasons that the Americans left Clark and Subic bases. Who wanted to be so close to an angry volcano?

"I like the food you make," I say, thinking about the dish we had the night before, bopis, made of chopped beef heart, sautéed onions, tomatoes, and peppers. Dr. McDonnell took liberal portions of it, and I asked him if he knew what it was. He chuckled and said his grandmother fed him a lot of organ meats when he was a child because that's what she could afford and that he liked kidney pie. I couldn't imagine a pie with organ meat and looked so confused he began to laugh.

I know people like Ms. Flor who prefer Western-style food and clean meats, trimmed of fat and with none of the innards that the poor had to make do with, like chicken feet, intestines, and hearts. Junior and I were hardly fed organ meat growing up—even this was scarce. "We'd be lucky to even have organ meat," Ma would say when we complained about how we'd be eating another can of Ligo sardines and instant ramen.

"I knew you liked it, Ading," Lucia says, smiling, using the Ilocano word for "younger sister." I ask her how she learned to cook all the dishes that I've tried, and she says that she likes to experiment in the kitchen, and that sometimes Ms. Flor's guests would teach her their dishes.

"Do you like working here?" I ask her.

She grows quiet and thoughtful and looks back at the television, and then starts fixing Ms. Beatriz's hair. The old woman lets Lucia play with her hair and adjusts herself a little bit so Lucia can comb it more easily. "I can't complain," she says so softly that I almost don't hear her. I want to ask her more questions, but something about her tone does not invite further conversation.

I continue to watch her. She is a shade darker than Michelle, with salt-and-pepper hair and a face lined with fine wrinkles. She is stronger and younger than Ms. Beatriz, who is so frail she looks like she would break if the wind blew toward her.

"I can't believe you're turning sixty-seven," I say.

"We all get old," she says.

"Don't you get tired?"

She doesn't answer me. I want to ask her what rest looks like, but I don't. I want to ask her if this is how she saw her life, aging this way. I wonder about our bodies, how they expand and contract in fear, in pain, in love, in hate. What we carry inside, which histories and stories, the ones we know and the ones we don't.

I see women like Ms. Flor, who would sometimes go to Zeus's

room and just stay there for hours with a bottle in her hand and a photograph of her dead first husband in her arms.

I see women like Lucia, who can make herself so small that sometimes no one knows she is even there. How tense her body is, tightly coiled and always ready to leap and dive into tasks.

I see women like Ms. Beatriz, who holds on to her former self without knowing that she is slowly disappearing, losing control, a prisoner of her own body.

And then there is me and my body.

The only parts of myself that I see clearly are the parts that I despise. My neck with its lined skin. My thick ankles, legs, and thighs. My wide shoulders. My short height. My skin that changes hues.

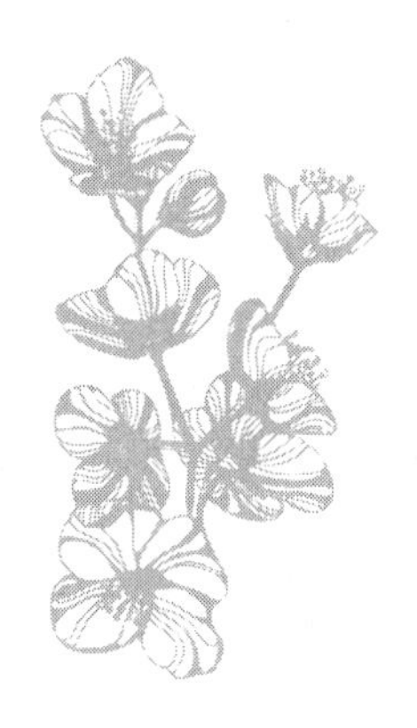

I call Yan's home number. The phone keeps ringing. I wonder what he's up to. He is usually the only one home at ten in the morning.

I hang up, wait a minute, and call again. This is the fifth day in a row that I've tried to get ahold of him. After several rings, I am about to hang up when I hear someone pick up the phone mid-ring.

"Wai," Yan says, breathless, as though he just ran.

"It's me. I tried calling you a bunch of times, but no one answers."

There is a slight pause, which is strange. Yan usually says what's on his mind. "I've just been busy."

"With what?"

A sharp exhale. "Work. You know?"

"But your ice cream job starts in the afternoon."

He makes a sound that communicates that he doesn't like my response. "What's this? An interrogation? I just do errands. I'm allowed to do errands."

His answer shocks me. Haven't we shared enough of each other to deserve loyalty? He knows he's been my anchor since coming here. He knows this American me—someone I don't even know—the most. Yan has never been this evasive.

"Why are you being so weird?" I ask.

I hear a long exhale at the other end of the line. "I'm sorry. There's just a lot going on." He doesn't elaborate. But I'm hurt that he doesn't even ask me how I'm doing. "I got to go, OK? We'll talk soon. When you get back . . ."

He hangs up before I can say anything. I stare at the receiver, listening to the dial tone. What is he hiding?

I lift Ms. Beatriz from the chair, straining, even though Michelle showed me how to pivot my hips as I lift. Before I can pull further, I feel strong hands wrap around her waist.

"Let me help you with that," Zeus says.

I startle but have the presence of mind not to drop the deadweight of Ms. Beatriz's body. That would have been disastrous. Zeus helps me move Ms. Beatriz slowly to the commode.

"Thanks," I say faintly.

Zeus watches me undress his grandmother, and she suddenly becomes charming, as if she's aware someone is watching her. She starts talking about her life as a young woman, then her life as a grandmother, the time lines blurring. My heart starts pounding from being so close to Zeus.

"You scared me."

"Didn't mean to," he says, and turns to his grandmother, speaking to her like she's a child, asking about her day and whether she remembers him.

"I want to do my business. No watching. Everyone's always watching. I'm a grown woman," Ms. Beatriz says in one of her most lucid moments, swatting us away. Zeus takes my hand, and we walk away to another area in the living room.

"Is this far enough, Lola?" Zeus asks, smiling at me while

restraining his laughter. He is still holding my hand, and I feel an obligation to keep holding it, and I hate myself a little for wanting to hold it. Taking a deep breath, I let go.

"I can still hear you breathing," Ms. B snaps.

Zeus laughs, and I also can't help but giggle at the absurdity of this. I imagine a bird's-eye view of this scene—an old woman with her nightgown over her hips trying to defecate, trying to assert control over the situation, while two youngsters stand with their backs to her fifteen feet away.

"Where's Michelle? Where's Lucia? Where's your mother?" she asks Zeus.

"Everyone's gone, Lola. Just me and her," he replies, pointing at me.

"I know you," she says, her eyes narrowing at me.

"Yes, ma'am," I say automatically. I almost turn around but decide not to.

"How do I know you?"

"I've been here taking care of you the past month."

"You're Nina."

"No, ma'am. I'm Queenie," I say.

"You look like Nina from the back," she says.

"She was named after the Queen of England," Zeus pipes up, and I look at him. He must have understood my silent question, because he explains to his grandmother that Ms. Flor told him that my mother named me after a living monarch.

"Queenie," Ms. B repeats, and I feel her eyes boring into my back. "Is she your girlfriend?" she asks her grandson, who laughs again.

"Do you want her to be my girlfriend, Lola?"

"No, she's a little too fat," she says, and my face turns red.

"But I like girls with meat on them," he says, and I can't tell by his tone if he is joking.

"What is she? A piece of steak? Please. You just don't have taste," she says, and I hear her struggle as she tries to push. She makes a satisfied sound and asks me to help her.

"I can help," Zeus says.

"No, you're a man. I can't have you see my apple," she says.

Zeus and I both laugh. I have never seen or heard Ms. B so alert. This must be the effect of having Zeus around. I turn to him and ask if she is always like this, and he nods.

"When I'm home, yeah," he says.

I go to Ms. B and ask her to stand and lean on her walker. She makes a disapproving sound and says she's not done. I take some wet wipes and slowly clean her.

I'd spoken to Ma a few days before and I told her about this part of the job. She laughed. "Get used to it," she said. "This is what's in store for you." I was angry and screamed at her, saying I would never do this for a living, and she screamed right back at me, saying how dare I look down on a noble profession, that this is clean and honest work. "Nothing about this is clean," I countered. She said this was the real world, where you cleaned up other people's shit. "So I'm cleaning up your shit by working to pay off your loan?" I said before hanging up. She called again, but Ms. Flor picked up and they chitchatted about the hospital. The few times Ma tried to call again, I pretended Ms. Flor or Dr. McDonnell was close by and that I couldn't talk much. She would then tell me to be good and to be extra nice if Zeus was around. "Why should I be nice?" I would ask. "He could be your destiny," she would say.

"All done," I tell Ms. B, and pull her dressing gown down. I ask her if she wants to sit, and Zeus turns around and interrupts.

"Lola, don't you want to go to the garden and get some fresh air?"

"It's too cold. Do you want to kill me?" Ms. B replies, but I can see she wants to go, because she's looking for her shawl. We all laugh. I've never seen Ms. B so full of sass. I almost like her. I hand her the crocheted shawl.

"I thought you said it was too cold, Lola."

"That's what blankets are for," she replies, her gnarled hands fixing her shawl.

We bundle her up, put her in her wheelchair, and head to the garden, where we sit on a wooden bench by the fishpond listening to the soft sounds of the water fountain.

I don't know what comes over me, but I ask them if they want refreshments, and I play hostess in someone else's house. Grandmother and grandson keep talking, and I cannot get over Ms. B's transformation. I wonder why Zeus doesn't just go to school here and keep his grandmother company.

This is what would have been done in the Philippines, but probably with poorer folks who couldn't afford to have help look after their ailing elders. For this family, they can afford to have so much, and I feel a pang at just how unfair life is.

I come back outside with a tray and three glasses of calamansi juice from frozen packets I found in the freezer, and a straw for Ms. B. I wouldn't have believed I would miss the tart taste of calamansi when we left the Philippines. I wouldn't have believed I would miss homemade sweet rice cakes with grated young coconut that we used to buy on the buses and at bus stops, sold by locals whose baskets were also filled with boiled quail eggs, shelled peanuts toasted and fried with garlic, fried pork rinds with spicy vinegar, sliced green sour mango with fish sauce, and balut.

The food tasted so vibrant. This is why, I imagine, Lucia uses the original ingredients in her dishes whenever she can.

I make sure that Ms. B's calamansi lemonade is lukewarm so she won't complain about the cold. Zeus takes her glass and lets her sip hers first. I listen to their conversation—they talk about school, and he teases her about her weight. Ms. B continues to be acerbic with her replies, but underneath her words, I hear a longing for a life, the center of the universe.

"You, why are you so quiet?" Zeus asks.

"I'm just listening," I say.

"She's quiet all the time," Ms. B complains. "I need a talker."

I look at her, surprised. She has hardly said anything to me except to complain when things aren't done correctly.

"I could read my book to you if you don't want to read anything from your library," I say, thinking about how they don't have a normal library here. Most people have a shelf of books, but they have a roomful.

I snuck into Dr. McDonnell's office once, in the middle of the night, but found mostly medical books and journals. There were, to my surprise, SAT books. I flipped through them, trying to see if I could get any answers right. Of course, I got more than half of them wrong, maybe even almost all of them wrong, especially the math section. I took the two books from the library and brought them to Ms. B's quarters.

What kind of life do they have without reading? I have never understood that about other people.

In my own family, books aren't appreciated unless they have a utilitarian purpose. "What's it for?" Ma would frequently ask about any of the books I brought home from the library on Fifty-Third or the paperbacks left on the street on garbage day. "As long as I'm not paying for it," she would say. She let me keep them and eventually took interest in some of the romance novels. She would skim through them but then forget about them since there were no pictures like the romance komiks in Tagalog she grew up with.

"I guess that's all right," she says.

"What is it?" Zeus asks.

"A Little Princess," I say, mortified that it is a children's book.

I tell them how I used to watch a Tagalog dub of the Japanese anime called *Princess Sara* and became so engrossed in the story that I hunted down the book it was adapted from and read it every couple of years. It's about a young rich girl who was born in colonial India, left at a boarding school by her widowed father to be cared for by a petty and jealous headmistress named Miss Minchin who openly fawned over Sara because she was wealthy. But when the father dies and loses his fortune, Miss Minchin makes Sara a maid and torments her. Despite all these hardships, Sara uses her imagination, pretending that she is a prisoner in the Bastille or a princess disguised as a servant. This all ends when her father's partner from India finds her and makes her rich again.

"Sounds like a Cinderella story," Zeus says.

"I appreciate her imagination. That's how she survived the horrors of her conditions," I say.

"Nerd," Zeus teases.

"Leave the girl alone," Ms. B tells him.

After another half hour, we take Ms. B inside. The day has exhausted her. She is fast asleep as soon as we walk into the house, so Zeus lifts her up and tucks her into her bed. We leave the room after he turns the light off. In the living room, alone, I turn to him, and we look at each other. His face is close enough for me to touch. I blush and back up, breaking the spell.

"Excuse me," I murmur, and run to the bathroom to splash my hot face with cool water.

By the time I return to the living room, I see Zeus flipping through the SAT books, a look of confusion on his face. "These are mine," he says.

"I found them in your dad's library," I say.

"He's my stepdad and that's his study," he says absently.

"His study," I echo, correcting myself.

"Are you studying for the SATs? I thought you were in college already."

"I'm supposed to be, but I just arrived here, and your mom asked my mom if I could come help with your lola," I explain.

Zeus said he got a 2100 on the SATs. It was good enough, but because he is also an athlete, he received a full scholarship. He didn't need it. His parents could obviously afford it. The world is so unfair.

"I don't even know why we have these lying around. Lucia must have put these in the study. You could have them if you want."

"Thanks," I say.

Zeus asks me point-blank what I'm doing here. I tell Zeus my story, and he says it's so messed up that I have to go through this. I make a small sound, surprised that he would even care.

"Why's your mom like that? My mom would never do that. She would probably walk across coals before asking me to do something like this."

"My mom had a hard life," I say.

"My mom always says that. You would think my mom was crucified, the way she talks about what she went through with Lola but especially with my lolo. I'm telling you, parents think they have it hard all the time."

Zeus looks so earnest that I wonder if he realizes just what he is saying. How could he possibly compare his mother to mine?

"Was your mom ever a prostitute?" I blurt out.

Zeus laughs and says, "You're funny. Of course not. Was yours?"

I don't answer him. Suddenly, there's a gulf between us. He would never understand what I am talking about. How could he? I talked too much.

"Wait. Your mom was . . . ?"

"Forget I said anything."

"But your mom is a nurse. Maybe you misunderstood."

"You think people who have a past can't make their lives better?" I say, my face hot.

"Hey, I'm sorry," he says. "I didn't mean anything bad."

But he is curious and asks me more. I don't know what comes over me. Maybe it's because I'm tired. Maybe because I just want to talk. I don't know why, but I tell him about Ma and Papa, about Olongapo, about Ma being a bar girl.

"Oh shit," he says. "Does my mom know?"

"I don't think so," I say. I can't imagine Ms. Flor, the proud woman who runs this house, knowing about Ma's past and letting her into her life.

I start crying. Why do I have to open my big mouth? He leans over and hugs me.

"I won't tell my mom," he says.

This makes me cry harder. We stay like that for a while.

Michelle will return from her trip in three days. Zeus comes to spend the night. Ms. Flor is happy and surprised that he is there. "You never stay anymore after leaving for college," she says, pinching his cheeks and surveying him and noting that he lost some weight. He replies that he's not losing weight but gaining muscle. He takes off his shirt and shows her that his torso is more chiseled now. As he speaks with her, he turns around and winks at me, making my heart jump, and his mother tells him to have some delicadeza and put his damn shirt back on. I pretend not to react to any of this, but I am aware that a change comes over Ms. Flor. She directs more thoughtful looks at me when she notices Zeus trying to catch my attention.

I read *A Little Princess* to Ms. B even though she doesn't remember where I left off or what she's listening to. Every so often, Zeus is there, and sometimes Ms. Flor is as well, watching how Zeus and I interact with each other. I remain cold and distant, barely saying anything to him. I just shake my head silently when he does something silly or outright dumb like wink at me when he thinks no one is looking.

He returns to school again on Monday morning, and as soon as his SUV leaves the driveway, Ms. Flor comes to Ms. B's quarters. I am in the middle of helping Ms. B stand up from the commode after she pees. I give her a wet wipe, and even though her hand is shaking, she wipes herself slowly. It feels like a small victory to both of us every time she does that.

"Front to back," I say.

"I'm not stupid. I know," Ms. B says as she hands me the used wet wipe. I forgot to put a latex glove on and grab the wet wipe from her with a piece of tissue and put it in the silver-colored waste receptacle next to the commode. I ask Ms. B if she wants to be cleaned more thoroughly and she grunts no.

Ms. Flor, with her hair piled up high into a coiffed hairdo, watches all this and doesn't even say hello to Ms. B as she normally would.

"We need to have a chat," Ms. Flor says.

"What's this about, Florencia?" Ms. B asks.

"Mama, this is not about you," Ms. Flor says.

"I want to know. I'm still alive and everything is still my business even though you're acting like I'm dead already," Ms. B says.

"Mama, I don't even know why you think that," Ms. Flor says, irritated.

Ms. B suddenly starts to scream at Ms. Flor, saying that she's the devil incarnate, and that as punishment for Kiriakos's death, Ms. B has to watch herself wither like a dried-up flower, and how she should have died instead. Ms. B becomes more and more hysterical. I have never seen her this way.

"Queenie, give her half a dose of the Haldol and Ativan. Make sure to crush them very fine," Ms. Flor says. I look at her dumbly. I have never had to administer any drug to Ms. B before, and the imperious Ms. Flor is acting like I'm supposed to know. Understanding my ignorance, Ms. Flor curses under her breath, saying punyeta and gaga. My ears turn red. How am I supposed to know something I have never been shown? Ms. Flor runs to the medicine cabinet, which I've ignored, and removes two childproof bottles. She takes a pill from each one, breaks them both in half, and crushes them.

"Make yourself useful and get some applesauce!"

I do as she says, and I hate myself for automatically doing her bidding because of the tone of her voice. I run to the fridge, frantic, and I put some applesauce into a bowl. I take this to Ms. Flor, and she puts the crushed half pills into the bowl and mixes them up. Meanwhile, Ms. B is still shouting in their dialect. Ms. Flor whispers and speaks to her in a singsong voice to try to calm her down.

"Eat this, Mama. You'll feel better," Ms. Flor says.

She coaxes her to finish the half cup of applesauce. Within half an hour, Ms. B's lids start to droop, and she falls asleep on her chair. Ms. Flor puts the bowl down and looks at me.

"You're a smart girl. I can see that," Ms. Flor starts. I don't say anything, so she continues, "When Zeus was a little boy, he found a stray puppy when we were vacationing in Crete when his father was still alive. He was from there. My first husband. Kiriakos wanted to share the Aegean Sea with us. At that time, Zeus was six or seven. This white puppy started following him on the beach. We looked for whoever owned him, but we couldn't find anybody. He wanted to bring the puppy home with us, but Kiriakos said no. That dog is a Greek dog and should stay in Greece. Do you understand what I am telling you?"

"Perfectly," I say, feeling my face turn hot.

She takes a blank white envelope from her pocket and gives it to me. It feels heavy. I know what's in it. Something to help me "understand."

She tells me I don't have to wait until Michelle comes back. I am free to go home and get some rest. She and Lucia can handle Ms. B until Michelle gets there. I look at the white envelope and wonder how much is inside. As if reading my mind, Ms. Flor says, "It's five hundred. Consider it a tip."

"Thank you," I say, even though I want to say other things and throw the money into her face. But who am I kidding? It is more money than I have ever had for myself. My greed overcomes my shame, and I smile and tell her thank you again.

"I won't tell your mother, so she doesn't have to take it. It's all yours. Your first American paycheck."

"Thank you, Ms. Flor. For everything," I say after gathering all that is polite inside me. "Why wait until tomorrow? I can leave now."

The white envelope with the five hundred dollars is burning a hole in my pocket. I have every right to each dollar—for every whiff of putrid stench, every humiliation, every moment that I had to spend chained to an old woman. I'm going to keep this money in my secret "piggy bank"—a letter-sized manila envelope taped to the back of the vanity mirror that no one ever moves. It's where I keep money I've pilfered from my mom's wallet—mostly ones and fives—while she was sleeping. I don't get an allowance like Junior, so I'll take one for myself. But I never take more than what she would miss.

It's only been six weeks, but the minute I return home, something seems off. The apartment is subdued. Stuffy. No sign of life anywhere. I look at the clock. Eleven in the morning on a Saturday. Where could everyone be?

I begin fixing myself a peanut butter and honey sandwich. I compare our home to the home I was just in. The difference is astounding. I look at the Jif peanut butter on the Formica tabletop. It's the same brand they have in that house. We also both have tins of Milo and the blue plastic boxes of SkyFlakes crackers, the pungent fish sauces in jars that have dried fish muck on the outside of the glass, bottles of soy sauce. But so many other things are different. In that house, the Jif container will be tossed when there are still a few spoonfuls of peanut butter left. In this apartment, we wipe a piece of bread around the inside of the container to make sure that all the peanut butter is gone.

Papa's high-pitched voice echoes through the hallway outside the apartment. I get up and open the door for him. He is surprised to see me, but I am more surprised to see him. He is disheveled and looks like he hasn't shaved in days.

"What are you doing here?" he asks.

"I'm done. They sent me home," I say, looking behind him to see if anyone else is with him. No one.

"Where's Junior? And Ma?" I ask.

"At Cynthia's," he says.

"Why?"

He comes inside and stands in the foyer—foyer, a new word I learned while staying at Ms. Flor's—and then plops down on the sofa. His pants, shirt, and jacket are all rumpled as though he's slept in them for days.

The summary: a standoff since Thursday.

Without him asking, I give him a glass of water. He grunts and stands up to go to the kitchen to grab a can of PBR. He drinks everything in one gulp, the beer foam spilling from his mouth. When he's done, he burps and throws the can on the floor.

I bite my tongue. "What did you do?" I finally ask.

He looks at me and says, "Your mother is seeing a younger man."

"That can't be," I say. Ma is always at work or at the apartment sleeping.

"You're gonna take her side?" he asks, his voice gruff.

He doesn't wait for me to react. He says that what happened was he clocked her with his south paw even though Papa is right-handed.

"I just tapped her in the chin. She's lucky I didn't hit her harder," he says, raising his left hand, showing proof that his nondominant side was weaker. Papa is shaking. He says that Ma deserved it because he saw her talking to a younger white man who was tall and handsome outside our apartment. She believed Papa was at work, but she didn't know that Papa had called out sick because, as he says, he had *that feeling*. Papa saw them lean close to each other, about to kiss . . . and then Papa came out screaming. The white man left, and when Ma went inside, Papa couldn't help his hand slipping. She stood there, holding her face. Then she took Junior with her and left.

"I tried to tell her I didn't mean it, but it was her fault," Papa says, looking at the wall.

I don't know how to respond to him. He asks me to talk sense to her.

"I have to know what I will say to her," I say.

"Mr. Park told me I should just let her be for a while. That women sometimes need a break from everything."

He explains that he went right to Mr. Park for advice about Ma and that Mr. Park said whenever his wife used to get angry, she would go to her sister's place in Queens. Then he would buy her a little gift and they would make up.

Pa nods to himself and looks at his hands. They are big and beefy, especially for a small man. They don't fit him at all. Even though he is muscular, his hands and forearms are large like Popeye's after he eats spinach. It's because, Papa says, he worked at a gas station when he was a teenager. Everything was manual. Pumping the gas and carrying hundreds of gasoline cans back and forth half a mile each way.

"How was your job?" he asks, changing the subject.

"It's OK. I survived," I say.

"Did she tip you? Show-offs like to tip just so they can let you know they're better than you."

"Yyy-eahh . . . she gave me something."

"How much?"

"Oh, not much," I say.

Papa doesn't say anything. The growing silence makes me uncomfortable, so I start telling him about what we ate in Ms. Flor's house and how Lucia knew how to make Greek dishes like moussaka. But Papa is only half listening.

"She's changed," he says suddenly.

"Who?"

"Don't be like her. Just because she's in America, she thinks she doesn't need anybody anymore, that she's independent." He says the last word like a bad taste he's spitting out of his mouth.

He talks more, getting flustered as he remembers past hurts, imagined or otherwise. He talks about how Lolo Manching asked for money for Ma when Papa went to see him after finding out that she was pregnant. He said he wanted to make things right.

"In a Chinese household, things are said with money. The groom pays a bride price for the woman," he says, "not the other way around. As far as the bride's family is concerned, she already belongs to the groom's family."

I tell him I don't understand and the irritation on his face grows.

"She's mine. She belongs to me. She's my responsibility."

"Because you paid for her?"

Papa's face darkens even more, and I know I've crossed a line.

"Are you defending her?" Papa asks.

"I'm not. I'm just trying to understand."

"The Bible says that you will know the tree from the fruit it bears."

I never took Papa for a religious man, but now he's spouting God and how God made Eve from Adam's rib. Women should remember that.

I let him talk and he talks for days to cut the tension in the house, circling the same issues like a song on a loop.

To pass the time, I reread passages from the novel I carried with me to America: *Madame Bovary* by Gustave Flaubert, its paperback edges fraying and its pages yellowing with age. In 1800s France, it seemed so normal to talk about what fortune the woman could bring into a man's household. Dowries were paid so girls could be married off. Love was nothing but a fantasy.

What is the difference between a bride price and a dowry?

I asked Papa once about dowries because I had read in a history book that Chinese people practiced this and because it was Papa who was Chinese and Ma Filipina, did this apply? "Did Ma's family give a dowry?" I asked. Papa scoffed. "Dowry? What dowry? I gave money to Manching."

How much a woman is worth and how attractive she is as a marriage partner boils down to how much her family could give and what she can provide in the partnership. That's what Papa said the first time I asked him about dowries.

"Why did you marry her, then?" I asked instead of saying that Ma sounded like a heifer put out to market.

"And make you a bastard child? Are you stupid like her?"

What could happen to a ruined girl? Papa had to convince Ma to get married because she was getting bigger. Soon she wouldn't have been able to hide. Ma was still waiting for her old lover to come back, a foreigner studying medicine in the Philippines. Papa said a bride price was a small thing to pay for his unborn child.

But what *is* the difference between a bride price and a dowry?

When my father's childhood friend married another girl from a Chinese family, her family demanded gold jewelry and a big sum of money. Just in case, they said. I asked my father what that meant, and he said that it was in case his friend reneged on the marriage. "It's insurance," he said. The groom gives money to the bride's family, a price to ensure her standing. A guarantee that she would be taken care of.

As for the dowry, I remember Papa and I watching a BBC documentary that focused on a poor family and a rich family marrying off their daughters. The rich family was all smiles. The daughter, who looked like a princess, looked nervous but glowing. Her father, a businessman and landowner, declared that this match was made by the gods themselves. By the time the program cut to the poor family's story, the darker-skinned daughter looked scared for her life even though she was adorned from head to foot in flowers, gold-plated jewelry, and a burgundy sari. Her father's interview was solemn. A farmer, he complained about having a daughter because he needed to come up with a sizable dowry. The bridegroom's family demanded it. He said the gods must have punished him with a daughter. His heart longed for a boy because life was already hard and bringing up a daughter was watering another plant in someone else's courtyard. In the same breath, he said that he was still a good man because he knew other families who either abandoned their infant girls, gave them away, or had them killed.

When Papa went to Lolo Manching, he told his future father-in-law, who wasn't that much older than Papa, that he was willing to give Ma a better life. Her stomach was growing; I was taking up space in her body. Ma pretended to spurn Papa's proposal talking about honor. Allegedly, Papa said that everyone must do the right thing by taking the high road and marrying a girl like Ma. He thought Ma didn't want to marry him. He had no idea that she had set a trap by getting pregnant on purpose to get him to marry her. But like Lolo Manching said, Ma got swindled. There was no money behind Papa's Chinese face.

I partially understand now why Ma was so adamant about becoming a nurse and why she thinks it's the path I should be taking, just like the rest of the Filipinos back home who would go to all the nursing schools that mushroomed in the past fifteen years. The profession lifted Ma, and others, and it also gave them a chance to escape the cycle of the endless money pit that is poverty. When you're poor, everything costs so much that even your soul is up for sale.

—

Papa and I both watch the time. It's been three days, and he knows that Ma will be at work today because she was called to do overtime, and Ma cannot resist making time-and-a-half money.

Papa, in a last-ditch effort to get Ma back, calls the hospital, at the unit she works at. His hand shakes as he dials the number. Someone picks up. "Hi. This is her husband . . . Mel's husband."

I hear someone on the end of the line saying, "I'm sorry, she don't wanna talk to you." Maybe it's the offhand way this person says it, like he's being written off, but Papa starts losing it. He begins to yell and say things like Ma is sleeping around and that she's a terrible wife and mother. He's not even at his second sentence when the woman hangs up on him. I don't know whom to feel sorry for.

He tells me that Sunday is the day when we have to confront each other.

"You mean *you* have to confront each other," I say.

"You're part of this family too."

Tita Cynthia's face moves between Ma's face and mine. Hercules is barking next to her as though he senses our discomfort. She picks him up and he calms down. "I'll give you a treat," she says as she takes a Milk-Bone biscuit from a plastic container.

Tita Cynthia's small living room is cramped from the balikbayan box she's been packing. Cans of Spam, corned beef, Hershey's chocolates, M&M's, Jergens lotion bottles, multipacks of Irish Spring and Ivory soaps, and hand-me-down clothes are stacked one on top of the other on the floor and on her table. In front of us are plates of rice noodles.

"We can't keep staying here," Ma says, her head and chin pointing to where Junior is in the corner, on the other side of the room, playing with his Game Boy.

"You know you can stay here as long as you like," Tita Cynthia says.

"You need to come back, Ma," I say, knowing that I can't go back alone to Papa, who is about to break.

"And let your father hit me again?" Ma says.

"He said he was sorry, but that you—"

"I what?"

I look at Ma and study her face. Dark circles under her eyes from lack of sleep and bruising on the right side of her face. I look at Tita Cynthia and wonder what she knows.

"If he's calmed down, then maybe you should go back, Mel. It's not good to keep things on hold. If you're going to leave him, you might as well do it cleanly," Tita Cynthia says.

"He's just not who I thought he was," Ma says.

According to Ma, Papa's conversation is uninspiring. His curiosity stopped growing as he grew older. He could not swim, dance, make her look good to other people, or even, as Ma says, "make money," and the day had come when Ma could no longer stand him. As a man, shouldn't he know more than her? Shouldn't he excel in everything else? Shouldn't he be able to provide for her? For all her wants, let alone her needs? Shouldn't he have some kind of passion leading him to better himself, to seek out some of the refinements that she longed for?

She repeats: "I can no longer stand him."

"He said he saw you with a man," I say.

"We were just talking!" Ma's face turns a deep red.

"He sent Queenie here, didn't he? That's a man who is sorry," Tita Cynthia says.

By the time Ma, Junior, and I arrive at the apartment, the place is quiet. We walk in gingerly, waiting for a trap. We half expect a dead body waiting to be discovered.

"Where is he?" she asks.

"I don't know," I say.

I see all the contents of dresser drawers strewn about. My eyes follow a trail of knickknacks and clothes on the floor. Then my feet carry me to the room where we all sleep, and my gaze pulls toward the vanity mirror. My heart stops for a very long second. I run toward the mirror, trying to avoid the debris on the floor.

"It's gone," I say when I put my hand behind the furniture, searching for the familiar feel of the manila envelope.

"What's gone?" Ma asks.

"My money."

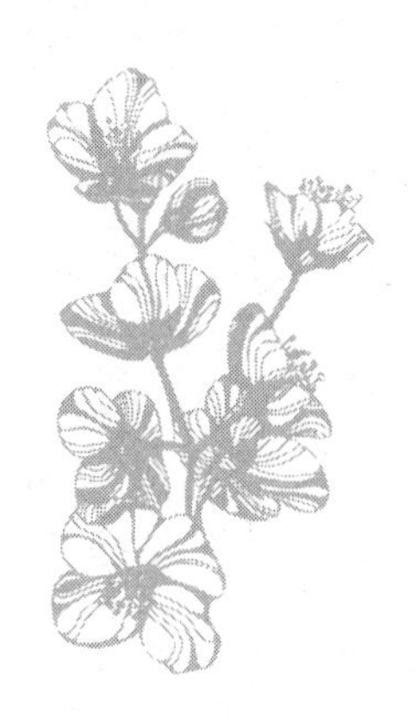

I take a pillow and start punching it, but it's not enough, so I push it into my face and start screaming until my voice is hoarse. I want to put things in my mouth. I run to the kitchen and open the fridge. I see Papa's PBR, open the can, and guzzle it down. It's not enough. I tear a bag of nachos and dump salsa on it. I grab a fistful and smash it into my mouth. I swallow as much as I can without chewing, feeling the sharp corners of the broken chips. I turn the faucet on and splash water on my face. It's not enough. I need air.

I need to get out and I do.

A familiar corner on Forty-Fifth Street. Wing Hua. The smell of deep-fried egg rolls and deep-fried chicken wings hits my nose before I enter. Inside, photographs of faded stock images of kung pao chicken, lo mein, and chicken and broccoli hang on the walls backlit by long fluorescent lights. Next to a stack of menus is a small statue of a golden cat with its right paw up. I asked Yan about it once and he said it's a good luck cat and most Asian businesses have them.

I watch the man in white chef's clothing tossing lo mein noodles and vegetables in his wok, the flames roaring underneath. The girl at the register takes a phone order and says, "Hello, Chinese food," as she dunks a batch of fried chicken wings into a vat of brown oil to refry them for another order. I hear the hiss of meat in oil, and I see the girl turn her face away to prevent the hot liquid from splattering her. I pull a takeout menu from the counter and sit on one of the plastic orange benches. The table next to me looks sticky from a collection of old sauces and spillages. I am careful not to touch it. I look blankly at the menu, my eyes straying between the prices, the descriptions, and the pictures.

I want an egg roll. It reminds me of lumpia, but we only have lumpia whenever there's a special occasion because it is such a time-consuming thing to cook. But here, if you want an egg roll, you just walk into any Chinese takeout restaurant. The convenience of it boggles me. We never had takeout in the Philippines. The Chinese food we knew was limited to the formal Chinese restaurants we went to with Pa's relatives, where round tables and lazy Susans were covered with more traditional Chinese dishes. Hong Kong–style or Amoy-style braised meats and seafood and steamed flatfishes with chopped scallions and black bean sauce.

"Hello, can I help you?" says the Chinese girl with a strong accent.

"Can I have an egg roll?"

"One dollar."

I pretend to look through my pockets, knowing I don't have any money. "Sorry, I don't have my wallet on me," I lie to save face.

"OK, no money, no egg roll."

I am suddenly very thirsty. I want to drink. "Can I have water?" I ask.

"Only bottled water," she says, pointing to the refrigerator filled with soda cans, iced tea, and Poland Spring bottles. "One dollar."

"How about tap water?"

"No tap water. You need to buy something."

I want to shout at her that I know Yan and that I'm only in this dirty little place because it feels like home, and I want to stuff my mouth with something that feels normal so I can feel normal. I want to shout at her because she reminds me of Papa and how all Chinese people care about is money and who owns what instead of helping someone who needs something.

Before I can say anything, the door opens, and a man comes in reeking of vomit, cigarettes, and alcohol. I recoil from the smell and hold my breath. He is drinking from a paper bag. He goes up to the counter and I back away.

"You serve dogmeat and cat, right?" he says, then laughs.

Have you ever eaten dogmeat? I want to ask him, remembering the old barangay where my family stayed and how the men who did the nightly patrols sometimes took strays, butchered them, and ate them while they hung out until the wee hours of the morning. They all reeked of drunkenness like him.

The girl behind the counter looks at him and doesn't say anything at first, then he repeats his question again, louder. She covers her nose. The male chef in the kitchen comes out and stares at the man. "You speak English?" the man asks the chef. The chef doesn't answer, and the man turns to the girl again. When she doesn't answer, he says, "You deaf too?"

He turns to me and asks, "You speak English?"

I nod.

"Well, can you fucking translate for me? I've been coming here so many times and this girl is new, and she don't know how to talk. Like cat got her tongue, you know? Probably 'cause they serve it." He stands erect and salutes to a small faded American flag sticker he sees under the counter. He then puts his right hand on his chest and begins to sing "The Star-Spangled Banner." His voice comes out in a surprising baritone.

"O say can you see by the dawn's early light, What so proudly we hail by the twilight's last gleeeeeamiiiiiing . . ."

"We call the police," the girl says.

"Oh, now you talk. Go right ahead. I'll call 'em for ya," the man says as he puts his hand down and takes another swig from his bottle.

"You disturbing customer," she says, pointing at me.

"Whatsa matter with you?" he asks.

"Nn-nnn-othing," I stammer.

He parrots what I say. "*Nn-nnn-othing*. Wow, you folks just like to fuck up English, huh?"

"I know English! But who wouldn't be scared when a drunk's screaming?" I yell, surprising myself and everyone else. The man looks at me for a while, sizing me up. I look back at him, mesmerized and afraid of what he might do next.

"Backbone . . . all right," he says gruffly, and starts laughing. He staggers a little bit and sits on one of the benches. "Give me beef lo mein and fried chicken wings. The combo. Don't be skimping on the beef, ya hear?" he says to the girl behind the counter. Within seconds she says, "Twelve dollars." We all look at the man and watch him take a stack of singles out of his worn leather wallet. He peels them one by one and counts out loud. When he's done, he puts them in front of her.

"See, I am a customer! I pay."

"What kinda soda you want?" she asks.

"You got ginger ale?"

She gives him a can from the refrigerator. He opens it up and takes a big gulp before letting out a loud, long burp. He looks at the can and smiles and then leans back against the wall and immediately starts snoring.

The girl behind the counter calls me: "Hey, girl."

I approach.

"On the house," she says as she hands me a bottle of water and the egg roll I wanted. She even threw in some fortune cookies.

I thank her and, suddenly, feel nauseated. I start vomiting on the street. Papa's beer and bits of salsa and chips.

By the time I get home, I am hollowed out.

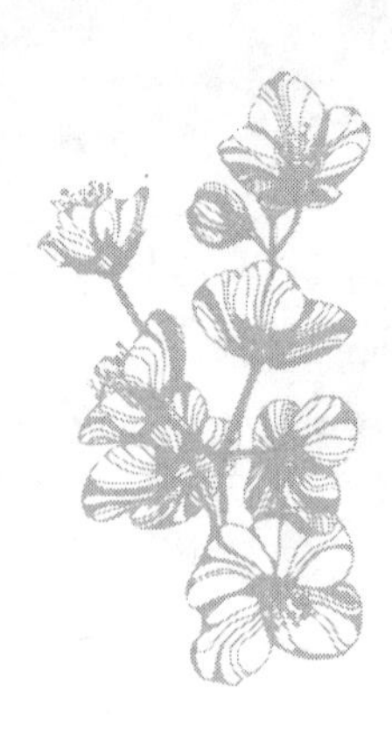

It's late when Papa gets back. He smells of cheap liquor and I'm reminded of the man in the Chinese restaurant. Before I can ask him where the money is, he presents to Ma a small red velvet box, the kind we've seen in Chinatown jewelry stores. Ma opens it and takes out a yellow pendant on a yellow chain.

"It's twenty-four karats," Papa says, explaining that Chinese like this kind of gold because it's shinier and yellower, which means that it is luckier. I realize that he's a man running out of luck and that he's trying to buy Ma back with an expensive trinket.

You don't buy a trinket to have luck.

You don't steal from someone and say it's your luck.

I laugh.

I want to kill him. There is so much white in my vision it's like my blood is seeping away and angry lights are hitting my temples. My breath comes out loud and uneven. Pitiful sounds emerge from my throat. My parents look at me, and their faces scream: *What on earth.* Even Junior starts to back away, but I control myself. I control the white spots I see. I control my breathing. I take a few steps back. The inevitable is coming.

"What's this for?" Ma asks, turning back to Papa.

"For you. You like jewelry," he says.

"Where'd you get the money? Did you steal it?"

"Why would I steal it? I've been saving," he says.

Liar! I want to scream. I want to bash his head and watch the blood ooze out. The white spots get bigger. I feel the air leaving me. I start shaking. That feeling of exploding inside hurts so much I start scratching my neck to prevent any sound from coming out of my throat.

I can suddenly see him so clearly.

They are speaking.

This old man and this young woman.

Him saying she used him, shitting on his head and flaunting a new man.

Her saying he used her for her youth, using her to come to America.

Shouting at each other, indenting the walls with their words.

I want to rip heads apart.

Was he the prince in shining armor, the champion, the rescuer he claims to be?

This man, groveling before a woman with a yellow necklace that I paid for by cleaning someone else's shit.

"You're nothing," Ma says.

"Say that again," Pa counters, trying to stand to his full height but failing a little because he had already started shrinking a few years ago.

She says it again, with more venom. She already feels the poison in her system. I could feel it for her. Her thoughts become mine.

"You call yourself a man? Shouldn't you provide for all of us? Shouldn't you make more money than me? Shouldn't you have been the one to get us out of the Philippines?" Ma screams.

"Where did I pick you up? *You* were nothing. *You* worked in a bar spreading your legs to every man who suited your fancy—"

"I had one boyfriend before you!"

"But you've had sex with so many. Don't tell me you're so pure. Don't tell me you didn't do that for money."

I try to cover Junior's ears, but he pulls his head away from my hands. I am sad for him, and sad for myself, and sad for everything that has happened, that is happening, and everything that will happen.

Papa is crying. Mama is crying. Junior is crying. My hands reach to wipe the wetness from my face—I am crying too.

Papa opens one of the larger suitcases we have and starts stuffing it with clothes. Without finishing, he takes another bag and starts doing the same thing—grabbing and stuffing.

I've never seen him so angry, so beaten. Even that time when we lost all our money in the world because he thought he was making it grow with people he trusted. "Never trust people who have nothing to lose," he said. We watch him quietly, not wanting to disturb his decision. I know he feels the need to be stoic to keep his pride intact.

And then suddenly, Papa is laughing. Laughing so hard, I become more afraid than angry, more afraid than sad. It's the sudden break from his previous expression that frightens me—hearkening back to a time long ago when it was acceptable and even expected for a man to kill someone who had wronged him, especially a woman.

"You're not even a real man," Ma says again. "Real men provide and don't wait for their wives to feed them!"

What possesses a woman to tell a man who is already feeling like a worm that he is a worm and that his worth is not even that of a worm? What good does it do?

We all look at Ma.

What is she doing?

What has she done?

"You want to see what a real man does?" he bellows. He runs to the kitchen, his whole body shaking. He pulls open the kitchen drawer and takes out a butcher knife. He turns to Ma and looks at her with so much malice. So much hate.

"I'll show you what a real man does," he says.

I blink several times. The white spots in my eyes grow larger, palpitating. A blindness consumes me.

He is in a rage, so angry that he can barely get the words out. He says he has never been as degraded as he has been in America. Almost seventy! At his age, he should be retired. Instead, he has never worked so hard in all his adult life, picking up people's garbage. His voice cracks.

"People look at me like I am scum," he says, slowly walking toward us while we back away with tiny steps, watching him and then watching the knife.

He accuses Ma of independence, unfettered by social boundaries that held our society in the old country with the old ways. He accuses her American self of being monstrous, aggressive, and foreign—just like this country. He says that he overhears her talk to her friends. How he should already be in a nursing home with other old people. That his flesh is beginning to hang and that it is an embarrassment to be around him.

"You're waiting for me to die. Worse than a dog," Papa says, the butcher knife swinging when he lifts his other hand to make a point.

In America, I am learning, nobody believes in the dead and they certainly don't care for the elderly. This is the land of the young who are ready to grind their way for the dream. But once their youth is spent, they become nothing. A burden who should just die already.

"In this country, if you work hard, you get somewhere. But you have to work hard when you're young. You know what they say to me at the hospital? At church? Ask anyone who sees me with you. They ask me if I lost my mind shacking up with an old man. Do you know how ashamed I am!" Ma says, her voice rising octaves.

Everything slows down and speeds up.

Our backs are to the bedroom door. Suddenly, Ma pushes us into the bedroom. She just barely manages to lock the door when he lunges after her. Junior whimpers and I am surprised when I hear a croak come from my throat.

Papa kicks the door. It doesn't budge, thank God.

Behind the door, he screams. It's a sound I will never forget.

The sound of a wounded animal. Pathetic and primal. Like goats going out for slaughter. The sudden pitch of pain. The volume rising. Then the loud silence after.

"You win," he says, defeated.

From where we huddle, we hear the shuffling of objects, the clatter of the knife on the sink—steel on steel. The air we didn't know we were holding releases from our chests. Junior and I cling to each other, and I think of all the what-ifs. What if Papa had burst through? What if he had stabbed Ma? What if he had stabbed me and Junior? What would have become of us?

We hear footsteps. Doors opening. Then silence. We wait like that, huddled together, sweating, crying. Five minutes. Ten minutes. Twenty minutes. A lifetime.

Ma opens the door.

The living room is a mess. Papa took none of his bags. We step around the mess and go into the hallway and see all the doors have been left open. Ma closes and locks them. On the table, we see Papa has even left his keys behind. Junior picks them up.

"What are we going to do?" I ask Ma.

"Nothing," she says.

Junior asks the question all three of us are thinking. "What if he comes back?"

"Are you afraid of your father?" Ma asks.

Junior doesn't answer.

I nod. "He's not in his right mind," I say.

"As long as I'm not responsible for him, he's free to do whatever he wants," Ma says.

"He's old and—"

"Incompetent?" Ma asks.

I want to tell her no, he's not. But my tongue stops as memories flood me. The time Papa felt insulted and punched another man for coming on to him. Or the time when he wouldn't wash Junior's diaper because it was "women's work." Perhaps Ma is right. Perhaps he is incompetent.

"If he wants to come back here, I don't think I can live like before. Not anymore," Ma says.

"A divorce?" Junior asks.

"I don't know yet," Ma says.

"Why did you marry him?" I ask.

"I thought he had money," Ma says plainly.

When I was ten years old, there was a woman who lived in our subdivision who slit her wrists because her boyfriend left her. She was so pretty, she got attention from many boys in the neighborhood even though her skin color was darker than anyone cared for. She was one of the many local college students from a barrio three hours away by jeepney.

That day, from the second-floor window of our house, I saw her being rushed to the hospital, her male roommate carrying her in his arms while she screamed "Just let me die" over and over again.

At first, we didn't know what was happening, but the story that went around the barangay was that she and her boyfriend had sex, the boyfriend found her lacking in some way, and then he left her for another woman who lived in Manila. The girl survived—stitches on both her wrists were proof that she once had the conviction to die by her own hand.

She kept her wrists covered with swatches of cloth bands but would, on occasion, show some of the housewives her scars. The housewives talked about her behind her back, saying that she deserved what happened to her because she gave herself to a man she wasn't married to.

"Only an idiot does that," said one of the women, and spat on the ground.

The girl stopped going to school and started working at the local department store. She eventually graduated from her studies and moved back to her hometown, never to be heard from again.

No one wants to be that girl, the crazy girl who didn't know she became a woman by having sex with a man who wasn't her husband when her only job was to keep herself pure and shame-free. Someone who lets her emotions rule her. The barangay women said she should have cut her losses and put the knife away instead of using it on herself, and that now, no man would want her. "But at least she didn't get pregnant," another woman said, carrying one of her sleeping children in her arms, her hip pointed to one side to support his weight. The other women murmured in assent.

Since I was just a child, the brood of clucking women disregarded me and the other children I played with. "Girls these days just open their legs for anyone," said one of the women, who sweated so much she always had a towel wrapped around her neck.

"Serves her right for being so loose," another woman said.

The women spoke openly about the blood that spurted out of the girl's wrists as she was carried—how it marked the ground—and the shame the whole incident incurred. As they washed clothes in the common area or hung them on the line, other tidbits of threadbare fact and fiction stitched together. Even a trip to the sari-sari store for a head of garlic became a place where the girl's story morphed from tragedy to scandal to a cautionary tale for young girls when the women decided that the children running around needed a story to put them in their place.

Papa and Ma told me to stay away from her, and I mostly did, except for that one time before we moved, way before Ma left for New York. The girl could no longer wash her own clothes because of her damaged wrists, so she washed them with her feet. She would put her clothes in a basin and step on them, just like how I saw, in a documentary I watched on a VHS, people in France step on grapes to make wine.

That afternoon, with no one around, I stood next to her and watched her, and she turned to me and smiled. Her body was heavy but with its innocence still intact, skin soft like the flesh of certain ripened fruits. Something about her was hard to grasp, as though she was an otherworldly being—that very something just made you want to kill her with your bare hands. Without breaking eye contact, she unhooked the large buttons on her blouse and freed her breasts the size of bread buns made of milk, her dark nipples the size of raisins. She began to swing herself back and forth, listening to her own beat as she stepped on her clothes.

My eyes swallowed her breasts, mesmerized, and my gaze licked her skin, and I felt a thrill of fear and desire run through me. She laughed and looked at me, daring me to join. To touch her in places. To cross a line. But before any of that could happen, voices sounded. The ones inside my head, layered with the things the barangay women said, and then in real time, Papa's voice yelling for me to stay away, and for her to keep her insanity to herself. The girl kept her clothes off, breasts hanging, and Papa's voice rose to scream obscenities, but he kept looking at her, staring at her breasts, with her exercising a kind of power over him. "Manong Sam, you want to touch?" she asked Papa, calling him by his first name. Papa forgot, for a moment, that I stood next to him. He blinked a few times, and she pulled him into her spell as she waved her hips, and she positioned her breasts for him to get a better view. For a moment, she conquered him, and he was at a loss for words, and I watched with great fascination how Papa blushed, then lunged at her as though he were going to hit her but stopped short when she hardly reacted. Her hands reached out to him, then he pushed her. She fell and her elbows broke her fall. I cried out, afraid that her wrists would start bleeding again. I looked at her and saw that she smiled, but it was a sad smile, and Papa dragged me away while calling her a bad woman. I turned around and saw that she sat up on the ground, touching her elbows, and with her hair disheveled and her breasts hanging like ripe fruit, she started singing an old folk song, and I watched as she put her blouse back on.

—

Sometimes, when I hear my parents fight, I think about that day and imagine Papa's face. It's as though this memory is preserved in amber. His look was the look of someone who desired both love and death at the same time, and I witnessed how desire can turn so quickly. What would he have done if I hadn't been there? Would he have loved her with his touch and tongue, or would he have murdered her with his hands?

The phone rings. Once. Twice. I pick up thinking it might be Papa. It's been almost a month since that fateful day. We talked about Papa at home, but in hushed tones, just in case our voices somehow had the power to manifest him back in our lives with the kind of rage he wanted to pour over our heads. We often wondered what we would say to him and how he would fit in the wake of this chasm.

I pick up the receiver from the wall and put it against my ear.

"Hello."

"It's me." I recognize Zeus's voice.

For a moment, I forget my father. I didn't realize how easy it is to forget to be rational, being completely overwhelmed by one thing that banishes all sense of reason. Zeus's voice. He asks me how I am, and I tell him I am fine. But I don't know what to say after. I feel guilty that I am so happy to hear his voice. But what the hell. It's been five weeks since we spoke. He had my number, and he didn't call. Not once. But too much happened. What was I going to tell him if he had called me then? That my father almost killed us all? He already knew about my family's past. What would he think of me now?

"You sound different," Zeus says.

"So perceptive," I say, keeping my voice light.

"Are you glad that I called?" he asks.

"Maybe."

"I want to take you out for your birthday," he says. "If you don't have plans with your family, that is."

"You remembered," I say.

There aren't going to be family plans. Ma is in a fugue state, working all hours. Junior is falling deeper into computer games and spends time playing at friends' apartments, which Ma has all but allowed because she's never home to say no. A few weeks ago he asked Ma if he could stay overnight for the first time at his friend Michael's house. Ma said nothing. Then Junior explained that Michael lived in our neighborhood and that Michael's mom invited him for dinner and to stay the night. Ma said yes before he even finished speaking, which surprised us all. She never says yes to these things since she believes, or at least she once did, that kids are supposed to stay home and do what they're told. After she said yes, that was it. He was at friends' houses like musical chairs and only stayed home when no one invited him for dinner or to stay the night. I had told him one time that he was spending too much time at his friends' houses and his response was, "You're not my mother." I never bothered him again after that.

We think we know loneliness, but after Papa left, a space opened that we didn't even realize could exist in our lives. We relied on television shows and Hollywood films to tell us the stories of American life. We thought that in America there would be neighbors or friends or family members always coming by unannounced, always friendly or too friendly, always curious, always a laugh track after every joke and every stumble, and always over moments when someone plays the fool. These people, in their American lives, live happily. None of this brokenness.

Zeus asks me if I want to see the new vampire movie. My mouth finally works and I say yes. I ask him about Ms. B, Ms. Flor, and Dr. McDonnell. I even ask him about Lucia's birthday and how they spent it and, after this kind of chitchat, hang up. I almost forget that Ms. Flor thinks I am not good enough for her son. Maybe she's right.

When I hang up, I feel a heaviness in my chest lift a little.

I take stale tortilla chips, a half-opened jar of salsa, and a can of beer Yan brought me. "To ease some pain," he had said. I was finally able to get ahold of Yan three weeks ago. He kept apologizing for not being around. "Work, you know," he said a couple of times. Beer was Yan's peace offering. "If you can't drink it, maybe your dad . . ." Then Yan's voice trailed off; he knew Papa wasn't around to drink what I wouldn't.

I don't like beer, but there is something desperate about my thirst, so I open it and drink it all in almost one gulp, liquid spilling through my lips.

"Are you sure you're the birthday girl?" Zeus asks, noting my disheveled outfit and my rumpled, frizzy hair. I only realize that I'm a sight when he looks at me from top to bottom. I lean back in the passenger's seat.

"Sorry, I didn't dress up," I say.

"All good," he says. "It's not like we're on a date or anything."

"At least I showered."

All the dates I've seen on shows involved flowers or chocolate or even a stuffed toy animal. My eighteenth birthday is a corpse resting in a coffin.

He starts driving and we sit in silence for a few minutes. He picks up speed a little and I notice how the sound from the outside doesn't permeate the car like it does in Tita Cynthia's, even when she plays her 1970s music, and I say as much to Zeus. "It's a luxury car," he says, as though that explains everything, and I remember that his mother drives a Benz. He has the radio station KTU playing dance music in the background.

"What happened to you?" he asks after a while.

"Do you want the long story or the short story?" I ask.

He asks me first for the abbreviated version. I tell him that Papa is gone.

"What do you mean gone?"

I explain that he just left after brandishing a knife and threatening Ma, telling her he would show her what a real man would do.

He double-parks the car a few blocks away from the cinema in Park Slope and leaves the engine running.

"That's terrible!" Zeus says. "Why would anyone want to do that to their wife?"

I don't answer him.

After a few seconds, he pulls a joint and a lighter from the glove compartment. He takes a drag and smoke comes out in a long O. He waves the smoke toward the open window and offers me the joint.

"This will help," he says.

I hesitate for a moment, then take it from him. I look at the embers at the tip of the joint and I inhale deeply. I start coughing, and Zeus laughs. I give it back to him—still coughing, throat burning. He takes another drag.

"Coughing's normal. Don't look so scared," he says, watching me.

"I don't like it," I say, feeling prickles in my throat.

"You have to wait a little bit for it to hit you."

He stares at the view through the windshield, and my eyes follow, and we watch cars pass.

"I hate it when adults fight," Zeus says. He takes another drag of his joint, looking at the smoke. "My dad died in a car crash. He had a big argument with Mommy over Lola and left the house drunk. He didn't see that he was driving on the wrong side of the road."

"I'm sorry to hear that."

"You've been here a little while. You must have seen her new husband and his nightcaps," he says, his voice low.

I had seen Dr. McDonnell passed out with an empty glass either next to him or sitting on his potbelly when I was at their house. All the empty liquor bottles.

"That's what he taught Mommy."

"I guess that's what real men do. Teach women something," I say, unsure if I mean it or if it's sarcasm.

"What's that supposed to mean?"

"I don't know. Do you know what real men do?"

"No. I bet nobody knows what that means. We have ideas, but who knows if those ideas are right. I mean, sure, I'm a Greek boy and a jock, but it doesn't mean I conform to those stereotypes. I don't drink till I drop. I have good grades. Is that the answer you're looking for?"

"Not really. I think some people have definite ideas," I say, thinking about Papa and Ma.

"Do you know what real women do?" Zeus asks, turning a corner.

The answer is a trapdoor. A girl wants to be a woman. She gets there, somehow—through directions, through maps, through stories. But when she reaches the destination, the ground shifts. Suddenly, what worked before no longer does. What glitters isn't gold after all. She has no choice but to change. She pulls out a different person inside herself, like a magician who pulls a rabbit out of a hat. A good girl now, a beggar woman later. Was that beggar woman always inside the good girl? The body holds multitudes.

Ma started out as a beggar woman. Was she ever a good girl? Free and innocent from the crime of poverty? To me, the whole world is filled with beggar women desperate to sell their youth and men desperate to purchase and live off them. Their youth prized, masticated, then swallowed. Where do the stories of these men and women begin? In the womb? As innocent good boys and good girls? In the desire that a man feels? Then, when these women have nothing left once their youth is taken, they grow up, and they shed their child selves. Are they nothing then? My mother, the woman. My father, the man.

"Do you think I'm pretty?" I ask Zeus.

"If you're fishing, I am not biting," he says. "I hate it when girls play that game. You still haven't answered the question."

I take a deep breath and exhale. "I don't know, to be honest," I say.

"That makes two of us . . . but are we supposed to know the answer already? Can't we just discover things?" he asks. Then he presents me with a small pink cardboard box.

"What's this?" I ask, surprised.

"It's nothing special. Just a small present. Maybe something a real man might do? Or better yet, maybe something a real person would do."

I open it and it's a chocolate cupcake with chocolate icing. He takes a striped pink candle, puts it on the cupcake, and then flicks the flint wheel of the silver Zippo lighter with his thumb. Little sparks fly like lightning bugs.

"Happy birthday, Queenie," he says.

I look at him and look at the cupcake in front of me. The ground shakes and my vision blurs from the lagoons in the backs of my eyes. I'm skydiving from my rib cage. I bite my lip, not knowing what to say.

"Make a wish."

He buys a large red-and-white bucket of buttered popcorn and an extra-large soda, most of it ice, and takes two straws.

"Coke OK with you?" he asks. I nod.

We find our seats in the crowded theater. It feels strange to be in a movie theater with Zeus. It almost feels like a date. As the film plays, Zeus whispers jokes in my ear every so often, and I laugh. The movie features a classic love triangle—a woman and two men. There's always unrequited love. Someone's always hurting.

"I really hate this story," I say.

"Why?" Zeus asks. "It's hilarious."

"These are all just teenage fantasies of happily ever after."

"You sound so jaded," he says.

The film ends, and we stretch our legs. As the credits roll, and as people exit the theater, he grabs my hand. It feels nice.

"We're close to the park. Want to walk a little?" he asks. I nod and we start our midnight stroll.

"You're holding my hand."

"I am, aren't I? You're so observant."

"Why?" I ask. Didn't his mother say that he's off-limits? I never agreed to anything, but still.

"I don't know. You're just so observant."

"No, I mean, why are you holding my hand?"

"You're holding it back, so we're both holding hands," he says.

I let him. Somehow, the act has a promise.

When we get to Third Street and Prospect Park West, I pull him behind a column at the entrance to the park. Although surprised, he lets me, following my lead. The intimate motion produces an image in my head. A girl and a boy locked in an embrace, their faces obscured. When I put my face on the girl's face, I feel a thrill. And I put Zeus's face on the boy's. Then an unbidden thought comes. Ma's face on the girl's and Papa's face on the boy's. Ma, a girl, and Papa, an old man. The image looks wrong. His white hair and his cracked skin and her black hair and her plump skin and they are both there standing and screaming. I imagine Ma biting her tongue and looking away as he leers at her. I push the image far away, but the more I push, the more distorted it becomes until I feel like I'm about to explode.

The image changes and it is me and Zeus again.

Here and now.

"Do you like this face?" I ask Zeus.

"You have a pretty face," he says.

I am suddenly aware as I look at myself in his eyes that I have two faces. The good girl face and beggar woman face. One face smiles while the other face has a litany of lamentations. One face is raised to smile because if this face doesn't smile, then she's the kind of girl that men don't like. The girls that men don't like suffer—they are punished precisely because they are the girls that men don't like.

Sometimes it's as simple as that. Then one face begins to eat the other face, like hatchlings fighting and pecking the weaker ones because, somehow, it is the circle of life.

"Your lola said I'm fat," I remind him.

"I like meat on the bone," he says.

I can tell he feels sorry for me—his eyes say it to my face. Something elastic is expanding and contracting inside me. My heart is growing and being cut apart with each breath. It hurts.

"You don't need to feel sorry for me," I say.

"Sorry for you? What makes you say that?"

"I don't need words to know. I can feel."

"Maybe you're feeling wrong."

I slowly put my hand under his belt loop, tracing a pattern on his jeans. My hand has become a dog on a leash, following a pull outside of its control.

"Don't men want this?" I ask.

"I thought you were different," he says.

"I am. I am so different."

"Why are you doing this?"

"Just kiss me."

He kisses me, and I kiss him back, and I am ferocious, and I can tell this stuns him as much as it stuns me. I want to swallow his face, but he is pulling back. I look at him and I don't understand. I want to share my pain.

"Not like this," he says.

"Fuck me," I say, a thrill running through me saying such words.

"What?"

"Fuck me," I say again.

I already know something, I realize. That it's not clothes or looks that make women beautiful or ugly. Attitude stirs desire. I remember witnessing that woman in the neighborhood, crazy with love and devastation. She knew the power of desire. Its force almost killed her. She had this intimate knowledge that it could kill and if she could wield it, it would not hurt her. When she turned her attention to Papa, to try to make him desire her, it was her way to tame the beast.

"No," Zeus says, pulling back even more.

"Why not?" I ask, faltering.

"This feels wrong."

I want to tell him it doesn't. Instead, I press myself closer to him, hoping that my body heat will persuade him to touch me back.

"Aren't you supposed to be innocent?" he asks.

"Am I?"

I think how I used to watch Papa's porn when I was twelve. With horror and fascination, I watched what people did when they didn't want anyone to watch. This is what the boys in school teased girls about. This is what boys want when they play doctor. This is what boys want so they feel good. What the boy wants, the girl wants too.

I think of Ma.

I'm surprised that he hasn't brought up my mother and her past. Maybe I take after her. Maybe that's why I feel what I feel right now.

"Maybe I should take you home," he says.

"You don't like me, then?" I ask.

"I do, that's why this feels weird. Look, I've got my share of loose girls, and you're supposed to be a nice Filipina girl, you know?"

"I'm half-Chinese."

"Yeah, that too, but you're Filipina and you're from there. Mommy says Filipina girls are supposed to be good. She wants me to meet more Filipina girls, and, you know, I think it's not a bad idea."

I laugh, remembering the white envelope she gave me. "Are you sure your mother wants you to meet more good Filipina girls? She must think I'm a bad girl."

"No, she likes you. She said you took care of Lola really well."

As help, she thinks highly of me. A blackness in my heart grows. Zeus squirms away and untangles himself from my body.

Several feet away, we hear another couple fighting. We turn our heads in their direction as they get louder. The other couple gets closer. Another boy. Another girl. The girl says she doesn't feel good and suddenly runs toward me, away from her boyfriend. She tries to hug me, a stranger, and vomits on my chest before immediately passing out. The bile on my clothes smells strongly of alcohol and acid. Bits of masticated meat land on the skin of my neck and on my clothes. I cry out in disgust, almost wanting to vomit myself, and I feel the saliva pool in my mouth.

The boy with her says, "Oh shit," and takes her from me, dragging her limp body toward him. Her hand is still on my arm as he pulls her away. "I want to go home," she says, her words barely audible. "I'll take you home, sweetheart," he answers in a way that makes me wonder if they are really together.

"Do you need help?" Zeus asks him, and the boy says no thanks and how he's sorry his girlfriend vomited on me, and that his car is parked right there, and he just needs to drive her home.

"But you're both drunk," I say, alarmed.

The boy laughs and says, "It's all right, I'm still sort of sober." He mumbles sorry and carries his drunk girlfriend away.

"Fuck," Zeus says under his breath.

"What?"

"I'll tell you later."

Zeus excuses himself and runs to the couple. He talks to the guy, who has just put the girl into the passenger seat. The guy pulls his phone from his pocket and shows something to Zeus. They talk some more, then shake hands. The guy drives off and Zeus runs back to me.

"What was that about?"

"I just wanted to make sure that was really his girl."

"Is she?"

"He had pictures of them together."

"She was passed out. What if they're not together?"

Zeus lets out a breath. "I know. But what can I do? Hold him hostage?" He notices my shallow breaths. "Are you OK?"

"Do I look OK? I smell like vomit and feel like shit." I start crying. My birthday has been a disaster.

"I'm sorry," Zeus says, pulling some napkins from one of his pockets and handing them to me. I wipe what I can from my denim jacket and my T-shirt.

"Let me find a deli to get you water."

"I'll come with you," I say, not wanting to be left alone, thinking that there might be more drunk girls lurking in corners.

We walk a few blocks and find a small deli. I tell him I'll wait for him outside, since I am feeling ashamed by how I smell. He nods, and within minutes, he's outside with two small bottles of Poland Spring and more tissues. He gives them to me, and I pour water over myself.

"Hey . . . I'm really sorry to do this, but can I just call you a car service? I just had my car cleaned." Zeus sounds apologetic.

"Yeah, that's fine." How could I dirty the beautiful interior of his car? That would be selfish of me.

During the car ride home, I pinch my face hard, the face of the other girl, the girl who is me but not me, the one who is the beggar woman in disguise.

I know the driver is watching me. I don't care. There had been no good-night kiss, but Zeus gave me money for the car ride.

And this makes me feel cheap and poor.

And I smell bad.

And I'm poor.

Good Filipina girls do not sit in a boy's car.

Good Filipina girls do not sit in a boy's car smoking weed.

Good Filipina girls have families who throw them parties when they turn eighteen.

Filipinos like to celebrate milestone birthdays, especially for girls. Eighteen is a big one. It's a sign that the girl is no longer a girl but a woman. The debutante selects eighteen members of her court, eighteen roses, eighteen everything to mark the passage from childhood to adulthood. Papa thinks that some Filipino traditions like debuts are wasteful and just another opportunity to show off what people don't have.

We knew families in the Philippines who scrimped and saved or even took on debt to give their daughters a lavish send-off to adulthood. "It's not even a wedding, what are you setting these girls up for?" he would say when people asked him if he was planning on giving me a big debut. Ma, already in America at the time, didn't care one way or another, as long as she didn't have to spend a dime.

Some of my old classmates wrote to me. They sent me pictures from their eighteenth birthdays, with their gowns and happy faces. In my jealousy, I burned the pictures.

—

Back at the apartment, the lights are still on. I look at the couch where Pa would have been sleeping if he were still here. Ma is at work for her night shift at the hospital down the block. Junior is awake and playing *Grand Theft Auto* on his PlayStation 2. He looks up from his game and sees me, taking in my rumpled hair and my shoes, which have splatters of dried vomit on them. He scrunches his nose.

"You stink."

"Really?" I answer dryly.

"I'm not even going to ask, but you're late."

"You don't care that I am late and that I stink?"

"I'm not your mother," he says, shrugging and returning to his game.

I try to respond with words, but the only syllable I can muster is a sound. His answer makes me sad. Does one of us need to be a mother for us to care? I smile at him even though he can't see. I don't have the heart to muss his hair like I normally would.

"Ma called asking if you're home."

"What did you tell her?"

"That you were sleeping."

I watch him play his game, his fingers navigating the controller fast. He lies without remorse for me. We are siblings, not mother and child. Maybe this is the best I can ask for. We stick together since no one else will stick around for us.

"Good. I owe you one."

I inspect myself in the bathroom mirror. I don't recognize my face; it looks like a stranger's. Long hair falling to the sides, the high cheekbones, the hollow expression in the eyes, the tightness around the mouth. I touch this girl's face and trace the area around her left cheek. She doesn't flinch. Tears roll down her cheeks. Fat translucent pearls. I try to shush her, but the sound garbles her mouth, making my chest hurt. I look away from the girl in the mirror. I take off my filthy clothes, throw them into a plastic bag, and shove the bag to the bottom of the hamper.

I shower and scrub myself clean with Ivory soap, letting the hot water wash off what it can—this shame from the night.

My brother is snoring. I envy him his peace.

My head hits the pillow. The smell of sheets, unwashed for a month, engulfs me. I take a deep breath and wonder just how much of the past I am inhaling. The sheets smell of everyone in the family. In a few days we will need to go to the laundromat and wash away the smell of old memories. Right now, I find comfort in the smell. I breathe. In. Out. The floor of my lungs moves in sync with my breath. I slow down. In. Out. Maybe if I slow down, I can slow time. I want to run from my thoughts. Travel into the forest of darkness.

I can't stop tossing and turning, so eventually I call Yan even though it's late. He picks up on the first ring.

"Are you crazy? My family is sleeping!" he says, whispering.

"Can you meet?"

"You realize it's two in the morning, right?"

"I knew you'd still be up."

He groans. "Fine, come on."

We meet at the Fifty-Third Street subway station. The clerk is sleeping. Yan swipes me in and instructs me to open the metal gate. We find a wooden bench and, finally, we sit.

"What's on your mind?" he asks.

I tell him about my night. He listens intently, laughs when he hears about the girl who vomited on me, and then apologizes half-heartedly when he sees me glare at him.

"That's sweet he didn't want to just fuck you, I guess."

"You're so crude, you know that?"

"You've seen one of these, right?" he asks, laughing. He takes out a small square plastic package—it could be medicine or candy—with a circle protruding from it.

"I use protection and have it with me all the time because you never know, so as your friend, I am giving you one of these."

A condom. I had only seen one once before. When I was in fifth grade, one of the boys from school brought a condom from his parents' stash and then tried to feed it to the school's pet chicken after the boys had their fill of laughing uncontrollably and touching it. Of course, all the girls scattered but watched from a distance, knowing that it was a bad thing but a bad thing that we must know about anyhow.

"Do you know how to use it?"

I shake my head no. Yan takes out a banana and another wrapped condom from his backpack.

"Why do you have a banana in your backpack?"

"It was my snack, dummy!"

"At two in the morning?"

"I carry it for emergencies."

He flips the banana so that the end of it sticks out, then he tears open the package.

"I'm sacrificing one to show you how it's done," he says.

Yan sounds so worldly next to me. He is only a year older, but how he looks and how he talks, he sounds like somebody's dirty uncle doing things the family would be ashamed of. He unrolls the rubber on top of the banana to cover the whole length of it.

"Voilà! Protection."

—

The R train comes and we get on and take it to the end of the line, to Ninety-Fifth. We cross the platform and hop on the next Manhattan-bound train. There's no one else around us. "Finally, alone," Yan jokes. We sit down. The train is one of the new ones. Gray and sleek. There aren't many individual seats, just a long uninterrupted row.

"I don't like this new design," I say.

"Yeah, it feels cold," he replies.

We exit our station on Fifty-Third and walk outside until we finally sit on a public bench next to an overflowing garbage bin.

"There's a guy I mess around with too," he says.

"What do you mean?" I ask.

"We fuck."

I don't know how to respond. I shouldn't be shocked by Yan's casual announcement, but I am. He's been hiding something from me, and now I understand. Can I blame him when all I do is talk about my family problems?

"How did you meet?"

"Craigslist. Men for Men section," Yan says. "That's how I meet all of them."

"All of them?"

"Don't judge me."

He knows me well. I tell him everything. But he chooses what to tell me and when. Not only was he a truant, but he was also a slut.

"Aren't you afraid of diseases?" I ask.

"That's why I always use protection. Duh."

"Does that mean that you're on a break or something? Instead of fucking another guy?"

"I think I'm in love, but he's been too busy to see me the past month and I'm just not in the mood for a casual fuck right now."

Yan had only been available, strangely, after Papa left. Now everything fits. Yan's love life took a nosedive and so he is here with me right now.

"Busy? But isn't he your boyfriend?"

"No. We meet when he has time," Yan says.

"Why is that?"

"People don't want any of your problems. The moment you open your mouth and show that you're a person . . . people don't want that. Not even your lovers. It complicates things. Especially when he gives you three hundred dollars every time you suck his dick."

Yan says that after messaging on Craigslist, they met in person at a seedy bar on the Lower East Side. He said he liked Jim the moment he laid eyes on him. He was tall with long blond hair and scruff on his face, and he was wearing a leather jacket adorned with a skull. Jim bought him three Long Island iced teas and they went to the bathroom to give each other blowjobs.

"That's quick," I say.

"It's different, I guess," he says, and shrugs. "But it's not all about fucking, you know? We did other shit. Besides, I found out in the bathroom when I took his head that he was wearing a hairpiece!"

We laugh loudly.

"I told him to just keep his hairpiece off because he looked sexier without it. After that, we went to Dallas BBQ, and I ordered a steak for the first time. Have you ever had steak? Like, real steak?"

I shake my head. The only steak I know is Filipino beefsteak cooked with soy sauce and onions.

Yan says the waitress asked them how they would like their steak and Yan was so confused. Jim said he'd have his rare, Yan asked him what that was, and Jim said that it means the meat is still bloody and it's at its softest and juiciest. Yan asked the waitress how else it could be cooked, and she said rare, medium, well-done. Well-done sounded good to Yan so he ordered his steak that way, but when he got it, he was so disappointed. The meat was so dry that it felt like he was chewing through leather. Jim paid for everything, then they went to the park and saw other men having trysts.

"He asked me if I was game," Yan says, "and said that there's nothing like cock to make me feel alive."

But Yan says he felt dirty.

He laughs, but it is a pained laugh.

Yan seems different. I want to ask him more, but the air shifts. I can feel him shutting down, nursing his own private hurts.

Another day at our American home, living our American lives.

In the year we've been here, we've slowly started living in an American TV drama and not a sitcom. What have I been doing? Ma has almost paid off what she owes from bringing us over, thanks to her doing overtime shifts and my meager contributions from part-time jobs cleaning for her friends, walking their dogs, and doing their laundry. They work all the time and hardly have the free time to do any chores. When they get home, all they want to do is veg out in front of their television sets to watch The Filipino Channel and their variety shows.

—

I try to walk away from Ma as she screams at Junior, her eyes afire. He hasn't been doing well in school and there was an incident. One of his teachers had asked to meet with Ma and Ma wasn't looking forward to coming in to talk about how bad of a parent she is for letting him fail. But the most egregious thing that the teacher said is that Junior has started to smell like the bums that hang out in the park nearby. Ma, already red-faced from the embarrassment of it all, couldn't handle that her kid smelled and how must all these strangers look at her—an unfit mother who couldn't even be bothered to bathe her son.

She turns to me and screams, "How could you let him go to school without showering?"

"It's not my job. I clean up after your friends' dogs and old people."

After working for Ms. B, I sometimes walked dogs for Tita Cynthia or one of her other friends. In the Philippines, we hardly knew anyone with pet dogs like Tita Cynthia's Hercules or Ms. Flor's Daisy. The dogs we knew were dirty, barked constantly, chained to makeshift dog kennels to protect their owners' property. Sometimes they didn't even have names.

"How dare you talk back to me?" Ma asks, her hand at the ready to smack my face.

I take my backpack and say I'm going to the library to research colleges. Being one year out of school is more than enough for me. I'm eighteen now. I should be in school.

"Don't walk away from me while I'm talking to you," she says. But I do, so she turns her attention to Junior, making her voice softer, more pleading, asking him why he would embarrass his mother like this when she worked so hard all her life after losing her mother, Lola Reming.

"Yeah, you worked as a whore," Junior says, and Ma slaps him hard, a shock to us all. She has never ever hit her golden child before. Junior starts to cry.

I stop listening and head out for a walk to calm myself. I'm afraid of what else might slip from my mouth.

At dusk, when I return to the apartment, Ma is still fully awake. Normally, she is just waking up to get ready for work. Junior looks the same except his hair is wet and smells faintly of Garnier shampoo. His eyes are locked on *Grand Theft Auto*. He looks like a tiny madman with fingers beating on his controller, making grunting noises when the game doesn't go how he likes it.

"What are you doing home?"

"I called out sick," Ma says.

"How come?"

"I need to spend some time with Junior since he's acting out."

On cue, there's a loud sound of screeching tires and then the crashing noise from the TV. Junior curses under his breath, saying a string of words, not in Tagalog but in English, audible and disturbing. Motherfucker. Bitch. Cunt.

"You want McDonald's?" Ma asks Junior.

Junior ignores her, his fingers pressing on the buttons of the greasy controller hard. Ma waits for a few minutes, her face almost still in its own confusion, a mix of anger and resignation. She turns away, heads toward the bedroom, and closes the door. A few minutes later, she is dressed in blue jeans and a white T-shirt with a full face of makeup. Even in crisis, Ma never fails to make sure that her lashes are curled and emphasized by mascara, that her lips are either glossy with tinted lip balm or highlighted with lipstick, that her face is even and contoured by liquid and powdered foundation, kissed by blush. When Papa used to ask her why she always had to have makeup on, she would remind him that it was a habit from her younger days. Then he would bring up Olongapo and tell her that her whoring days should have been long over and then they would fight. But Papa isn't here to say those things to her anymore. The silence is filled with Junior's video games and the occasional grunts and curses.

Ma looks at Junior for a few seconds, takes a deep breath, and exhales. Without another word, she heads for the door and leaves.

"Why do you have to be such an ass?" I ask Junior.

He mimics me, his voice cracking, since he's in that in-between stage of boyhood and manhood, a chick hatching through an eggshell.

"You're not my mother—stop acting like you know me like that. Why don't you get a life? Go do something and leave me alone!" He doesn't even bother to look at me as he says this, like I'm not even worth it.

He's right. I'm not his mother.

"You want to know what a mother *fucker* is?" Junior asks, still playing his game.

"What?"

"It's when a guy fucks your mother."

"What are you talking about?"

He tells me about how when he played hooky a few weeks ago. He went inside the apartment and heard some strange noises. Curious, he went to the bedroom and saw a white man on top of Ma. That guy. Junior said he froze for a few seconds and then left quietly. They didn't hear him, since they were too into what they were doing.

"She was supposed to be at work," Junior says.

This isn't a surprise to me, but Junior looks like he's expecting me to react and be as outraged as he is.

"Is that why you're acting out?" I ask instead.

"You wanna hear how I got suspended this time?" Junior asks, changing the subject. He doesn't wait for me to answer and goes right into the story, telling me how he was on his way home from school and was at the Fort Hamilton subway station. Because it's an outdoor station, he and his friends knew that they could see the train coming from a mile away, so they sat on the platform with their legs dangling over the tracks. It wasn't the first time they'd done it, but that day, it was the first time that one of his friends, a tall skinny Chinese kid they all nicknamed Mormon Bobby, wanted to show off and decided to moonwalk on the third rail, the live rail, which everyone knew was stupid, but they egged him on anyway. There was always news of somebody getting electrocuted on the third rail. Somebody with an adult voice, a woman, saw them from across the tracks on the other platform, headed to Coney Island, and yelled, "What the fuck are you all doing?" and they all laughed, and she thought they were laughing at her.

"That's incredibly stupid," I say.

"Nobody asked for your opinion," Junior says, turning back to his game. Then he added, "Do you want to hear the rest of the story or not?"

I nod.

They got called to the principal's office the next day, and Ma was called in too. All five boys were there with their parents, the parents all yelling at their kids in different languages: Arabic, Chinese, Spanish, and English. Ma was quiet. The parents went home, and all the boys were sent to the detention room, but the teacher was cool with them, and the only punishment they received was to write an essay about what they had done wrong. They completed all their classwork, and instead of going to the lunchroom like they would normally do, the lunch lady came and dropped off their lunches on sectioned foam plates. Junior trails off.

"And that's it?" I ask.

"What did you want to hear?" he asks.

If it were me doing something stupid like that, I know Ma would have reacted differently. Yet Ma is just watching Junior fall. She's not even here. She might come back from her trip to McDonald's tomorrow for all we know. She sometimes did that. She'd say she'd be back in a few hours, but it would be much longer. Sometimes she was out the whole night. Sometimes, we'd hear the door open at four in the morning.

"What did Ma say?" I ask.

"What can she say? She said don't do that again."

"It's been a while. How are you?" Mr. Park asks me.

For the past several weeks, Ma has been taking the laundry to Mr. Park's laundromat. "I need to think," she says. This time, because of the vomit on my clothes, I took them to the wash myself.

In the Philippines, we had a woman launder our clothes by hand. Only rich people had washing machines and there was no shortage of women who would wash clothes for money. Some women would beg to wash clothes for money. When we arrived, and I asked Ma if she expected me to do the laundry by hand, she scoffed and said, "We have machines for that here," as though I were so naive and so backwoods for not knowing this.

Mr. Park is staring at me, waiting for an answer.

"Good, thank you," I say, and apologize for spacing out.

He nods again and looks as if he wants to say something but changes his mind.

"How's my dad?" I ask.

"You know he's with me?" He seems surprised.

"It makes the most sense."

Of course Papa would go to Mr. Park's, even if his home is far away, in Flatbush. He is Papa's only friend here.

Mr. Park lets out a big sigh. "It's no good not to have a family together," he says.

"You know what happened!"

"I know, but your father doesn't mean it. He feels sorry. He feels shame."

"Why doesn't he even call? It's like he has no children."

"Not yet. He will when he's ready."

Ma sits on a stool in the kitchen, cursing under her breath. It's her day off and she is preparing to make chicken caldereta. She has all the ingredients lined up on the counter: a whole chicken carcass in a plastic bag, a small plastic container of chicken livers, a small can of tomato sauce, red and green bell peppers, a yellow onion, a head of garlic, three carrots, and five potatoes.

"Don't let men give you anything," she says, even though she's kept the necklace and pendant that Papa gave her when he was still courting her. She launches into how she was once so beautiful that a man from another town offered her father a building in exchange for her, and her father considered it. They were so poor he even let his children steal eggplants and tomatoes from other people's gardens.

"Your grandfather would have let me go," she says.

She puts the whole chicken on the cutting board and hacks each limb with a butcher knife. The cleaving leaves the cavity intact.

"So what happened?" I ask her.

"What didn't happen, you mean. It was your grandmother," she says. "Your lola Reming said she had a dream that the man is actually married, but the woman is made out of clay from his backyard. This clay woman did everything he said. She told your lolo that the building the man offered was not a real building and—"

"How did she know that?" I ask, cutting her off.

"Can you let me finish? You're just like your father." Ma shakes her head as she washes chicken pieces under running water. "Your lola interpreted the dream to mean that he was actually a married man and what he was offering was not his but his wife's family building."

"Was that true?"

"They asked around about the man and found out that he had another mistress from three towns over. He was so good-looking that people hid their daughters in case he decided he wanted to make them into his lovers. His wife would get so jealous, she would turn to a local mangkukulam to cast a spell on the girls he liked. She was a rich woman. She could afford to have someone like him." Ma starts sautéing the aromatics, the steam hitting her face. "The moral of this story is I listened to my mother, and I didn't marry that man," she says, wiping sweat off her brow with a towel. "That was the last thing she said before she passed away."

I calculate in my head. "How old were you?"

"Fourteen? Fifteen? I don't remember."

"That's gross. Why is an older guy chasing a teenager?"

"That's just how it is."

I look at Ma and wonder whether this was how it was when she was growing up. Was there a string of old men chasing her? Was that how she ended up working in Olongapo?

"How is this related to Papa?"

"Why don't you make yourself useful and peel and cut the potatoes," she says, changing the subject as usual.

"How many potatoes?" I ask, annoyed that she is not answering my question, even though deflecting is not an unusual thing for her to do.

"Whatever's on the counter," she answers.

Ma doesn't usually cook. I watch her out of the corner of my eye as she hacks the rest of the carcass into smaller bits. She used to say that in her village, everyone could handle a knife or a machete by the time they were eight years old.

"There was a man from Laguna who was visiting our village and he didn't have much money, but he knew how to tell stories," Ma says. She stops what she's doing and has a faraway look in her eyes.

"Have I ever told you about the mother dog story?" she asks.

I shake my head.

She says that there was a king with a pet dog whom he treated so kindly—like a queen—that the dog followed him with all the loyalty in her heart. One day, the dog gave birth to three puppies, but what was incredible was that these puppies were human girls, and the king, overjoyed, had them all baptized. When they grew up to be beautiful young women, each of them was married off to a prince from a different kingdom. When the king died, the dog, who no longer had the protection of the king, was cast out of the palace, abused by boys in the streets with kicks and sticks and stones. The dog went hungry for several days, driven away from every house where she tried to find shelter. With her pitiful appearance, she looked for her first daughter and found her. The first daughter, who lived in luxury, found the dirty matted dog outside her window trying to climb a ladder to get inside. Horrified, the daughter shooed her mother and said that she didn't want her husband finding out that her mother was a dog. As if that wasn't enough, she kicked the poor dog until the dog tumbled down the ladder. The dog then went and searched for her second daughter in another kingdom. She found her second daughter and her husband exiting a church and she ran to her daughter for help. Horrified, the second daughter whispered to one of the guards, instructing him to catch the dog and tie her up in a forest far away so she could not see her mother, whom she was deeply ashamed of. Exhausted, wounded, and grieving, the dog wailed. Not too long after, her youngest daughter and her husband came riding through the forest. Recognizing her mother, the youngest daughter leapt from the carriage and untied her mother, covered her with her own veil, and took her back to the palace. At the palace, she unveiled the pitiful dog and told her husband that this was her mother and would he please take her in. The husband just said, "Thank God!" Upon hearing these words, the youngest daughter ordered the kitchen staff to make the best food and told her servants to prepare the best room so her mother could sleep in comfort and luxury. When the youngest daughter, her husband, and the dog all dined together, a light shone everywhere. Where the dog was, a beautiful woman with fine clothes appeared. She turned to the youngest daughter and said, "I am the dog, your mother. God bless you, my child!"

Ma tells the story like she's in a trance, remembering a time when the story was told to her.

"What's it supposed to mean?" I ask.

"That you're supposed to listen to your mother," she says, her trance broken. She rubs her eyes with the back of her wrist and resumes cooking, throwing onions into the sizzling-hot pan. "You're lucky your mother is still alive, so you should listen to me."

She starts talking about how when Lola Reming died, life became harder for her family. Lolo Manching didn't know what to do with life and it showed. He stopped going to work and paying bills. He started drinking, placing bets with jueteng kubradors, and frequenting sabong joints to see roosters fighting. He lost the family home to pay for his gambling debts and alcohol addiction. Someone else had to take the lead and it fell on her.

I wanted to change the subject. "Did you like this man who could tell stories?" I ask.

Ma doesn't answer me immediately, but when she does, she says, "He had no money. What use are stories? You can't eat a story."

I want to tell her that there are stories that keep us up at night. We can't eat stories, but stories can eat us up inside.

We both listen to the sounds of the kitchen. The knife hitting the cutting board. The simmering water in the pot. The beeping of car horns outside. The occasional cooing of pigeons. The scurrying feet of mice in the walls.

"Why didn't you tell us you knew Papa was at Mr. Park's?" I ask her, finally, after so much time stewing, waiting to see if she would say something, anything, to fill the silence.

"It didn't seem important," she says.

I stop mid-peel and put the potato down. "Why not?"

"He has his life now. I have mine," she says.

"What's that supposed to mean?"

"I didn't report him to the police. I didn't tell any authorities. We're talking. What else can he ask for?"

"Talking about?"

"His papers."

I ask her if he plans on coming back, or if he is just going to stay with Mr. Park in his apartment like two old bachelors.

"He's too ashamed to see either of you, and I want out," she says.

"Meaning?"

"I told him I would still help him with his papers so he can stay here and make something of himself. But I'm done. I want to get on with my life." Ma chops hard for emphasis. She puts the chicken pieces in an empty basin and washes them with a mixture of white vinegar and water. "I'm done with this. Can you finish and cook? I have to go to sleep now," she says, washing her hands in the sink.

"What about Junior?" I ask.

"What about him?"

"Aren't you going to tell him?"

"He's still a kid," she says.

"Why are you telling me now?" I ask.

"You're not a kid anymore. You need to be responsible for your life. Make money and pay bills," she says with her back to me. She goes into the room and closes the door.

I cut myself with the paring knife. The shock of the pain hits me and it stings. I watch the ooze of red liquid from where the skin broke. This is what it means to be alive.

As I look at the blood, I recall the old women in the wet markets in the Philippines. They weighed freshly harvested pig's blood by the liter so that they could sell it to people who would use it with marinated pig's innards, and then sauté these with onions, long green peppers, and garlic to reduce the gaminess. The dish is a delicacy that is eaten with sweet and soft rice cakes. The rich people never go to the wet markets. They have their maids go and haggle with the shopkeepers, butchers, and other vendors. The maids will walk away and pretend that they won't buy, but they return later after they have walked and asked around. The rich people go to the clean supermarkets, where everything is washed and covered in plastic. If they go to the wet market, the smell gets to them, and they cover their noses with their fine handkerchiefs. I think of Ms. Flor. I can't imagine her going to a wet market, her perfume mixing with the stink.

I put the cut to my tongue, tasting the blood. Then I smear it on my lips with my fingertips.

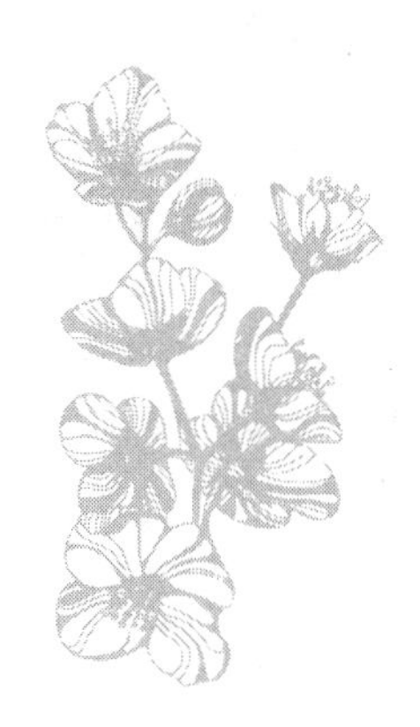

The phone rings. It rings and rings until the answering machine starts.

"Hey, it's me," Zeus says.

My spine tingles, making my legs move on their own, and I run to the phone. But before I pick it up, I stop, frozen.

"Did I do something wrong?" he continues.

No. It's me, Zeus, I want to tell him. The heat rises to my face. I am the dog in Ma's story.

"Can you call me?"

He hangs up.

My finger hits Play on the answering machine and his voice repeats the message. I think about Ms. Flor and the way she talked to me. Tears come as I press Delete. Ma can't hear this. What would she think?

"Three polyps from my colon! Two years ago, none!" Tita Cynthia says to Ma. "You've got to start doing it once you hit forty, Mel."

"I don't have time for that," Ma says.

Ma never has time. As she tells her friends over the phone, she's a single mother now and needs to work to feed her babies.

Six months have passed since Papa left.

Six months of Ma's freedom.

"You say that now, but sometimes you just have to do things when your body stops working," Tita Cynthia says.

We're at Costco. Every third Thursday of the month is Costco day. The day that Tita Cynthia has off to do her errands. We always go with her so Ma doesn't have to pay the membership fee.

"Take three more," Ma says, pushing me toward the food samples—toasted pita slices with Gouda cheese. The old woman at the stall pushes her thick black-rimmed glasses up her nose and scratches an itch underneath her blue kitchen cap. "Just take one," she says with a high-pitched voice. I point to my mom, my brother, and Tita Cynthia. She nods while I take more toasted pita slices.

"Why aren't you eating?" Ma asks, noticing that I didn't take one for myself.

"I'm not hungry."

"Don't worry about it, Mel. She wants to watch her figure," Tita

Cynthia says. Then she checks her lipstick and applies a fresh coat. She presses her lips together and rubs them back and forth, then licks the red from her teeth.

"Aren't you excited that Queenie is finally going to school?" Tita Cynthia asks. I had told them earlier that I was going to sign up for a class at BMCC to start college.

Ma shrugs. "As long as I don't have to pay."

Ma's response is expected, but I still feel disappointment that she doesn't seem to think that this is a big deal.

"You should take nursing," Tita Cynthia admonishes me for the tenth time today, as though she is saying it again for the first time. I smile in response. There's no use opening my mouth. Before more words spill out of her, Tita Cynthia gets distracted when she sees workers putting freshly baked rotisserie chickens on the shelves. "Look, Mel, the chickens are coming out now!" Ma and Tita Cynthia walk ahead, hurrying to pick up the chicken. All this time, Junior is playing Tetris on his Game Boy console. When he loses a round, he turns his attention to Ma and Tita Cynthia heading to the rotisserie section.

Junior runs after them and pushes the shopping cart brimming with bags of rice, oils, meats, and boxes with all his might, but the weight is too much for his thin body with the speed he's trying to use to maneuver the cart. Several cereal boxes fall to the ground. He picks them up. "Cunt," he says under his breath.

"You curse too much."

"Why don't you push the cart, then?"

"You're the man of the house now, right?"

"Why does pushing a cart have anything to do with that? I'm tired."

I tell him he needs this as exercise, that he plays too many video games.

Ma calls us over to the shoes section. She beams at the $24.99 price tag and tells Junior to try the sneakers on.

"Can we not get these?" Junior asks Ma, saying that everyone else in school would make fun of him.

"They're not paying for your shoes. We get these or you don't get new ones," Ma says.

"All my friends have Nikes. Why can't I get regular shoes like them? Why are you being so cheap?"

"Excuse me. Do you think I'm made of money?" Ma asks him, putting the box of no-name-brand sneakers in the cart.

Junior starts causing a scene, saying, "This isn't fair!" He stamps his feet and crosses his arms like a little boy. "You buy yourself things all the time!" Everyone around us starts looking.

Ma looks around, feeling the gaze of the other shoppers. "Stop embarrassing me," she hisses. "You're almost twelve. Act your age."

"That's all you care about. Whether you're embarrassed or not! Papa would have gotten me the shoes."

"If you like him so much you should go live with him and see how much you like that," Ma hisses.

Tita Cynthia pulls on Ma's arm, and I tell Junior that he's out of line. He glares at me and sticks his tongue out.

"Stop acting like a baby," I say, irritated at him for being so unreasonable. Doesn't he see that we can't afford what his friends have? Doesn't he see how lucky he is that he at least gets to go to school?

"Stop bossing me around. You're not my mother," Junior says, scowling. I want to hit him so badly. He used to be so quiet and pliable. Now I don't even know who he is anymore. He has become a brat.

"OK, I'll buy you Nikes. Your birthday is coming up, right, hijo? It will be your birthday present," Tita Cynthia says. This appeases Junior and he grunts a thank-you. Tita Cynthia takes a five-dollar bill from her overstuffed wallet and gives it to Junior. "Here, go buy yourself a hot dog and soda downstairs and just wait for us."

Ma, of course, is horrified. But before she can say anything else, Junior scampers off toward the food court and I know he will get more than the hot dog and soda. He will probably get the churro and the berry ice cream sundae too.

"I don't want to spoil him, Cynthia. He has to understand that he can't get everything he wants because that's life," Ma says.

"He's a boy, Mel. You have to spoil them a little bit."

—

At the food court, while Ma is in the bathroom, Tita Cynthia lets information slip in between bites of her hot dog. "Your mother has a boyfriend now . . . a doctor," she says.

Junior stops playing his Game Boy. Junior and I both look at her. Junior is shocked. I am not.

"It's that guy," Junior says, piecing together that the man he saw in the apartment is Ma's boyfriend. He lets out a string of curses that alarms Tita Cynthia, who tells him, "Language, hijo." She shakes her head in disappointment.

I've noticed some changes with Ma. Slow but steady, like watching a puppy turn to a bitch in heat. The clothes and the makeup. Trying to look better than usual. I want to ask Ma if it's the guy Papa saw outside that day. Ma returns, sits down, and before she takes a bite of her hot dog, Junior speaks.

"Does Papa know?" Junior asks, as if reading my mind.

"Know what?" Ma asks.

"Nothing," Tita Cynthia interjects.

"You have a boyfriend," Junior says.

"Who told you that?"

Junior points at Tita Cynthia.

"You shouldn't have said anything yet," Ma scolds Tita Cynthia. "It's none of your father's business and none of yours."

"I'm sorry for telling your kids, but you're not divorced yet and the church doesn't believe in divorce—"

"Ate Cyn, I'm separated, and the church doesn't pay my bills. No one needs to know," Ma says.

"Is it that guy Papa saw?" Junior asks.

Ma flutters her eyelids several times, a tic of hers when she's uncomfortable, and laughs nervously. "It's him, but nothing was going on that time, OK? He's one of the residents."

Tita Cynthia jumps in and tells us that it's a thirty-five-year-old Romanian man named Radu. Ma glares at her, but Tita Cynthia keeps eating her hot dog and sipping her fountain soda, unperturbed.

"That's what people from the hospital said," Tita Cynthia says.

"It's none of their business," Ma says.

The table is silent. Junior retreats into his video game. I feel awake but strangely sluggish. Papa would say that he was right, that he had a sixth sense about these things. A man half his age with twice his accomplishments. I excuse myself and make my way to the bathroom. When I am done, I feel like destroying something. Instead, I remove the toilet paper roll attached to the metal hood on the wall and put it in my backpack. There is something satisfying about stealing it, even if it's a small thing. When I step out of the stall, a middle-aged woman with big dyed-blond hair with dark roots tries to come in after me. "There's no toilet paper," I say with no guilt. She nods and chooses another stall.

By the time I get back, the mood has shifted. Everyone is calm and laughing as though nothing happened.

We pile into Tita Cynthia's beat-up gray Toyota and make a few pit stops. Instead of Fei Long Supermarket on Eighth Avenue, today we'll head to Woodside, Queens, to a small specialty grocery store to buy Filipino goods that we can't get in regular American groceries. After that, we will go to one of the Filipino carinderias and turo-turo to eat Filipino dishes—some too complex and too time-consuming to make when all people want to do is rest.

According to Tita Cynthia, food solves everything.

Yan already signed up for classes at BMCC. "To pursue higher education," Yan said, sighing while explaining that his boyfriend persuaded him to do so if he was going to stay in his apartment. Yan told me it was easy to sign up, and I also found out that my H-4 visa allowed me to be taken in as a regular in-state student. I wasn't considered an international student, and it makes such a difference with what I have to pay.

The first day of class at BMCC is strange. I'm in a trailer with the rest of my classmates, since the building we were supposed to be in is still under construction because it was destroyed during 9/11. I've never been in a trailer before. It reminds me of one of the Pantranco buses we took when we traveled from one province to another, but the trailer is slightly smaller. I'm surprised that twenty students fit inside, although it feels a bit tight. Some of them look bored.

When the teacher, a tall, spindly white man, enters the classroom, I stand up and say, "Good morning, Mr. Teutonico"—the instructor in the class, according to my program card. I hear snickering and look around. I hear someone say, "What the hell is she doing?" I turn around and realize that I am the only one standing and feel like an idiot. In the Philippines, we had to stand up and greet the teacher. But here, even Mr. Teutonico looks at me with eyebrows raised and tells me that I may have a seat. I vow never to speak in the class again.

A dark-skinned girl with slicked-back hair leans over and says,

"Don't sweat it." Mortified, I mumble thanks and turn my attention to the teacher.

Mr. Teutonico writes *English 101* on the whiteboard and hands us our syllabus for the term. After going over it, he asks us to pair up and do introductions. "Make sure to tell your partner something interesting about yourself and what you're thinking of."

I turn around to my neighbor and introduce myself. "I'm nervous. This is my first time in an American school." She nods and says her name is Mercedes and that she is originally from the Dominican Republic. "I'm thinking about breakfast," she says. On cue, her stomach growls and we both laugh. She's wearing a polo shirt with a patch that says *SECURITY* and dark pants.

"I wouldn't be wearing this right now, but I gotta go to work after class," she says.

Mercedes explains that she works for a security agency and that she had to get her license. When I ask her how she got into it, she explains that her uncle was a security guard and encouraged her toward it because she would be stationed in one place and could do her homework when it was quiet.

"It's especially useful to get those overnight shifts. No one's watching and you can do almost whatever you want."

After class, I walk with Mercedes to the Chambers Street subway station. "Hey, if you ever want to try this out, let me know. I can refer you to the agency I work for." She takes a piece of paper out of her book bag, scribbles a number, and hands it to me.

I meet up with Yan at a café outside of campus on Duane Street and tell him about my day while he is sucking on a boba tea. He chokes laughing—liquid running out of his nose—when he hears that I stood up and greeted the teacher.

"That's such a fobby thing to do," he says.

"What does 'fobby' mean?"

"FOB . . . fresh off the boat."

—

At home, Junior hears about my morning and even he makes fun of me. He then tells me that the same thing happened to him on his first day of class. I ask him why he didn't say something about it before, and his response was "And what would you do?"

When I say "Nothing," he says, "Exactly, so there wouldn't be a point telling you anything." I wonder if Junior told Ma or Papa. But what could they have done anyway?

A year has passed since my parents' fight. The violence in his eyes on that day should prevent me from wanting to ever see him, but it doesn't. Didn't I want to kill when he took my money too? But I didn't. And he didn't harm anyone. The knife hit no flesh. Do we judge intent or the actual action? I don't know. All I know is that time has passed, and time is supposed to heal all wounds. Ma thinks differently. "It was my life on the line," she said. "You can forgive, but not forget."

I worry about Pa. He's never been by himself before, without women around him. Is he eating well? Does he remember to take his blood pressure medication? I mention this to Mr. Park, and he arranges for my father and me to see each other at a Chinese bakery on the corner of Fourth and Sixtieth that sells pastries and homemade comfort food. Why does it take someone else for Papa to say yes to see his child?

I buy myself a Hong Kong–style tea and a pineapple bun. When I first had a pineapple bun with Yan, I was so confused since I expected that there would be pineapple inside like in the Philippines. But this was just bread with a sweet topping. Yan laughed at me then. But I didn't get it. The people who invented the bun had clearly not grown up with pineapples.

A woman in an apron and a bandanna over her head is wiping

down an empty table at the end of the café. When she finishes, I sit down.

Should I tell Papa about Ma's love life? That seems like a bad idea.

Mr. Park and Papa are at the door. My throat dries. Papa looks older. The once-smooth face of his seems softer and lined with faint wrinkles I never noticed before, and his hair is longer and grayer. His face is gaunt and haggard. He grew out his facial hair, but he obviously didn't care to keep it neat. There are strands that point in all directions like he just tumbled out of bed.

They nod at me, and Papa asks me if I want anything else. I shake my head and they each order coffee and a bao. They sit across from me, and it is awkward.

"The red bean bun is good here," Papa says.

"The bao too. They put a lot of meat filling," Mr. Park says.

Instead of letting silence settle, they continue to talk about how a lot of places don't serve food well and how we are all fortunate that there are still places that understand the needs of the working class. They name places, both in this neighborhood, on Eighth Avenue, and in Chinatown in the city.

I clear my throat. "Are we just going to talk about food?"

Papa looks at his coffee cup and Mr. Park shifts in his chair. After an awkward minute, Mr. Park stands up and excuses himself, saying that he should be getting back to the laundromat.

Papa and I are left behind by ourselves.

"Are you eating well?" I ask, stupidly, not knowing what to say.

"I eat when I'm hungry," he says. "You're getting fatter."

I don't have the heart to be angry. This is as normal as it's going to get.

"Do you have a boyfriend yet?" he asks.

"Why do you ask?"

"You're nineteen now. I met your mother at that age."

"I'm going to be nineteen in less than a month," I say.

"It's the same thing."

Almost nineteen. This is a revelation to me. I knew it in the back of my mind, but Papa stating it so plainly gives it another dimension. Was I like Ma when she was nineteen?

"Not everyone has a new boyfriend," I say, feeling guilt about Zeus.

"Like your mother," he says, his voice thickening and his eyes watering.

"So you know about him, then."

"I saw the bastard."

I am surprised that he hasn't completely lost his composure talking about Ma like he did that last time. "Yeah. So, what's your plan?" I ask.

"What do you mean?"

"With life. What are you planning on doing? Are you going back to the Philippines?"

"Mr. Park convinced me not to."

"How'd he do that?"

"He said my children are here."

"Even if you're not really talking to us?"

"I'm talking to you right now."

"You should talk to Junior. He's not doing well."

"That's not what your mother said," he says.

"Since when did you ever believe her?"

He decides that Junior and I should visit him at Mr. Park's place. Mr. Park was only off on Sundays, when he went to church in Queens.

"You and Junior should visit me then," he says in between bites. He finishes his bao and drinks the rest of his coffee. "How about your school?"

I tell him that I've started taking a class at BMCC and that I've been paying my tuition by working odd jobs. I remind him that I spend a lot of my free time at the library and reading books. Papa nods.

"That's good. You need to be a wide reader," Papa says, and starts talking about the crate of books that his Australian business partner left behind.

I feel a twinge in my chest hearing him like this. It's something I've heard him say before. It's something with the semblance of normal.

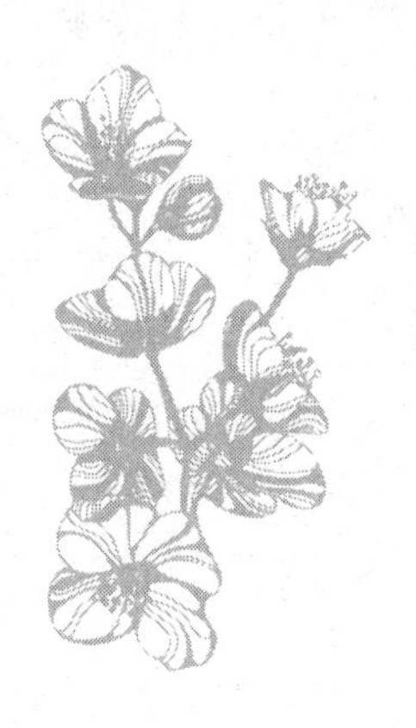

At the library, I am reading a novel about honor killings in the high mountains of Albania called *Broken April.*

All the highlanders' lives revolved around an ancient book called the Kanun, which focuses on concepts of honor like besa, keeping one's word, and hospitality—all of which are ruled by the family. Any sign of dishonor leads to death, even by their brother's or father's own hand. There is a side story of a woman who was raped. Her own family killed her for "dishonoring" them. During the autopsy, it was discovered that she was carrying a boy, so the rapist's family considered him theirs and decided they would avenge the unborn child and a blood feud began. These killings were a way of life.

I jump out of my seat when I feel a tap on my shoulder. It's Yan. But he's not looking like his usual put-together self. His hair isn't gelled and the skin under his eyes is red and slightly swollen.

"What's wrong?" I ask. I'd only seen him like this when he was upset by something that happened at home, usually with his father. But today must have been something even worse.

"Come with me," he says.

He starts walking toward the exit before I can pack all my belongings. I hurry after him, pulling out my library card and taking the novel with me. Yan is standing outside, smoking a cigarette.

"Since when do you smoke?"

"I just picked up the habit recently," he says.

His long legs are moving fast. I ask him to slow down but he doesn't, so I jog to catch up with him. We're headed toward the brick row houses on Forty-Fourth Street where he lives. We climb up to his apartment. I've never been here before, although I've passed by a few times. I never questioned this because, even in the Philippines, I never went to my classmates' or even friends' homes unless my family knew theirs.

Anyone would know right away that a Chinese family lives here. Outside their door is a red and green hexagon bagua mirror with the I Ching trigrams painted in gold yellow. In the Philippines, almost all the Chinese homes Papa and I visited had the bagua mirror hanging on their doors to ward off sha chi. We had one on our apartment door, but Ma took it down when Papa left. "Do we even know what it means?" she had asked.

"Make yourself at home," Yan says.

Yan's family's apartment has clean wood floors, a large twenty-gallon fish tank with several large emergency-orange goldfish and black mollies, and Chinese newspapers stacked on a small dining table with an assortment of pens. It smells of incense. Without looking, I know the scent comes from the ancestral shrine. The shrine is typical of what I've seen in other Chinese homes: a carved wooden miniature temple the size of a milk crate with framed black-and-white photos of an unsmiling man and woman inside, a bowl of mandarins in front of them as offering, and an even smaller figurine of a red-faced god.

The setup reminds me of home altars in the Philippines where, instead of photos of ancestors and Taoist or Buddhist deities, there were images, icons, and statues of saints like Saint Francis and Saint Anthony or those of the Holy Family—Santo Niño La Suerte in green, Jesus of Nazareth with a black face and a cross on his back, and versions of the Blessed Virgin—Our Lady of Perpetual Help, Our Lady of Manaoag, Our Lady of Lourdes, Our Lady of Fatima. Ma decided we didn't need a family altar. "The saints can live in the church," she said to Papa when he wanted to set up one in the apartment. She wouldn't even let him put Angkong and Amah's pictures, let alone novena pamphlets or rosary beads, in our apartment.

Yan takes some Yakult bottles from the fridge, hands me one, then disappears through one of the doors. I sit in the dining room and leaf through what looks like a Chinese fashion magazine. Yan brings me a black binder covered with Hello Kitty stickers. Inside is a collection of cut-up photographs of beautiful young men with fair skin, most of them smiling.

"Hong Kong actors and singers," Yan says.

"Pretty boys," I say.

Yan nods, motioning for me to keep flipping the pages. Halfway through the binder, the contents change. They're pictures of half-dressed or barely dressed men of all colors, their features chiseled. Some have hands on their crotches, their heavy-lidded eyes closed or half-closed, their mouths partly open with the suggestion of excitement and pleasure. The next page has black-and-white naked pictures of Yan in similar poses and expressions. I look up at Yan, who is watching me.

"I got paid for those," he says.

He tells me he went to an apartment in Park Slope after seeing an ad on Craigslist. It was an expensive prewar brownstone that was refurbished so that the hardwood floors were made from actual wood and not some man-made knockoff; every piece of furniture had cost thousands of dollars. The man who took his pictures was a family man in his forties or fifties, smooth-skinned, and Black. Around the house were photos of his older white wife, their two biracial kids, and their orange cat named Fidel. The wife and the kids were at the man's in-laws' and the man had the afternoon to work on his hobby. His hobby was photographing what he called "objects of lust," and Yan was one of them.

"'Object of lust' is so cliché," Yan says, but I can see that he finds pleasure in this. He says that the husband took pictures of him, nude, and then approached him and started to caress his skin.

"Then it happened, and it was hot," Yan says, his face changing.

The husband gave Yan some of the images from the shoot two weeks later in a manila envelope. When Yan called him to see if they could hook up again, the husband told him he didn't want to see him, that the "object of lust" should remain an object in the past in order for it to live through its potential and nostalgia, which the husband called the "sepulcher of memory."

"'Sepulcher of memory'? Who talks like that? What a bullshitter," Yan says.

I look at Yan's black-and-white photos again, seeing another part of him. His face, without guile, pleads with the camera, screaming *look at me.* He looks much thinner and younger in the pictures, almost like an underaged kid. This changes as I flip through the binder. His expressions and body language transform with his dick in different stages of erection.

"He would jerk me off a little throughout the session and then take pictures," Yan says. "I told him I could do it myself, but he took off his own pants and I could see he was hard already, and he told me, 'Don't be nervous,' and then he came to me and touched me a little."

I close the binder and wonder why Yan is telling me all this. Looking at Yan right now makes me nervous. His image is distorted, like I'm seeing him through a tinted glass.

"My dad saw the binder," Yan says.

"What did he say?" I ask.

"He said that he didn't come to America to have a son like me, that in China, this *problem* would never have happened. He also brought up my brother . . . Why couldn't I be more like him? Normal and always the good son."

"Doesn't he know that you're going to college now?"

"So what? I'm not his golden boy. My brother got a full ride. My dad always talks about him, saying he's so perfect."

We're both quiet, taking in the silence around us. My eyes wander to the ancestral altar. Yan's eyes follow my gaze, and he sighs.

"My father told me to get out by the time he gets back from work and not to come back," Yan says.

"What did your mother say?"

"What's she going to say? If he told her to jump, she's going to jump. If he told her to shit on the kitchen table, pardon my French, she's going to shit on the kitchen table. That's just the kind of relationship they have."

"What are you going to do?"

"What else can I do? I'm going to go."

"Where?"

Yan takes a deep breath. He's thought of this. Since I've known Yan, he's been methodical. "I'm just going to call Jim. He just bought a place in the city. He said I could crash there anytime. No strings."

At least he has a lifeline.

Would Yan have survived in the high mountains of Albania? He would have dishonored his family. No one would have taken him in for refuge unless they wanted to start a blood feud.

If we were anywhere else, Yan's father might not just ask him to leave. Anywhere else, lives are at stake. I think about Papa and his rage. Why must men kill when they are angry? What is this bloodlust that comes out that makes them want to hurt the closest thing to them?

Ma puts some baby oil on a cotton ball and begins to wipe her makeup off, starting with her cheeks. She looks at her own reflection in the mirror, examining her skin for any blemishes. She even looks at her smooth neck.

She came home late. When I asked her where she was, she said she went out with a friend. I tried to ask more questions, but she shushed me and said that it wasn't any of my business.

I watch her make small circles with the cotton ball, removing the red blush and then the brown foundation, marveling at how her skin changes with each swipe. The pressure of her fingers and the circular motions give her skin a natural glow. Ma stops wiping her face and begins massaging oil into the flesh and bone under her brows, then she dabs another wet cotton ball to the places she missed. She stands up and heads to the bathroom, and the sound of running water on one side of the apartment accompanies Junior's snoring from the other side of the apartment. Ma returns to the vanity mirror and sits down. This time she applies her Eskinol toner and Eskinol skin-whitening cream. She turns her face left to right and right to left, surveying the landscape. Ma, once again, appears like a young good girl growing into her skin.

Without looking at me, Ma says flatly that people have three jobs assigned to them at birth no matter who they are or where they come from: go to school, get married, and have children, and then, when you've done all that, take care of your parents. She finally turns to me and says, "That's what they told me. I've done that and it's still not enough. Do you think you come to this world to do what you want?"

That man with pale skin, her new shadow, conjures all the other shadow men she's been with. I remember Papa saying all white men want is sex. They think someone like Ma is exotic. They cannot take their eyes off her. They say to Ma, *where are you from what are you what's your background where are you really from why are you so beautiful how are you forty when you look twenty-five* and *no you really look like a nineteen-year-old fresh-faced girl* and *why are you here* and *where are you really from.*

"A girl doesn't yet realize that she's a novelty," Ma says. "By the time she does she's no longer one. Her sad story is not sad anymore. It's just a story. Like everyone else's."

I think about the stories of girls who are young and whose lives are lived for someone else's dreams. Ma reminds me her own father said nothing when she told him she was off to Olongapo. He wasn't dumb—he knew that girls go to Olongapo to do one thing, and that is exactly what she did. What's a girl to do when the life of her family is in her hands? When everyone around her is crying because life has thrown them all a bone that is dry and brittle and already gnawed through?

Ma says men shape reality and women bind themselves to that reality because we think a woman's essence is already contained in her body. The essence is trapped in her many versions, pressured by boys and men, by society, and by life. Then the boy-men fill her hole with their seeds. Then these seeds grow and then there is life, unwanted life, another mouth to feed and that mouth feeds on the girl-woman's pendulous breasts whose peaks rise with her breath, her skin sagging with the weight of motherhood. By the end of it, her breasts and body sag and kiss the ground after giving birth again and again, drying them up of milk and youth. A history written on the body like a house of matchsticks ready to be set aflame.

Ma goes out a lot more with Baldie, the unimaginative nickname I give her boyfriend. She calls him honey, sweetheart, and darling—endearments that make me think of rotten teeth. This man caused Papa to go berserk. This man caused Ma to go so weak in the knees that she's practically crawling in subservience to him. I had never seen her lose herself in her senses. "He makes me feel like a woman," I heard her say once to one of her friends on the phone. As if to be made to feel like a woman makes one forget that the world, and anyone else in it, exists.

Ma said among the most useful things she learned when she became a nurse were vital signs. Her job is to monitor them: body temperature, pulse rate, respiration rate, and—although not a vital sign—blood pressure. "You start knowing a person's body, how they breathe, how the blood vessels contract and expand based on situation, circumstance, and genetics," Ma said once. Knowing these things makes Ma feel smart, and this had thrown off Papa. He was used to being the smart one, and his knowledge came from being the older one. Ma had deferred to him once when she was still younger, before she came to this country. "She's harder now," Papa said, recounting how Ma didn't even pass her board exam the first two times. Once she did, she slowly changed. He should have known that was just the beginning. "She doesn't need me anymore," he said.

Now that she's dating a doctor, she wants to show more guile, more softness. I can hear it in her voice when she's talking to him on the phone, laughing in that girlish way and letting her voice diminish to an imperceptible whisper. "You can't let a man think you're smart, because men want to be the smart one in the relationship," Ma would say to her friends—usually Girly or Juliet—over the phone, and they would laugh. Papa, when he was still around, never liked it when Ma called them or when they called Ma to catch up. "They're not really your friends!" he would scream at Ma.

One time, I heard her tell one of them: "I'm a nurse and I am proud of it. I know things. People respect me. I make clean money." The talk of clean money made Papa laugh. "Doing shit and cleaning shit . . . it's all the same."

—

Ma's boyfriend brought several Cadbury chocolate bars for me and Junior and a bouquet of long-stemmed red roses with baby's breath for Ma. She took a deep breath and let the air out of her, her lips parted, as though she had never gotten flowers before. She reminded me of an old balloon—deflated and hanging too low on the ground. He kissed her on the cheek. At least he was prudent and didn't kiss her on the mouth. He offered me a handshake, and in my hesitation, it took me several seconds to shake his large hairy hand, a tight smile on my face. "I'm Radu," Baldie said to me. He was tall, hairy on his arms, and although thin, he was fit and had lean muscle that showed through his tight clothes. I supposed he was a little handsome in his own way. Junior totally ignored him and slammed the bedroom door so loudly, the apartment shook. Ma turned to Radu, apologized, and then banged on the door, screaming at Junior that she didn't raise rude kids and how was this making her look. "You didn't raise us!" he screamed back.

—

It started like that, uneasy and with little compromise. Then—

I watched her transform again. Flushed cheeks, giggly, breathy voice. A lovesick schoolgirl. That's what made me hate him the most. That he could reduce this thorny woman to this mess of a human. Too soft, but only for him.

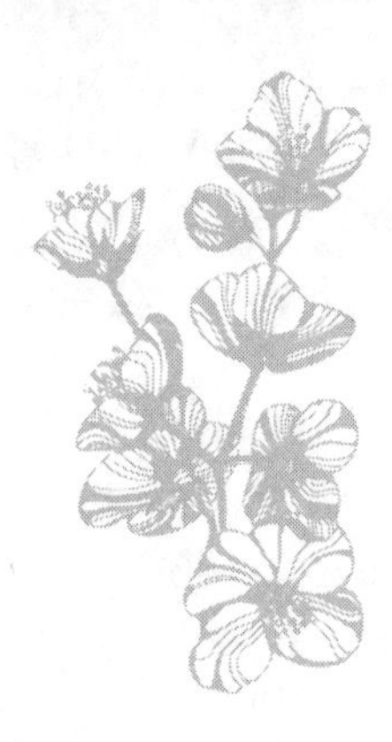

"What do you mean you're going to send him to California?" I ask Ma.

Junior, who used to be Ma's angel baby, is now sullen. He has grown his hair long in opposition to Baldie, telling Ma that he has hair longer than her boyfriend's. To Ma's horror, he refused to go to the barber shop. He even came up with the excuse that he was saving her money every month. "Para kang babae," Ma complains, saying that long hair is only for girls. His hair now reaches past his shoulders—the length of time Ma's been with Radu, a year and a half. In that time, Radu already looms over us—as though we are observing the weather news and the skies to know if a typhoon is coming or not, so that we know how badly our lives will be flooded. I watch as Ma defers to him as though he is her superior, like she is his maid. She was never this way. Not even with Papa. She cooks complex dishes for her new man and dolls herself up. I overheard her tell one of her girlfriends that his precious compliments send shivers from the nape of her neck to her coccyx. If she had a tail, she would have been wagging it.

Radu didn't like that Junior disrespected him. One particularly bad offense happened last month when Junior called him a name even worse than gago. "Where did he even learn that word?" Ma asked.

Baldie was offended, therefore Ma was offended.

This is the beggar woman crazed with love.

Ma looks at me and Junior and says that she and Baldie have decided it is best for Junior to live in California with Ma's cousin, Auntie Violetta, and her husband, Uncle Roland, because they're a military family with relatives who are in either the army, the navy, or the air force. No one's a marine, since everyone knows marines are the first ones sent in and last ones out during any conflict, which increases their chances of death, and America is always in a war.

They think this will help shape Junior up. He would go to school there, then join the ROTC when he turned seventeen, and then sign up for the air force or the navy. Something like that. The plans were both vague and certain.

She says she pities Papa, but that there's only so much a woman can do when given a choice, and besides, she says, a boy needs a father figure who can knock sense into him. Someone like Papa is too unyielding, too nostalgic, too old-school to get with the times.

"It's too soon for Radu to support you like a father," Ma says.

"But it's not too soon for him to help you make decisions about your kids?" I ask.

"Don't talk back to me! Remember who brought you to this country. With my own blood. Wala kang utang na loob."

To be ungrateful for what she'd done and what she'd sacrificed is like being Satan himself. I seethe and bite my tongue hard until it bleeds. I taste blood and my eyes water at the pain.

I hold it all in.

"Your auntie Violetta said her husband is happy to step in."

I had heard about Auntie Violetta, who had married a retired army lieutenant, a Black man almost twenty-five years her senior with four full-grown kids almost her age in Oakland, where he's originally from. The story was that he saw her walking on the road selling sampaguita flower garlands on a Good Friday and he bought everything she carried. By Easter Sunday, he took her back to the base on a date to eat a real cheeseburger with fries and root beer, which, in turn, made Auntie Violetta fall for him.

"How do you feel about this?" I ask Junior.

"As long as I don't have to see Baldie," he replies. "And that guy . . . he's useless."

Junior doesn't even bother to call Papa "Papa" now. He just refers to him as "that guy" or "he" or "him." When we went to visit Pa at Mr. Park's apartment, Junior balked at how cramped the room that Mr. Park and Pa shared in Flatbush was. It was a studio, and they slept on bunk beds. Kitchen appliances spilled onto tables. There were electric wires everywhere.

"It's so far," Junior complained when we had to take two trains to get to the apartment. Papa offered us tea biscuits and coffee. Junior didn't want to touch any of it. "I heard you're not doing well in school," Papa said. "What do you care?" Junior replied. Then they were screaming at each other. We were all shocked at Junior's behavior. Even Papa agreed with Ma to send Junior to California.

"Maybe he'll find a better family there," Papa said.

Junior leaves without much fanfare. One piece of luggage and his backpack, a quiet trip to JFK. He doesn't even turn back to wave. It's just forward momentum to the other coast. No farewell party, only silence. Like when Papa left. Except Junior really had no choice in the matter. "Call me when you get there," Ma said. Junior grunted, which was all he could do without exploding.

It's just me and Ma now. But Ma isn't here. Not really.

PART TWO

Yan invites me to visit him at Jim's apartment in Tribeca. It's a too-clean duplex with high ceilings and large windows, an expensive showroom with no domestic atmosphere except for the large potted palm in the corner of the living room. There is also an enormous tank with plants where an albino snake is resting. Yan notices me looking at the tank.

"I know. That's the first thing that caught my eye too and, no, I have not touched the snake. Not even for curiosity's sake."

I'm not sure which shocks me more: Yan's new place or the snake. The only time I had seen a snake was at the Manila Zoo. Snakes should only live in zoos or jungles, not in people's homes.

"Does the snake have a name?"

"Bowie, after David Bowie."

I approach the tank slowly and feel the warmth of the heat lamps. I'm afraid the tank will break and Bowie will bite me. But he's resting, and I marvel at the magnificence of the reptile. I have never seen one so close.

"Why is it hot? I thought snakes were cold-blooded."

"Bowie's a tropical species. He likes it comfortably warm. I'm sure Jim will explain more. If you get him talking about snakes and primates, he won't shut up about it."

"Where is Jim, anyway?"

"Brussels. A 'family trip,'" Yan says, his voice heavy with sarcasm.

The last time Jim was away, Yan said Jim was in London. Also for a "family trip." Jim has two families that Yan refers to—*the* family, the one he works for, and then there's *his* family, the one he isn't out to.

When I asked Yan if Jim was single, he was tight-lipped at first. But he caved and revealed that Jim has a complicated relationship with another man, much older than him, and wealthy, and that Jim is usually in Connecticut because he has to be on call for when the old man needs him for business or for pleasure. To the older man's family, Jim is just another one of the many assistants/lovers who help him run the family businesses, including commercial real estate, yachts, antiques, and even racing horses. The old man flies Jim at his whim, partly to parade Jim around and partly because of work. Jim was not only good-looking, but also smart.

Yan moves with confidence around the space, like a lithe cat patrolling his territory. He opens the chrome fridge, wrinkles his nose at something in the freezer, takes out some ginger ice cream, and pulls two spoons from a drawer. He hands me one.

"What's with the face?" I ask.

"You don't want to know."

"Now I need to know.

"It's a frozen mouse."

Yan explains there's a vacuum-sealed pack in the freezer that usually holds a frozen mouse to feed Bowie in case Jim can't go to the pet store to get a live one. But he usually gets a rat so that he only has to feed the snake once a month. "I have to do it when Jim isn't around. He loves this snake more than anything."

"Don't the mice know they're about to be eaten?"

"They do, I think. They're usually frozen in fear in the corner of the tank. I look away. I don't watch. I usually leave the poor things at night. By morning, it's just Bowie." He shrugs. We both find this disgusting, so I change the subject.

"How's work?"

"I quit. Then I bought a few pints of ice cream on discount."

Yan quitting isn't a surprise. From the looks of it, he doesn't need to work anymore. He just needs to feed a rodent to a reptile every few weeks. I savor the ginger flavor of the ice cream, trying not to think that the frozen rodent was next to it in the freezer.

"I have to thaw the mouse for a few days, you know. Bowie can't have it straight-up frozen. I don't want to even touch the plastic. I use tongs."

"Have you tried to give him a frozen one?"

"I thought about it. Too risky. If something were to happen to Bowie, Jim would flip out. He's had this snake for ten years already."

I put the ice cream down, losing my appetite.

"I know, sorry," Yan says, still scooping ice cream and eating it. "I kind of got used to it. Cycle of life and predator and prey and all that shit, but it doesn't mean I don't find it gross. But then I don't want Bowie to starve because he's not out in the wild, and Jim said if Bowie were out in the wild, he'd be eating rodents. Jim thinks it's silly that I find it disgusting. One time, he made me watch Bowie feed and it was quick. But because Bowie is an albino, I could actually see the mouse going through his system. I saw it struggling until it stopped moving. I gagged and vomited in the bathroom, and Jim laughed, calling me a snowflake."

According to Jim, Yan says, humans believe we're civilized and relegate the animal kingdom to a different category, but all this is just an extension of our attitudes and taste, to claim physical and psychological territories—to show power.

Yan talks about how he fills his days after quitting his dead-end job at the Chinatown Ice Cream Factory. The most he could hope for was to be the store manager, but even that was just a few dollars more than the minimum-wage pay. Now, he doesn't have to work. He's basically, as he says, "a kept bitch."

The plan is for him to finish with an associate's degree and then transfer to one of the senior CUNY colleges, perhaps Baruch or Hunter. Jim had suggested this, telling Yan to get it together because he can't have someone around whose only qualifications are being Chinese and gay.

"That's a bit much," I say.

"He doesn't like small talk. It's not like what he's saying doesn't make sense. He went to Yale, then Columbia, I think. Some PhD shit in social science or something."

"I'm sure he likes your potty mouth."

"Sometimes," Yan says with a grin.

I tell Ma that I'm going to stay at Yan's because BMCC is within walking distance and it would save me money on subway fare. I also tell her that I've just gotten a job at the Blimpie on Chambers Street serving subs and panini sandwiches.

Ma looks at me but not at me. Her eyes are unfocused. She puts the steam iron in a standing position on the ironing board to avoid burning her hospital scrubs. "I used to stay at a dormitory to go to nursing school. The dormitory was for girls only. No boys allowed. Not even to visit. I moved to a boardinghouse near the school where the landlady didn't care what happened as long as we were quiet, made no fuss, and paid her on time every month."

She starts ironing again as she tells her story, paying attention to the creases and corners of the scrubs. The boardinghouse was run by a widow who had her own troubles. Her drunk husband had died when he stumbled down the cement steps. He fell and hit his head on the ground, cracking his skull open. After his death, creditors would come by every few days demanding money that her late husband owed from his gambling, and the sari-sari store around the corner refused to let her buy anything on credit before she paid what she owed for the month.

"You know how she ended up like that?"

I shake my head, folding my clothes, making mental notes of how I would pack everything in one suitcase.

"The husband was a neighborhood boy. He got her alone in a corner one day. She got pregnant at fifteen. Their parents made them marry."

This wasn't surprising. I'd heard so many stories of young girls in the Philippines falling prey to boys and men. It wasn't uncommon for the girl to wed her rapist.

"Just don't get pregnant," Ma says.

"Yan likes boys."

"That's good then."

"I don't know what's wrong with Bowie," Yan says, his voice an octave higher. He's running his hands through his hair so ferociously he's pulling out strands of it.

For the last week, the snake had been slowly changing color to a bluish hue, and his eyes were clouding up, turning opaque. He hadn't eaten the defrosted mouse and it was starting to smell, decomposing from the heat. Yan put on thick rubber gloves to remove it and triple-bag it. We google *snake turning gray not eating* and find out that Bowie is molting, which could take anywhere between one and two weeks depending on the snake's size. Bowie is five feet long, so we expect that this would take closer to two weeks.

"Do you think Bowie's in pain?" I ask Yan.

Yan shows me an article that says skin shedding is a necessary but very uncomfortable process for snakes.

"I thought Bowie was already all grown up."

"It says here that they also shed skin to get rid of parasites. I guess all animals shed their skin, even humans," Yan says. We shed millions of skin cells every day and these cells look like dust; in the shower, they rolled into little gray worms underneath our fingers. With snakes, it is one continuous process. Bowie will leave his old skin behind like a discarded sock.

"I wonder if we can change our faces like that, like when we age.

I mean, clearly that's true, right? Because a person who's seventy isn't going to look like a twenty-year-old."

Yan nods distractedly, watching Bowie, his mind far away. "At least I don't have to tell Jim that I'm killing his snake."

"When's he coming back?"

"Next week."

By then, maybe Bowie will have sloughed off the entirety of his old skin.

Jim pours himself some Courvoisier and asks me if I would like to try it. I have never tried cognac before. The closest thing to this is the bottle of Chivas that Papa kept in the house when we were still in the Philippines for impressing some bigwig who came over. I nod, curious.

Jim asked Yan to go to the pet store to get Bowie's food, so I'm alone with Jim. My heart beats like a flying hummingbird. This whole setup feels like an interview. I'm sitting down, legs crossed and hands folded on my lap, while Jim walks back and forth, opening his cupboards to find another lowball glass for the cognac.

"How old are you again?"

"Almost twenty," I say.

"Almost isn't quite, though, is it?"

I shake my head, my cheeks turning red. He still gives me the glass and I try to drink it in one gulp, but as soon as the amber liquid hits my throat, I sputter and cough. The alcohol burns my tongue and throat.

"Slow down. This is not something you chug."

I feel heat rush through my chest. We both look toward Bowie's tank.

"Do you know why I like reptiles? They're different from us mammals—specifically primates—we need to be in groups, and within those groups, there are hierarchies."

He's right. Even in kindergarten there are pecking orders and groups within groups—the elite cool kids who are cool because they feel like they have nothing to lose. All they care about is getting what they want even if it's at another kid's expense.

Jim takes another sip of his cognac. "The first time I saw a reptile was at the Smithsonian National Zoo when I was eight. I'm guessing that you've never been."

I shake my head.

"The Smithsonian Institution is an incredible structure, the largest complex of its kind in the world. Multiple museums and a zoo in our nation's capital, Washington, DC. You should go one day. My mother took me there and we spent a weekend looking through the museums, but I loved the zoo. The highlight was watching the handler during feeding time. It was fascinating. One swallow was all it took, not even a bite."

Jim had waited a few years until the breeder could find an albino rainbow boa. Albinos are rare. Jim likes rare things. He likes handling Bowie every now and then but generally leaves him alone since rainbow boas don't like being touched all the time. "That suits me fine," Jim says, "since work keeps me occupied.

"What do you want to be when you grow up?" Jim asks.

It's a question I've heard all my life, but I don't know how to answer him. When I was in grade school, I thought I would become a doctor. That's what most of us said. It was either that or engineer, lawyer, or UN ambassador. We wanted to be UN ambassadors because it meant we would get to travel, to go to exotic places like Mount Kilimanjaro and Tahiti or the Red Square. I started becoming unsure in high school because biology, chemistry, and physics were difficult subjects. But I could never tell my mother I didn't want to be in the medical field.

"Yan tells me you met at a public library. How quaint," Jim says. "I didn't know people still meet at libraries."

"We both like reading."

Jim snorts. "Yan likes to read hard romance. Nicholas Sparks. Nora Roberts. Anne Rice. Maybe some suspense and mystery. All genre material."

"What's wrong with genre?"

"Nothing. But it shouldn't be the only thing in one's intellectual diet. Humans—we're omnivorous creatures. We're meant to consume almost everything, and our reading habits should reflect that. Have you heard of Manichaeism?"

I shake my head.

Jim explains that it's a cosmology of duality—life is a constant struggle between the good spiritual aspects of light and evil material darkness. It's through the activation of choices in human history that these aspects compete for the light to return to its source. From this concept of duality, another practice was born—gnosis, or knowledge from personal experience and learning from it as one would learn from a textbook. One uses this knowledge as a map to navigate through pitfalls and tribulations, but also joy and, possibly, meaning.

This so-called map is not concrete, however. It's also a ghost. Its sepia and blue tones mark boundaries and names of rivers and oceans, continents, and nations, layered with people and places that change through time. Lands change hands through blood and deceit. Empires fall. Maps change.

"There's nothing more dualistic than a mixed person. It's the literal manifestation of dualism," Jim says, explaining that nature favors balance between the so-called good and so-called evil and that humans favor imbalance since we tend to be obsessed with purity and absolute goodness. "We're in a material world. Nothing is perfect, not even goodness."

"Don't we all have good and evil within us?" I ask.

"Precisely. This is why we need to constantly reflect on ourselves, detaching from premises of absolute good and absolute evil. Everything is relative."

Jim makes everything sound so simple yet so complicated. Everyone has a worldview that anchors their lives. When that worldview crumbles, like Papa's, chaos ensues.

"Yan tells me you're half-Chinese," Jim says.

"Yes. But he doesn't consider me Chinese, since I don't speak it, and he says I don't really look Chinese either," I say.

"What does he consider you as?"

"Filipino. I mean, I'm from there. That's the language I know. That's where I grew up. That's where my life was before here, even though it was my dad who raised me."

"Your dad is the Chinese one?"

"Yeah. But he was born in the Philippines, and he was considered a foreigner and actually had a Taiwanese passport. He had never been to Taiwan, but most people considered him a foreigner even after he changed his citizenship to Filipino."

Jim laughs and pours himself another shot of Courvoisier. "You sound like me. I'm half-Jewish, but that doesn't even make sense. Is Judaism a culture, a religion, or an ethnic group? Even Jews are conflicted about who's who. In my case, it's my dad who's the Jew. But according to halachic law, one only gets their Jew card from their mother. Do you know how matrilineal lines came about?"

I shake my head.

"Some say that it was during the time of the Roman Empire. The father could've been a soldier who raped a Jewish woman, and the woman would give birth to a Jew because everyone knew her bloodline. Of course, sometimes erasing heritage can be convenient, but we can't change what's in our blood. Even science says that. You can't hide. Generations later, what's in the blood rises."

I tell him about what I know of mixed people. From my high

school history class in the Philippines, I learned that mixed people were a caste of mestizos who led the revolutions. They knew the Spanish ways because their fathers were the ones who either raped or had affairs with local women. The mestizos also knew the ways of their indigenous Indio mothers. The term *Filipino* was widely used by the most famous Filipino national hero, José Rizal. He himself had mixed racial ancestry, being Chinese, Spanish, Japanese, and Tagalog.

"We half bloods get around," Jim says, raising his glass and draining the remaining liquid.

The door opens and Yan comes in with a small cage, saying that the usual pet store didn't have the mice and he had to go to another one. "Honestly, I just don't know how we can be such willing partners in aiding and abetting the murder of a creature."

"You're so dramatic," Jim says.

"Did he tell you about how he had an orgasm at eight years old watching a snake eat a rat? I mean, that should tell you everything about this man," Yan says, putting on slippers by the door. He places the small cage by Bowie's enclosure. The two small white mice look timid, barely moving, disoriented. "The poor dears know what's up," Yan says, watching them and cooing.

"I told you not to get attached," Jim says.

"What were you two talking about anyway?" Yan asks.

"Half bloods changing the world," Jim says, smiling.

For dinner, Jim orders Indian takeout—potato-filled vegetable samosas, garlic naan, saffron-flavored basmati rice, butter chicken, dal, aloo gobi, creamy raita, and saag paneer. He sets everything out on white ceramic plates. We begin eating with our fingers, dipping the naan into the curries and scooping the rice with it. I watch Jim and Yan, and I follow their lead. Seeing Yan eat with his hands doesn't surprise me as much as seeing Jim do it. Jim says this isn't the best Indian food he's had; the best outside of India was from a hole-in-the-wall in London he used to visit when he lived there for a summer as a student.

"Why don't you transfer to Brooklyn College? It's allegedly the poor man's Harvard," Jim says.

"Allegedly?"

"Hey, why don't you tell me to get out of BMCC?" Yan interjects.

"I have, but you just want to be in business administration. Dull, boring. You'll go to Baruch eventually," Jim retorts. Yan smiles and nods, agreeing with Jim.

"I haven't confirmed it myself, but the other public colleges should still be better than a community college even if they are all in the same system. If you look at the faculty list, you'll see that a lot of them were trained in Ivy League universities. Not that Ivy League graduates are smarter. It just shows they have the means to be there, and they want to show the world they're special. Just tell anyone that you've graduated from Yale and they'll look at you differently than if you say you've graduated from some community college."

Jim has a point. During one of my Blimpie shifts, I overheard a group of snarky students from Stuyvesant High School make fun of each other by saying they're so stupid they wouldn't make it through BMCC. But they were talking about people like me and my classmates, who are hardworking people—some of whom have families and children to look after, along with working one or two jobs, doing what they can to survive by getting a degree.

When I told Yan about this, he scoffed and said that he lost friends from middle school who took the SHSAT exams. The ones who made it through went to Brooklyn Tech or Stuy. Once they attended those high schools, his world and theirs never seemed to meet again.

I never would have thought that Jim was gay. He's so masculine. In the Philippines, most of the openly gay men I saw on TV or on the streets dressed like women and were so flamboyant. They were the loudest and most expressive, but also the funniest and most dramatic. To see someone like Jim, who is so reserved, manly, and subtle, it is hard to believe.

One time, while watching *Dirty Dancing* and talking about how Patrick Swayze was still very masculine even though he was a dancer in the film, Papa talked about the Hollywood icon he liked, Rock Hudson. Papa was such a huge fan because of Rock Hudson's suave presence in films, especially in *Giant*, which he starred in alongside James Dean and Elizabeth Taylor. Papa thought that if Rock Hudson could get a woman like Elizabeth Taylor in the film, he must be like that in real life, so Papa tried to emulate him. Papa even showed me old pictures where he copied his hairstyle. "But Rock Hudson got AIDS. Bakla pala siya," Papa said, disappointed. "Sayang," he would say, "lalaking-lalaki pa naman." Because Papa thought it reflected poorly on him that he was fooled. He assumed that Rock Hudson was the man's man.

Papa also liked Marlon Brando as Stanley Kowalski in *A Streetcar Named Desire*. He wore a thin white cotton ribbed sleeveless tank top, like the ones almost every male in the Philippines wears since they are cheap and good in hot weather. They go out wearing wife-beaters, shorts, and slippers, drinking and talking to men also in wifebeaters, shorts, and slippers. They act more like boys than men, playing games and ogling women in the streets and eating fish balls, betamax, and chicken innards from stalls. Salty sweat runs down their spines and is absorbed by the thin white fabric of their shirts. When I found out why it is called a wifebeater, I wondered if it's because of Marlon Brando as Stanley. How many women fall for men like Stanley? How many women are stuck with men like Stanley?

I've seen Jim wear a wifebeater, but only as an undershirt. Yan is so attracted to Jim, especially his leather jacket. It makes Jim look suave and cool. I am drawn to Jim too, though not necessarily in a sexual way. Jim has his appeal.

Yan once mentioned how jealous he would get when he found out that Jim occasionally slept with women. "To keep up appearances with his family, the real one," Yan said with sarcasm. Jim had a certain type of woman from what I understood. Tall and thin and very flat-chested, almost androgynous. I am none of those things. Attraction to me was out of the question.

"Don't stay up," Jim says, winking at me, as he and Yan leave for a date.

"She's not a child," Yan retorts.

The next morning, I smell freshly ground beans percolating in the coffee machine.

"How long is she planning on staying here?" I hear Jim ask quietly.

The question takes me by surprise. I didn't realize Jim was uncomfortable with me staying here. What about all the talks we had?

"Until she gets on her feet."

"When's that going to be? Months from now? She's been here for two months already."

"Five weeks. You're not even here most of the time. You hardly stay here except to feed the damn snake, and now you're only here longer than two days because he's shedding his damn skin!"

"Do you know how often he molts? I want to save his skin. It's very delicate and you might rip it and then I'll have to wait months before he sheds again."

"What the hell?"

"It's for an experiment. I want to make a meditation tool from his skin."

"That's the weirdest shit I've ever heard of."

"It's for meditation. You wouldn't know anything about it."

"Are you calling me stupid? You always call me stupid."

"I do not. Stop changing the subject. I didn't get to where I am today to house runaways. There's the Covenant House in Times Square for that."

"I'm a runaway," Yan hisses.

"I don't mean you. I mean—"

"I know what you mean. She's a friend and I invited her to stay with me because I am lonely. I'm not some damn snake. I need people around me."

They keep talking, vacillating between silence and loud whispers. Jim's initial question still rings in my ears, ricocheting in the crevices and folds of my brain. I think about how in the last week, when he came back from a particularly grueling outing with his employer's family for an event with a big fashion house, he was quiet and grumpy. He sometimes stared at me, and I would catch him looking at me. When I did, his expression would change, and his eyes would crinkle, and the corners of his mouth would rise in a small but genuine smile.

I should have known. It's the American way of hospitality. In the Philippines, you could stay at people's houses for months at a time. At least, this was true in the provinces. I know because Papa grew up sleeping in other people's homes.

Yan makes an exasperated sound, his voice rising. "When I came back you were talking like she was your best friend."

"Unlike you, she's interested in books other than romance."

Their voices trail off to the bedroom and then there is silence. When the door closes, I hear only my own breathing. I make up my mind to go back to Brooklyn and live with my mom. I won't be where I'm not wanted.

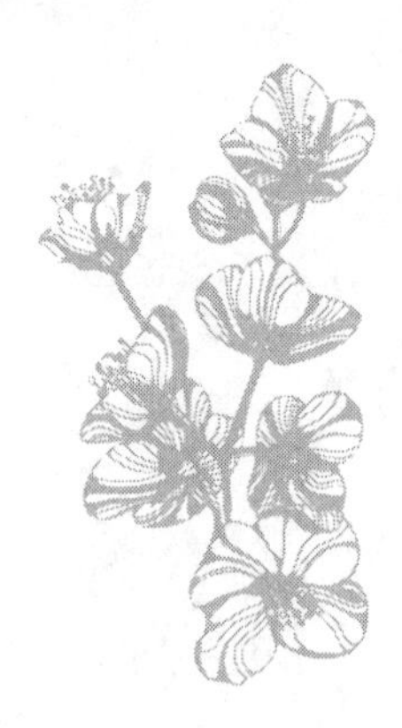

I spend a restless night thinking about going home.

Here, I can forget. But when I go back, I don't know what I will face. Even Papa once told me, "Once a whore, always a whore."

I found out from Tita Cynthia that the Filipinos in the hospital think Ma is a whore, and they don't even know about her past. They say she's still a married woman, that she's going around with a younger man without a care. "Walang kahiya-hiya," they said. I asked Tita Cynthia if she thinks Ma is shameless too. She sighed.

Tita Cynthia told me, "Anak, don't be like your ma," and to heed what it means to be a good Filipina woman because "a good woman is hard to find." Tita Cynthia also said that others were jealous of Ma. So young, so pretty, all the men flock to her. They pitied her when they found out she was with an old man, but now they are also jealous.

As the night progresses, I dream that I am a white dog being chased by women throwing sticks and stones, yelling "whore."

The apartment in Sunset Park is dark, quiet, and empty. The key still works. Almost everything looks the same, even how the furniture is arranged, but I can feel Junior's absence. No video games, no consoles, no notebooks, no clothes scattered around. I'm surprised Ma hasn't moved out yet with her lover. Then I would be homeless.

I see Radu sleeping on the bed, slightly snoring, nude, his buttocks in full view. I back away and walk quietly to the bathroom.

When I finish in the bathroom and open the door, there is Radu, standing naked with a leery grin on his face. I scream and back away from him. He stops and squints at me.

"Mel?" he asks.

"I am not."

His thick European accent blurs in my ear. "Sorry, I don't have my glasses on . . . I didn't know anyone was here."

We both stand there like idiots for what seems like an endless minute, or perhaps it was a mere twenty seconds, not knowing what to say to each other. This is the guy Ma is fucking.

He quickly returns to the dark room where he was sleeping and puts on his pants. I hear the front door open. It's Ma. She sees me standing like a petrified creature.

"What are you doing here?" Ma asks, setting down bags of groceries.

As if I need a reason to be in this apartment.

"Radu?" Ma walks forward, looking for him.

"I'm here," Radu says, exiting the room, barefoot but with a shirt and pants on.

We stand there in silence for a few seconds. Ma breaks it by going to the kitchen with the shopping bags. I follow her and begin unbagging them. A brown paper bag spills out from one of the plastic bags, and Ma, upon seeing it, tries to take it from me. A box of SKYN condoms falls out. We both look at it, and then Ma looks at me before quickly stuffing it into her handbag.

Neither of us says anything.

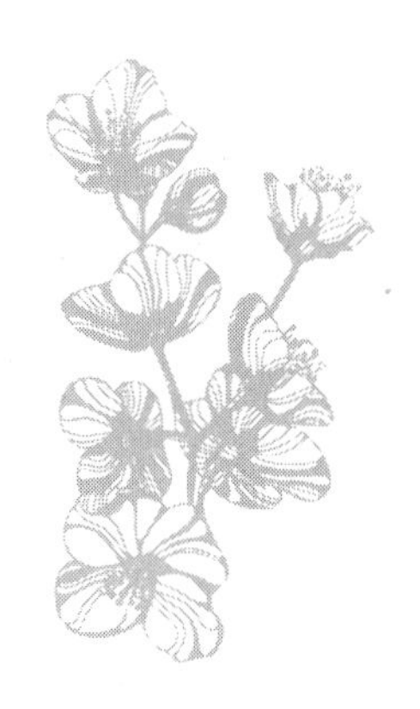

"Ms. Beatriz died," Ma says, putting the phone back on the receiver after we pass an uneasy night together. I slept on the living room couch; Baldie went back to his apartment in Bay Ridge. Ma didn't want to live together, but Baldie suggested it so that they wouldn't have to pay separate rents. "I don't want the gossip," Ma said. As if that mattered at this point.

I didn't want to fight with her, so I didn't tell her that I already knew what the other Filipinos were saying about her.

"Flor wants us to come to the funeral next week in Queens."

I hadn't heard Ma talk about Ms. Flor in a while, not since Papa left and Junior was sent away. Ma, unlike Papa, doesn't like to air out what stinks in the closet. She will smile and tell you she is thriving. "Never let anyone know you're weak," she would say. "You only show them you're defenseless, so they feel sorry for you and give you what you want."

Ma sits on the edge of the couch, her eyes far away.

"Ms. Beatriz was a good woman. She didn't look down on people and she lived a long life," Ma says.

"How about Lucia?" I ask.

"What about her?"

"I don't know if she was nice to her all the time. She screamed at her."

"That's what happens when you're the help." Ma shrugs. "You think no one screams at me at the hospital? You think all the residents respect me just because I'm a nurse? They think they know everything just because there's an *MD* slapped onto the end of their name."

Ma complains about the time when one of the first-year medical residents looked at a patient's chart and berated her for not giving him pain medication stat. He threw the patient's chart across the nurse's station and stormed off. When Ma picked up the chart, the metal rings of the binder opened, and all the papers fell to the ground. The unit ward clerk helped her put everything back in order.

"You screamed at Tessie when you were growing up," Ma says, reminding me of Ate Tessie, our live-in nanny, housekeeper, laundress, cook, and surrogate mother all rolled into one.

"The difference is that I was a kid," I say, feeling guilty.

"Ms. Beatriz was old. Sometimes old people scream like children."

Like Ma, I am surprised that Ms. Beatriz held on for as long as she did.

Once, when I was looking after Ms. Beatriz, she was napping, and I pictured what she would look like dead. I pictured a distant future in which her face would droop like a deflated balloon as the last breath escaped her lungs. I imagined bouquets and garlands of flowers around her body and the heavy scent of roses sprayed around her and photographs of faces she would join on the other side to keep her company. Together, they would make an orchestra of objects—lifeless and waiting to be forgotten.

I heard from Ma that Zeus was too busy with law school to visit Ms. Beatriz and that she might have died of a broken heart, waiting for her grandson to appear.

Baldie drives me and Ma in his Toyota Land Cruiser. Ma wears a sleek black dress she just bought from Macy's, black high heels, and black stockings. I'm wearing black flats and a hand-me-down dress from her. Ma did my makeup as if it were her own. Side by side, we could be mistaken for sisters, a compliment Baldie gave Ma that made her cheeks redden more than the powdered blush she put on my face.

This is the second funeral I've attended. When I was nine, the father of one of my playmates died. He went to work in one of the Benguet gold mines and got crushed by falling rocks. They were able to recover his mangled body after a day of digging. He had a closed-casket funeral since his face was unrecognizable. I remember his widow climbing on top of the wooden casket, her voice hoarse from screaming and cursing God for taking the very life out of her and their three children, who were just in grade school, and that now they had nothing. The priest had to calm her down. Most of the people who came were people who hardly knew the family. They were there for the food. Sotanghon noodles, rice, puto and kutsinta rice cakes, dinuguan, arroz caldo, SkyFlakes, instant coffee for those who wanted it, Zest-O juice packs, gallons of Tang with ice were served. Not long after the funeral, the family moved away, back to the widow's family on a farm in the Ilocos region.

—

Baldie barely finds parking in the lot. We go inside and I'm struck by the red velvet and wall-to-wall sconces. The room is filled with flowers in every arrangement imaginable: wreaths, sprays, bouquets, and crosses. Everyone here is from all intersections of Ms. Beatriz's life. I see Ms. Flor, Dr. McDonnell, Michelle, and Lucia, but I don't see Zeus, which brings me both disappointment and relief.

Ms. Flor, her chest heaving with sobs, cries over the body of her mother, holding on to the coffin to steady herself. The priest has a hard time getting her attention. He hovers over her and says "Mrs. McDonnell" a few times and clears his throat. Lucia taps her gently on the shoulder and whispers to her. Ms. Flor looks up, her eyes red, and dabs a piece of Kleenex around her face to avoid ruining her makeup.

"I'm sorry, Father," she says, composing herself, looking around and remembering there are other people here too.

"Sorry for your loss," Ma says, and gives Ms. Flor a hug.

Ms. Flor hugs Ma back, but her eyes are on Baldie, who also gives his condolences. Ma and Ms. Flor disentangle from their embrace and Ma introduces him.

"This is Radu, my friend."

Ms. Flor smiles and inquires after my father.

"He is fine. Couldn't make it today because he had to work."

A total lie. He wouldn't have come. I overheard Ma tell Papa about it over the phone and she asked him to come, because without the money Ms. Flor lent, we couldn't have come to America when we did. I heard Papa yell something to Ma, and Ma pulled the phone away from her ear. "It's up to you," she said.

"It's fine. Thank you for coming," Ms. Flor says, and turns to me.

"Sorry for your loss," I say.

Ms. Flor inspects me from head to toe, scrutinizing the changes in my body. Perhaps she smells the perfume I sprayed on myself—Ma's gift from Baldie.

"Such a pretty young woman," she says.

"All grown up," Ma says.

"She looks more like you now," Ms. Flor says, and Ma thanks her.

"I thought about calling for you every time Michelle went back to her country," Ms. Flor says, "but your mother said you're going to school."

We all know this isn't true. Ma would've pushed me to keep working for Ms. Flor had Ms. Flor asked. She excuses herself and speaks to a group of people who are just walking in. We turn our attention to the casket.

I am surprised at how ethereal she looks wearing her traditional cream-colored Filipiniana dress with puff sleeves, her hair brushed and styled, her face covered with powder and blush. Black eyeliner has been carefully applied with seamless strokes across her eyelids, and her lips are pink and glossy. I'd never seen Ms. Beatriz wearing makeup before. Even in death, she is stunning. A corpse bride, sleeping, waiting for her prince from Hades. Even her fingernails are painted pink.

Ma and Baldie go off and talk to the people they know from the hospital. I am left alone.

Suddenly, the air changes around me and the hairs on the back of my neck prick and I turn around.

"How long have you been there?" I ask.

Zeus doesn't answer for a while. He just watches me. His face seems leaner, and there's stubble on his chin. "You never answered my calls."

"I'm sorry," I say, looking around until I see his mother. Now she looks like the woman we both know, imperious and certain, with no trace of the display from earlier.

"She hides it well, but she's devastated," Zeus says.

"She's a great actress then," I reply.

"She could have been. She used to say that there were film directors who approached her to star in their movies, but she refused all of them."

More people arrive and I begin to feel claustrophobic. People approach Zeus, giving their condolences. Some of them look at me, probably wondering who I am. Zeus turns to me and asks, "Can we talk after all this is done?"

I nod, then find a seat and watch everyone pay their respects to the woman in the casket.

After the funeral, we all go to a restaurant not too far from the cemetery. They serve a buffet lunch with a mixture of Filipino staples like adobo, pancit, lumpia, and empanadas, as well as some American dishes like chicken tenders, beef brisket, and french fries. There is even a table with cookies and some pastries. The only thing missing is a celebratory cake.

Michelle seems to have shrunk a little from when I saw her last. She cries as we stand in line for pasta.

"I'm going to need a new job now that Ms. B is gone," she says.

"Maybe you can go back to your country and look after your family," I say.

She looks at me as though I've grown horns on my head and clucks her tongue and shakes her head. "With what money? There are no jobs there. You stay where the job is. Besides, do you know the headache I went through to come here?"

She's right. It was thoughtless of me to say that.

We look over at Lucia, who is approaching us. She seems to have aged from when I saw her last. Her back has a slight bend that I never noticed before, as though she bent down so much that she forgot what standing up straight was like.

"At least she's still working," Michelle says.

Lucia stands next to us, and I see our reflections in the mirror, holding our plates in this buffet line. Side by side, even though we are all different ages, we are all connected, and for a moment, I think about the three fates and their sisterhood tied to the natural order of things—the girl, the woman, and the crone. We're all here because we served Ms. Beatriz at different stages and different times.

We finish piling food on our plates and sit down at one of the tables. Lucia and Michelle reminisce about their moments with Ms. B. I can't contribute much since I was only with her for a few weeks.

"That woman loved her grandson so much that nobody was good enough for him," Michelle says, and proceeds to talk about the time Zeus brought a girl to the house when Ms. Flor and her husband were vacationing in Aruba.

I see Ma and Radu at another table talking to some people from their hospital. They look like a cozy pair, with Radu putting his arm casually on Ma's seat. I can see Ma's hand on his knee. I feel a lump in my throat. I cannot remember a time when Ma and Papa were ever as close as this in public. They both had reservations about displaying any kind of affection; Papa because of his conservative upbringing, while Ma felt the shame of not being able to do better than marry an old man with no money.

Zeus walks toward our table and says he needs to borrow me for a few minutes. Michelle's eyes move back and forth between him and me. Lucia looks away as though she knows the trouble we are about to start.

"Let me tell my mom I'm leaving with you," I say.

"Tell her I'll drive you home," Zeus says.

I approach Ma's table and whisper to her not to wait for me. Ma looks behind me and sees Zeus standing several feet away. They wave at each other. Then Ma turns to me, smiling.

"He's a good catch," she says.

"We're not having this conversation," I say.

Baldie looks at him with disapproval. "Isn't he supposed to be with his family at this time?"

"They're kids, darling. Let them have their fun," Ma says, squeezing his hand.

"You should talk," I say under my breath.

"What did you say?" Ma asks.

"Nothing. Have fun." Before they can say anything else, I walk back toward the other side of the room, where Zeus is waiting for me.

Zeus and I leave before coffee and dessert are served, away from the prying eyes of the crowd.

Zeus parks the car in a discreet cul-de-sac in a nice neighborhood with large houses and lawns littered with garden gnomes and mini fountains. "One of my classmates from high school lives here," he says, pointing to a colonial mansion. "No one's home. Family trip to the Bahamas."

"Have you done this before?" I ask.

"Done what?"

"Take a girl out after a funeral."

"It's a first."

We both laugh.

"Ma's boyfriend wasn't happy that you're not spending time with your family right now."

Zeus's face darkens. "What does he know? Who the hell is he to judge somebody? People grieve differently. You wouldn't know it, but my mom's been drinking heavily. Following in the footsteps of her husband. It's a hobby they share now."

"Don't you like your stepdad?"

"He's all right, but he's not my father and he never will be."

"I hope he doesn't drink while he works. He's a doctor."

"You think doctors are holy? They're human just like the rest of us. I think he almost got caught drinking at work one time, but he's friends with a lot of people, so they let it slide."

"Why does he drink like that?" I ask.

Zeus pushes his seat back and loosens his necktie. He puts his hand behind his head and closes his eyes.

"He thinks he killed somebody. Malpractice. He worked at a private clinic and then at a hospital. He prescribed the wrong medication or the wrong dosage. Something like that. But the court couldn't prove anything. Guy left behind a family. Pregnant wife and two kids. A mortgage."

"It sounds like it was an accident."

"Accident or not, he thinks it's his fault and that he's going to pay for his sins one day. That weighs on him."

I feel close to Zeus in that moment. My hand finds his knee, connecting my body with his. He opens his eyes and takes my hand. Our fingers interlock.

"What does your mom see in him?"

"Who knows . . . After my dad died, she was a mess. This guy was there. I guess that's what it takes sometimes. Just being a body in the right place at the right time."

I blush at the way Zeus looks at me, as though he is searching for something inside me that I am not even aware exists. My heart beats wildly in my chest, an origami crane tearing its own paper wings to fly.

We lean toward each other. My face falls into the sphere of his gravitational pull. We kiss.

Zeus leads me to the back seat of his car. We both kick our shoes off. Our hands grope each other, feeling the curves and angles of our bodies. His long arms envelop me.

"Help me," Zeus says, crying. I hug him harder.

His tearstained face is so soft, so near my face, I want to suckle on his cheeks. My mouth searches for the scent of his sadness, freshly baked bread and musk, and I lick his face gently. My mouth eventually finds his and then he kisses me back; his own sadness escapes him and makes room for desire through tongue, through mouth, through fingers touching my breasts through the fabric, through tongue snaking down at the urging of its own gravity until it excavates what I am ashamed of and brings it to light, to moist, to wet, and the walls inside me break at the force of the tide crashing into me.

Zeus stops and fumbles for something in his glove compartment. There's a box of condoms. He tries to fish for one, but when he shakes the box, it is empty.

"Shit, I ran out," he says.

I hesitate and find the condom that Yan gave me. I'd left it in the pocket of my purse, forgotten.

"I have one," I say.

Zeus looks at me and says, "It's OK. I want to feel you."

I want to feel him too, even though I don't know what that means. I just want him in me.

—

Even though it feels like eternity, it doesn't take long.

—

"I love you," I say, because this is what girls tell boys after. Zeus's eyes open, a startled look that turns feral, when he realizes what we have just done.

The next day he calls.

—

"When are you ovulating?"

—

"I don't know," I tell him, my voice small, a little brown sparrow jerking its head and body, ready to take flight.

—

He makes me count the days with him, and in the background, he asks questions like:

"When was the first and the last day of your period?"

"Are you sure?"

and when he is satisfied, he says, "I'll get you something."

Three hours pass with me looking at the phone until it rings again. When I pick up, he tells me to come outside.

The air in his car feels stale and I feel feverish thinking thinking thinking but not thinking hard.

Rap music plays.

"I didn't know you liked rap," I say, numb.

He doesn't reply and instead pulls out a paper bag from the glove compartment. Plan B pills he bought from somewhere. His hands are so sure, and he's so composed, that it seems like he's done this before.

I look out the window and see a man and a girl, about four or five years old, come out of a deli holding hands. The man carries a bottle of blue dishwashing liquid. They stop outside and he gives the child a lollipop.

"Hey," Zeus says, touching my hand. His eyes follow mine and we watch the child peel off the wrapper.

"Take one now," he says. "Then I'll call you to remind you to take the other one twelve hours later."

He twists the plastic cap off a water bottle and hands it to me. How thoughtful. Our fingers touch and my fingers shake, and I spill a little water on myself. He pushes the thin aluminum covering to free the tablet, puts it in the palm of his hand, and waits for me to take it.

It's so small, like a piece of candy nesting on a miniature skin pillow. *Don't get pregnant,* I hear Ma's voice whisper in my head. But what if I want to? Did she want it? Did she want me? Did she have a choice? Ma's body housed mine when she was nineteen. Her life flashes before me, a kaleidoscope of moments where a scared girl like me crosses a line that she can never return from. I understand Ma for an instant. Tears pool in my eyes. This fear seems as old as time.

"It's for the best," he says.

I say nothing and continue staring at the pill. He loses patience and takes my hand and opens my fingers and tries to put the pill in my palm. My palm shakes. I close my hand again. He lets out a loud exhale.

"Open your mouth," he says, exasperated.

I do as he says, and he places the pill on my tongue. I taste the bitterness, far from the sweetness of candy. He points to the water bottle.

"Swallow," he says.

I do.

PART THREE

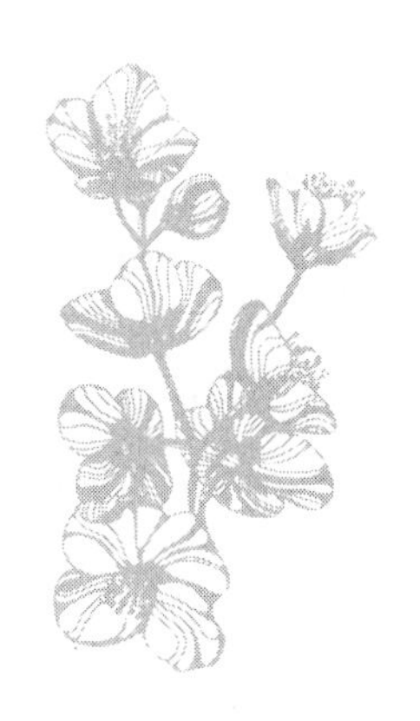

I was made to read the Bible in my religion class at my Catholic high school. Mr. De La Cruz, a stiff-lipped unmarried man in his fifties rumored to be closeted, would repeat the verses from Matthew 7:16–20 again to everyone:

> *Beware of false prophets, who come to you in sheep's clothing . . . You will know them by their fruits . . . A good tree cannot bear bad fruit, nor can a bad tree bear good fruit. Every tree that does not bear good fruit is cut down and thrown into the fire.*

Mr. De La Cruz called women wolves in sheep's clothing, reminding our all-girls class that it was Eve who presented Adam with the temptation that caused him to fall from God's grace. He focused on verse eighteen and told us all that no good comes from contact with Eve. Mr. De La Cruz would look at us and say, "The apple does not fall far from the tree and God help us all."

One time, when Ma was still in the Philippines, we went to midnight mass before attending Noche Buena at our neighbor's. During the sermon, the priest was in a rage. He said there was talk about how servants of God were found in a house of ill repute because they were tempted by Eve's, and thereby the devil's, minions. He spoke at length about these jezebels. How they were bad fruit from bad trees. Then he took a deep breath and talked about the birth of the savior. I remember turning to Ma because she was shaking and making a scene. Papa shushed her and pinched her arm. She glared at him. On our way to Noche Buena, they argued. Ma said that there was no place in this hellhole for her.

Ma doesn't go to church unless it's a big holiday like Christmas or Easter. She doesn't even like keeping any saint statues or pictures in the house. "I don't like them watching me," she used to say.

—

All I can think of is Zeus and how exposed I am.

There was so much bleeding after I took the pills. Forced bleeding. There could have been a life there absorbed by menstrual pads or flowing down the drain when I showered. Or it could just have been blood at that time of the month, heavier, as if it also contained my shame.

But maybe I want to come from Adam's rib, to know the place of my origin was from below his heart.

—

The thought of Ma and Radu together flares such jealousy.

—

A beggar woman pleading *love me* as she opens her legs to a man in the hope that he will never leave.

—

How about me?

—

Would I understand her more if I were in her place, desperate?
Worse yet—am I the same as her?

The apple doesn't fall far from the tree.

Twenty-one and fallen. Where did the time go?

This is how beggar women begin to know they are beggar women. The feeling of falling into an abyss, screaming for deliverance. The desperation clings to them like perfume. Everyone smells it, and people are either repelled by it or attracted to it.

Then, somehow, through the numbness, when they think they can't fall any lower, they claw their way out to some kind of light.

What did I come to America for? What did we all come to America for? Wasn't it for a better life? Junior in California, sullen and rebellious until military school and living with an ex-military uncle, has trimmed his edges. Papa, living in limbo at Mr. Park's with a job that he despises, laments his life in his twilight years. Then there's Ma, who is living her American dream. What about me?

After my first class with Mr. Teutonico, I stopped for a semester. No, it was after Zeus that I stopped. I barely finished the term, and when I did, everything was a blur after. I took a pair of scissors and cut my long hair until it was just jagged ends. When Ma saw, she screamed at me, saying a woman's beauty is in her long hair. "What is wrong with you?" she asked. Radu told her that I was just acting out and to leave me alone. For once, I appreciated him. She shut up and left me alone.

I just kept working at Blimpie until exhaustion took over. I got orders wrong sometimes. People yelled at me and sometimes cursed me out. When I wasn't working, I walked endlessly, blocks upon blocks, in Brooklyn and Manhattan. One Saturday morning, I walked from Sunset Park to the Manhattan Bridge, crossed it, and ended up in front of Jim's apartment in Tribeca without thinking. I rang the bell, but no one answered. I kept ringing until, I don't know what came over me, I started to cry. I sat there, bent over, huddled in a corner, and wept until an older woman tapped me on the shoulder and asked me if I was all right. She offered me a bottle of water and said, "Everything will be fine," before hurrying to the subway.

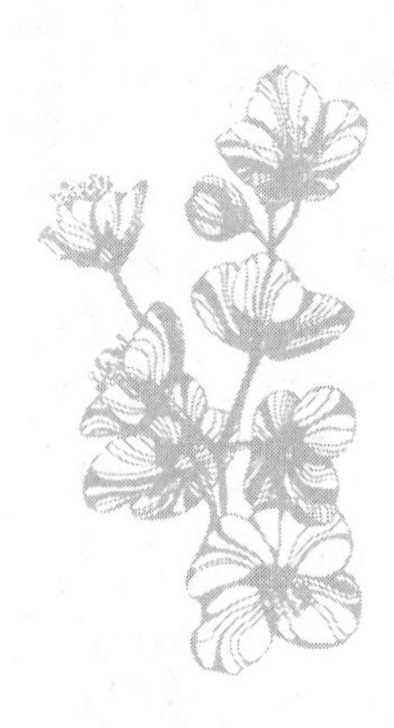

My old classmates write to me less frequently now, if at all. In the beginning, everyone wrote, interested in connecting with me just in case I make it big in the Big Apple. The promise of success and knowing someone in America who might one day return and take them to a restaurant to eat expensive food appealed to them. But I stopped responding after a few months. My old classmates have moved on. Some of them are graduating. Some of them are about to get married, pregnant with some boy's kid. Some of them are planning to go abroad and work in Dubai. Maybe some will end up as domestic help in the Middle East.

Everyone has a future to look forward to except me.

Mr. Park tells me he's been taking Papa to his church and many widowed Korean women talk to him because they say he is handsome and that, with his chiseled square face and baby-soft skin, he looks like he is in his fifties instead of his seventies. I find this hard to believe since he aged so much. I suppose to others who don't know him as well he still looks youthful. Ma did say that Papa was a good-looking man in his prime.

"But isn't he old and short?" I ask, folding the clothes I'd just washed.

"If he is, then you're also saying I'm old and short." Mr. Park grins. He and Papa are almost identical in height, though Papa is a little shorter.

"No, I didn't mean that . . . I mean . . . shouldn't they be looking for someone younger?" My face turns shades darker.

I know Papa just goes to please Mr. Park. He said so himself the last time I talked to him.

"How's Junior?" he asked, and I told him to fly to California and find out himself. "How can I face him?" he asked, his head low and his eyes on the paper cup of coffee in his lap. I wanted to throw my drink at him and scream, *How about me?* Instead, I rolled my eyes and then he said, "Your mom used to do that when she was upset," and I stopped, horrified that I was becoming like her, even in this small way.

"What did Papa think of the church ladies?" I ask.

"He says they're too old for him," Mr. Park says, chuckling.

"He would say that," I say, smiling in spite of how I feel, telling Mr. Park how Papa always seemed to have a flock of women after him. In the Philippines, this had mostly been poor girls looking for someone to give them help.

"He can't marry them anyway. They're not divorced yet," I say.

"Yes, your mother mentioned," Mr. Park says. He stops what he's doing and hesitates, then says, "Your mother is still young and beautiful—"

"But?"

"No but. Just that people come here, and they change. This country changes you," he says. "My daughter is too busy with her schoolwork and her job to come visit. I don't blame her. I didn't make the time."

He tells me that she wrote about him in her college applications. How he never came home after her mother died—because he was always at the laundromat. He smelled of bleach, fabric softener, and detergent, and the fresh-clothes smell never went away, even when he sweated. He spent so much time washing and cleaning other people's laundry that the smell became part of him.

"I guess that got her into school," Mr. Park says.

I say nothing and imagine myself writing about Papa. What is there to say about him? He used to tell me a story about how all he did was work growing up, but when he could, he escaped his chores to play with the neighborhood Filipino boys. He said he was so good at the games boys played—basketball, jackstones, shooting with marbles—that they called him Sharp Shooter Sam. He beamed with pride until his mother would show up with the wooden stick she kept behind the counter of her store, chasing after him with her little feet to beat him.

In the Philippines, Papa liked to watch American films that he would rent from a store on Session Road. We watched Alex Haley's *Roots* from one of the pirated VHS tapes he borrowed.

"See how they were taken as slaves," Papa said, pointing at the TV and shaking his head in disgust when a white man kept whipping the hog-tied Kunta Kinte to get him to say the name Toby.

Papa pontificated about poverty after war when we watched *Gone with the Wind*, especially during the scene when Scarlett O'Hara tears down the curtains and says, "I will never go hungry again." It reminded him of how he grew up and how everyone was afraid and hungry after World War II and how his mother would sometimes not give him and his siblings enough to eat even though she owned a store. All the neighborhood kids teased him because he was supposed to be rich. They dared him to steal food from the store, and once, he stole a piece of warm bread. His mother beat him when the inventory didn't add up and she found out he'd taken it. She kept beating him until welts formed and he bled.

He said the world back then seemed simpler. Go to America and all your dreams will come true. You will never go hungry again. You will never be sad. You will never be lonely. You will never suffer.

One of the drying machines rings loudly, its cycle finished.

"We should all go eat dinner today. Your father wants to go to this new place near his building," Mr. Park says, interrupting my thoughts.

The new place near Papa's building is Vietnamese. It looks cleaner than the dingy Chinese takeout places we usually frequent, where the employees are so harried that there isn't even time to wipe the grease off the Formica tabletops before other customers come in, so the surfaces are thick with piled-up old grease and sauce turned dark gray. But this Viet place feels rich, each table covered in not just a dark forest-green tablecloth but also glass. There are holders for chopsticks and condiments in glass jars: chili oil, sliced jalapeño peppers, sriracha.

Mr. Park and Papa are already sitting and drinking tea from small white cups when I arrive. As soon as I take my seat next to them, Papa's hair stands out. His hair is dyed black. My mouth opens in shock.

"You look different," I say. I have never seen Papa with dyed hair before. He used to say that he had no one to impress.

"You like it?" he asks.

I hate to admit it, but he looks younger than his age. I nod and tell him that he looks great. He beams.

Papa pours me tea. They've already ordered, and the waiter, a short, squat man in a dark green T-shirt, comes over and asks me if I'm ready to order. I ask the waiter for his recommendation, and he says pho without hesitation, so I nod and tell him I'll get the number one special.

When the food comes, we eat in silence. Neither Papa nor Mr. Park likes to talk when eating. They believe it's sacrilegious to open your mouth to speak when grace through food is trying to enter. When they are almost done eating, Papa and Mr. Park exchange glances and Mr. Park slows down chewing, clearing his throat and taking a sip of tea.

"What do you think of me having a girlfriend?" Papa asks.

As soon as I hear these words, I choke on my food. Papa gets up and tries to pat me on the back, but I move away and indicate I am OK even though I'm not. When the coughing stops, I ask him to explain. He tells me he is in love with a girl my age. A girl he met on Facebook. From the Philippines.

"Are you serious?" I'm so angry. I don't even know where to begin. He couldn't even support his family, let alone himself, and now he is *in love*. This is sick. This is crazy. I look at Mr. Park and he looks away, barely making eye contact.

"Did you know?" I ask.

He nods hesitantly.

I turn to Papa and ask him, "What did you promise her? Do you send her money?"

He doesn't speak.

So many words crowd my throat. Words that would disrespect him, that would show him how he's a poor excuse for a father and a man.

Instead of saying anything, I get up and leave.

At home, Ma puts on her makeup and arranges her hair into a braid that reaches her waist. She went to the salon a few days ago and got her gray covered with black. Just like Papa. She only had an inch taken off to trim the split ends. "Short hair is for tomboys," she would say.

When Ma takes her time to put on her face, she looks like she's just stepped out of a lifestyle magazine. She invokes the women from a long line of women who are going to hunt. Their choice of weapons: cabbage soup to lose weight, lemon water in the mornings, the master cleanse, eating only between the hours of ten and six. Then, after these hunting rituals, the result: the face of a woman, airbrushed and ready for the kill.

When she returns tonight, if she returns, her hair will no longer be in a tight braid, but loose. She takes a bottle of perfume, a gift from Baldie, and sprays it all over herself. This reminds me of Ms. Flor. The smell of too-ripe flowers overwhelms me, and I start sneezing.

"Are you getting sick?" Ma asks without looking at me. She holds a bobby pin between her teeth as she examines her reflection in the mirror.

I don't answer and turn on the TV. It's a rerun of an *Oprah* episode where she's talking to a writer, an old white man, who says his postapocalyptic novel about a harrowing father-son journey to a desolate wasteland after some unknown cataclysm is actually a love story he wrote to his son.

"I asked you a question," she says, irritated.

"What?" I ask, and she repeats her question. "No. You smell . . . it's just too strong," I say, thinking about Baldie on top of her and screaming her name, or perhaps she's screaming his.

She says I have no taste and tells me it's one of the most in-demand perfumes in the world. She drones on about how worldly she is and what she *knows*. I try not to laugh out loud.

I wonder if she *knows* that Papa is *in love* again. I wonder if she would even care. I have questions, but they remain in my throat. They have their secrets. I have mine. I suddenly feel lonely.

"Have fun," I say as she walks out. A lady dissolving into the night.

My feet slowly go to her vanity. I don't know how long I stand there, feeling like an old person confused by this image of a girl. The creams, perfumes, ointments, salves, and makeup tempt. I watch myself transform as I rub cream into my skin and put makeup on in imitation of Ma's ritual. First foundation, then eyeliner, then eye shadow, then lipstick, then blush, then a poof of powder for the makeup to set.

I open her drawers and find black lace underwear and a push-up bra with their tags still on, and the image of her sagging breasts held up and wrapped in the lace and how she would use them to seduce a man makes me uneasy. But then couldn't I do the same with my painted face and perfume and black lace?

I call Yan's parents' house to see if he's there. He sometimes comes by his old apartment to visit his mom when his dad isn't home. Yan hasn't told her about Jim. She thinks he's staying with a friend and that he's doing well and going to school.

Yan's there, and he comes over when I ask him to. It's his first time in this apartment. He looks around and I can already feel him judging.

"I know it's not your palace in Tribeca, OK?" I say, irritated.

"I didn't say a word."

"You don't have to. Your eyes say it all."

We go to Ma's vanity, and he inspects her perfume. "Hmm . . . expensive," he says, spraying his wrists. He looks through Ma's makeup, opening bottles and containers, and wrinkles his nose when he's dissatisfied with a product she's using, especially now that he has access to the top-shelf items Jim buys for him.

"Pretty soon that guy might be your stepdad. Is he hot?"

I punch him in the arm. He knows I don't like it when he jokes about the man my mother is fucking. I lift my chin toward a photograph of Ma and Baldie. Ma had replaced photos of her and Papa, as though paving the way for the new future she wants. Yan picks up the photograph, examining it.

"I think balding men are cute," he says.

"That's not moral support," I reply.

"Jim is balding, but he shaved off his hair, so now he just looks like a bad boy, so that's hot," Yan says. "And when he wears his leather jacket . . . meow. Better than when he wore that damn toupee."

Behind the photograph is the old one of Ma and Papa, its edges torn. Ma is still a girl, barely out of school, already pregnant with me, her smile cracking from the weight she was beginning to feel. Next to her, Papa is beaming with pride, his smile strong and reassured that the tide of the future would carry them forward.

"Your mom is such a looker," Yan says over my shoulder.

I put the photograph down and ask Yan if that means he would fuck her.

A flash of annoyance flits across his face as his eyebrow shoots up. "Excuse me?"

I repeat the question with no inflection in my voice.

"I don't get hard thinking about it, OK?" he says. "It's like looking at a Barbie doll."

For him, a beautiful woman is to be admired.

Even boys like Yan cannot escape. They admire pretty women because they envy them. Maybe they want to be them. They want to be admired as well by men. They want to be the face that launches a thousand ships. And so some of them do the next best thing. They fuck the pretty women. If they can't, they worship them like idols.

I call the number I find on Craigslist.

Just like Yan, I want to be carefree.

"Hello," the woman says with a rasp. My voice is just above a whisper when I answer her. I don't even bother telling her a fake name. I tell her my real one. Queen Elizabeth.

"Is that your real name?" she asks, unable to hide her incredulity.

"Yes."

"Uh-huh."

She doesn't believe me. It doesn't matter.

"I'd like a job in your agency," I say.

She gives me an address and I write it down with an unsteady hand. She sounds out each syllable like I'm hard of hearing, stupid, or someone whose first language she doesn't share. She hangs up.

—

The next day, I arrive at a tall building in Midtown. I pass by a uniformed security guard sitting behind a desk, looking bored, as he reads a newspaper. He doesn't spare me a glance. This is just as well. I don't want anyone looking at me. When people look at you closely, they judge you.

—

"Men, women, both, threesomes, orgies?"

Her question takes me by surprise. The audacity of it is blunted by her flat expression. I nod. I say yes to everything even though I have no clue what it really means. I'd only been with Zeus, once, and that was enough to make me feel nothing. There was also Papa's stash of porno that I'd watched long ago, in the Philippines.

She stops to take me in. To really look. She takes another puff of her cigarette. Her long black hair is braided. Her dark skin reflects the pink glow of the light next to her. Her lips are thick and red. She quickly eyeballs me from head to toe. I am wearing jeans and a T-shirt. I feel plain. I don't move.

"You sure—?" she asks again. She puffs her cigarette.

I watch the gray smoke filter through her lips. "Yes," I say.

Because how will I make the pain inside go away if I don't try? I don't want to be innocent anymore. Innocent people get into trouble because they get tricked. But I don't tell her this. I remember the things my mother has said about fear and opportunity, that risk is our daily bread, and how you need to be aggressive in America. I push her away from my thoughts. This is not the risk she has in mind. That much I know at least.

"We're an agency. Men call. Or women. Or whoever."

"Whoever," I echo.

"Yeah. You know. Money is money. We don't discriminate. Of course, we're walking a fine line, you understand? We have our boundaries and it's up to you to set those for yourself. You just have to know what you're getting into. This is just business."

This makes sense.

"There's also whatever, if you know what I'm saying," she says.

"Whatever?" I ask.

"Sometimes clients ask for some kinky shit," she says.

"So how do you—?"

The phone rings, cutting me off. She answers. I let my mind go blank for a second and look around. The room is dark, and the haze of her cigarette smoke hangs in the air. There are no pictures of naked girls on the walls. Just pieces of paper all over. There is, however, a photograph of the new Black president. He is smiling and waving. Next to this is a photograph of him, his wife, and their two girls. They are all smiling.

She reads something from her notepad. I notice her nails as she takes a sip from her mug. They're so long they remind me of talons, each one painted a bright red.

"The room number is five-oh-nine and it's at the Sheraton," she says to someone on the phone. She hangs up, then turns back to me. She dials a number. Someone picks up. She tells whoever is on the line an address. She turns back to me after she hangs up.

"I was about to say the cut's fifty-fifty," she says.

She eyeballs me again. I feel self-conscious.

"Thirty-six, twenty-four, thirty-six," she says out loud.

I look at her in surprise. The numbers do not match me at all, especially the waist. I'm about to say something, but she raises her manicured hand and motions for me to come to her desk. I approach and see she has an assortment of headshots of smiling young women. Her ashtray is filled with caramel candy wrappers, chewed gum, and cigarette butts. There is a cane leaning against the desk. I quickly look down at her legs. Something is misshapen. I can't quite tell. She notices my gaze, and she quickly shifts a shawl on her lap over her legs. I feel like I am caught doing something I'm not supposed to.

"It's not polite to stare," she says.

"I'm sorry."

She points to the computer screen. I see she has uploaded the picture I sent to her. My smiling face looks back at me beside the smiling faces of all the other women. Some look innocent, while others have expressions that telegraph they're ready to devour someone. The screen looks like a page from a senior yearbook.

"What name do you want to use?" she asks.

"I don't know," I say.

"Well, don't give your real name, but I guess even if you give that name no one will think it's real," she says. She stands up to reach for something and I see her legs. One is deformed and larger than the other. She sees me looking. Our eyes lock for a second and she lets the shawl fall on the floor.

"There's a reason you never give your name," she says.

"What's that?" I ask.

"So people can't hurt you. Names have power," she says.

I want to ask her about this, and about her leg. Whether Amber is her real name or one she uses so that no one can hurt her. But it doesn't matter. There's an air about this place that says no questions are allowed.

She gives me a credit card reader made of dark blue plastic. It's small. She shows me how to work it, ripping a sheet from a booklet of receipts and a credit card on the table.

"Now you try," she says.

I copy the movements she showed me. I make the receipt exactly as she did, even though my hands are clumsy.

"You got it on your first try," she says.

I smile, weakly clutching the paper. Even call girls have to give receipts to show the transaction is complete.

"Do you need any paperwork from me?" I ask.

"We're strictly a cash-only business. With our girls, I mean. I don't need anything from you. No name. No social. If the clients use credit cards, you use this," she says, pointing to the small blue plastic machine. "When you use the card reader to charge, we give you your cut at the end of the day once we clear the funds," she adds.

"What happens if it doesn't work?" I ask.

"That's why you wait till it's cleared. You don't want the card declining on you once the deal is done. Otherwise, you're just giving a freebie."

I'm told to stay within the vicinity of the Midtown Manhattan office or around Columbus Circle. "Most of the clients are in the area," Amber said. "But don't be in an area that's too crowded. You'll stand out." I pick Columbus Circle.

I wear jeans and a jean jacket, a Maybelline lipstick color called Mandarin Rapture I found on Ma's dresser, and black eyeliner from a ninety-nine-cent store. I don't know how I look. It's cold and raining. I get wet. I am a drenched rat.

God is coming down on me, crying. Here are all the tears of the world, and I am about to drown in them. Everything makes me cold deep into my bones. The only thing that warms up is my feeling of shame.

My phone rings. It's Amber. "Hey, you got somebody."

I take the train to Chelsea and enter one of the apartment buildings on Ninth Avenue and Twenty-Second Street. Amber told me this john wants a special experience, and no sex. She said she decided to give him to me instead of one of the other girls who liked doing kink. "It's hard to fake innocence, you know?" Amber said. Although I agree, I am confused. What does this person want if he doesn't want sex?

I ring the doorbell to apartment 3F, and I want to vomit. The door opens. It's a very thin guy with glasses, wearing a plain white cotton T-shirt and jeans. He is very pale, and his eyes are sunken underneath the thick glasses.

"Hey, I'm . . . Emma," I say, thinking about Emma Bovary, and how, at this very moment, I, Queenie, as Emma, am on a spiraling descent to fallen-woman status even though I don't think I would go so far as to kill myself like Emma did. I don't owe the kind of debts she accumulated. I take a deep breath and smile.

"Hey, Emma . . . I'm Chris . . . uh . . . do you wanna come in?" he asks nervously, and steps aside to let me into his apartment. There are boxes everywhere, opened, unopened, and half-full. Some of his belongings are shabby—old and mismatched furniture—but the apartment is clean. He's so skittish that he's talking nonstop, saying it's his first time calling an agency, that his parents just died three months ago, and that he's been sad. He wanted someone new, the newest girl the agency had.

"I'm sorry," I say, and mean it. He leads me to a worn leather couch covered by a crocheted, brightly colored afghan. I smile at him, and when he looks away, I scan the rest of the apartment. It's my first time being in an apartment only occupied by one person.

"Do you have roommates?" I ask.

"I live on my own now," he says. A large tuxedo cat appears from one of the boxes. He meows at me and parks himself at my leg. "Except for this little guy."

The sight of the cat calms me down. Maybe I won't be killed by this man because he has a pet cat.

"What's his name?" I ask, stroking the cat's fur.

"Henry," he says. He explains that he's a history buff and the cat's name is based on Henry VIII, who created the Church of England just so he could have many wives.

"Didn't he have one of them beheaded?" I ask.

"Don't worry. This Henry won't behead you," he says, chuckling, and I swallow hard.

I think of Jack the Ripper from London, the infamous serial killer who killed prostitutes.

"I know you're on the clock," he says, "but I want this experience to last for a few hours."

"Sure," I say. "What do you want to do?"

"We'll just talk for now . . . and what I would really like is for you to treat me like a baby," he says.

I nod. It doesn't seem like a hard thing to do. He leads me to a closed door in his apartment, and when he opens it, I see what appears to be a crib large enough for a full-grown man.

The rest of the room is filled with large plush toys and toy blocks. Everything is in soft pastels. Chris opens one of the drawers and shows me a collection of pacifiers, and from the bottom drawer he pulls out a cute apron with a fleur-de-lis motif.

"Can you wear this?" he asks.

"Over my clothes?" I ask, nervous.

"I would really love it if you could wear it with nothing underneath," he says.

"It's your call," I say, forcing a smile.

—

"I'm sorry about your parents," I say. I am thinking about my own parents as I slowly stroke Chris's scalp. He drops his baby talk for a little bit and talks about how his father was dull and quiet, sterile and serious and more interested in his failed inventions than in humans. When Chris was growing up, they'd pass each other in their own kitchen like strangers. The only good thing he did was buy an insurance policy that afforded Chris a small fortune.

"What about your mom?" I ask.

Chris looks up at me and says that his mom was a housewife who did nothing but complain that they lived so country that she couldn't go to museums and cultural events. "She wasn't very smart, though," Chris says, explaining that she liked to talk of culture this and culture that, but that she read nothing but cheap romance novels and watched daytime soaps.

"She wanted a girl," Chris says, "and from the moment I was born, I had already disappointed her."

"It's different for us. They want boys to carry the family name," I say, and he nods.

I feel sorry for this quivering bald man whose head is on my lap, wearing nothing but an adult diaper and a light blue pacifier necklace. He can barely see me without his thick glasses, and he frequently squints, reminding me of baby moles I once watched in a Discovery Channel documentary. He looks up at the ceiling.

"There was a time when my mother babysat a few kids who were still in diapers, and she paid more attention to them than I'd ever seen her pay attention to anyone. I was twelve, and seeing all these innocent, small creatures mewling in diapers made me so curious. I stole a couple of diapers, and I went upstairs into my room and tried one on. I just wanted to see what it would feel like. It was small, but I wasn't that big at the time. Then I sat down and played games on my computer, and I just forgot that I had it on. When I remembered, I was really excited, but I didn't want to get caught. After sitting there for a while, I needed to go pee, and I actually considered going to the bathroom and doing it the regular way, but then I thought, here I am wearing a diaper, shouldn't I just use it? So, I just peed. Right there." Chris stops and turns his face up at the ceiling. He closes his eyes while his slim, pasty fingers touch the diaper and then he squeezes the fat on his inner thigh.

"It felt weird, but as soon as it started and I felt that flush of warmth, it felt so comforting, you know? That might sound strange, but that's how it felt. I didn't even realize until half an hour later that the diaper was meant for a toddler, so it couldn't hold everything coming out of me and it leaked onto my clothes and the chair, but I enjoyed it. At the same time, I was thinking there must be something wrong with me. But now I know there's nothing wrong with it. I'm not hurting anyone. It just gives me so much comfort, you know?"

After he finishes speaking, he looks up at me, waiting for approval, and I understand how this person found his bliss, and is willing to go to great lengths to get it, and this is something I can respect despite how odd I find him. Not knowing what to do, I tell him he's a good boy and pat his head like I would Hercules or Daisy. Chris seems to like that, because he closes his eyes and smiles.

I suddenly smell something terrible and see that Chris is continuing to smile, but that his smile is full of mischief.

"Baby had an accident," Chris says, and starts making baby noises.

I have a sinking feeling about what he wants me to do. Chris starts to become more agitated and points at me to play my role more seriously. He points to a collection of wet wipes, paper towels, and latex gloves, and I try not to let my face reflect the turmoil I feel inside.

"Does Baby want Mama to clean him up?" I say, trying to keep my voice bright.

I think about the days and nights when I had to clean up Ms. Beatriz—this feels much dirtier.

After three hours, with my pocket heavy from the cash Chris gave me, I call Amber from my blue-screened Nokia. The line on the other end rings once.

I tell her: "I can't do this again. I don't think so."

"Uh-huh," she says with no hint of surprise in her voice.

I make a sound in my throat. I don't even know that I'm doing it. It's a gurgle. But somehow my resolve is coming across because Amber is answering me.

"If that's what you want," she says.

"I don't know what I want," I say.

"I can't help you there."

I hear another line ring, and Amber says hello and please hold before turning her attention back to me.

"Listen, you know where we are if you change your mind. You have to come by to drop off the money. Make sure you bring it because I'm going to count . . . I don't want you shorting me." She hangs up without bothering to say goodbye. Just like that, it's done.

—

I open the door to the empty apartment and feel cheap and dirty. But also exhilarated. I did something bad. Like a grown-up. But just because a girl knows she did something bad, it doesn't make her a woman.

I answer another Craigslist ad. It seems safer. All you need to do is massage people. That I can do. I can massage. I think about the Chinese shampoo girl at the hair salon that Ma goes to as well as the faith healers in the Philippines who use their hands to heal. What they do seems easy enough.

The ad asks for a photograph, so I look through images of me smiling. Everyone likes girls who smile. I pick two images, attach them to the email, and send.

An hour later, I receive a reply. *We like your picture,* the e-mail says. *Come meet us.* There's an address in Gramercy Park with an apartment number. I hesitate only for a moment, but that moment passes, and my resolve brings me to the door of the apartment.

I don't know what I am expecting. The exterior of the town house seems normal—a place where normal people live. A cast-iron veranda and small white Greek columns frame a solid door. Big pots of evergreens line the clean pavement. I almost feel like I'm not in the New York I've come to know.

I put my hand on the door handle and press down on the lever. It opens, so I let myself in. An empty hallway. A staircase. There is no one to ask me where I'm going, so I take the stairs to the third floor.

I ring the doorbell. My heart is pounding. Someone opens it. I see a distinguished-looking man a head taller than me in a blue silk robe and slippers. His face and skin remind me of smooth pebbles bleached white by water.

"I'm Jin," he says.

I barely squeak a hello back. My mouth is dry. My whole body wants to run. He holds out his hand. I take it.

"Your hands are so smooth," I say in awe.

"I moisturize," he says, and smiles. His teeth are perfect, unblemished, straight, and pearly white. "Let me show you around," he says.

The living room looks like any other living room. Large, comfortable sofas with throw pillows. A coffee table with magazines I have seen on newsstands. I look to see if there are ones that cater to men. Jin notices.

"No girlie magazines if that's what you're thinking," he says, and winks.

He takes me around the apartment, briefly pointing to the doors of the three bedrooms. One of the doors is wide open and I see a group of three girls lounging on a bed. Two brunettes playing with their phones and a blond woman reading a book. I try to read the title, but I realize it's in Cyrillic. They all look up and give me a nod.

"Some of the girls come here to relax when they're not working," Jin says.

I see two girls chatting in the kitchen. They smile at Jin but only give me a once-over and go back to what they're doing.

"Be nice," Jin says as he fills up a glass with water. He touches one of the girls on the shoulder and she flashes him a smile.

"Would you like some water?" he asks me.

I shake my head. He motions for me to come with him into one of the bedrooms. I follow. The queen-sized bed takes up most of the room.

"Have a seat," he says. "I'll be right back."

He goes into the bathroom. I hear a faucet turning and then the sound of running water. I look around the room and notice a framed photograph of a single person, naked, standing next to a black Corvette in a villa. I look closer. It is Jin. His skin is bronzed and muscled. I can't tell how old this picture is. The running water stops. A few seconds later, Jin sits across from me on the bed, leaning against the headboard.

"Do you go to school?" he asks.

"I was. I took a break. I'm going back soon," I say.

"Where?"

"I was at BMCC for a bit, but I'm probably going to transfer to Brooklyn College."

"Oh, one of the girls studies at Brooklyn too. There's a few who go to Baruch. Hunter. All working girls," he says.

I'm surprised. All these girls are here and they're going to school.

"What are you studying?" he asks.

"Literature," I say.

"So, you're a reader."

"Yeah."

"Do you want to do this to pay for school?"

"Yes and no . . . not really," I say. "I could get other part-time jobs to pay for school, I guess. But I'm looking for something I don't quite understand."

Jin raises an eyebrow, surprised, it seems, by my candor. I tell him there's a lot going on—how there's no one at home, how Junior was shipped off to California. Jin listens and nods.

"Everyone's got a story," he says.

I am comforted that he understands.

"You don't look like the pictures you sent," he says, examining me.

"Oh," I say.

"You looked happier."

"You heard my story. I got sad."

"Sadness is not a good look," he says. "But what we do in this business is more about your hands. Let's have a try, shall we?"

He lies down and opens his robe. He is naked. I see his penis like dead skin hanging in front of him. He closes his eyes.

"You can start whenever you want," he says.

I place my hands on him and look at the length of his body. I touch other parts of him with one hand while the other takes care of the limp skin. His face begins to turn red, and he squirms a little bit, but it's not as violent as I expect. My breath begins to thicken. My throat dries up, and I swallow to try to get some fluid into my mouth. It's still dry.

My hands slow down, and Jin notices. He opens his eyes and sees me staring at the glass of water.

"Go have some water if you want," he says.

I reach for the glass and gulp the water greedily. The liquid spills from my mouth.

"Careful you don't choke," he says as he grabs a tissue from a box next to him and hands it to me.

Somehow, his tenderness and concern for my well-being move something in my chest. Jin closes his eyes again, and I resume with more intention. I knead him as softly as I can, and I am surprised by the deftness of my fingers. The flaccid thing becomes erect and alive. I look up at his face. It is redder than before. His eyes are open. He is watching me. He takes his hands and puts them on mine. I stop.

"You're gentle and that's potential," he says.

I glow at his compliment and feel a little strange. Am I so starved for an older man saying "good girl" to me? Is this how Ma felt when she worked at the bar?

"I don't mind what you wear, but you have to put care into it. It's not about the clothes. It's about the look," he says.

I nod even though I'm not exactly sure what he's talking about.

"You're clean-looking. That's important," he says, drinking more water and touching my face. He offers me water. I take it and drink.

"It's important for you to hydrate. For your skin," he says, touching his face. "I know what men want . . ." he says while he looks at me. He cups my face and looks at it as he turns it to the left and to the right. He looks at my body and I feel naked. I wait for him to finish what he's saying. He doesn't. He lets the words trail off, as his fingers trace curves lightly into my arms until he clasps my hands, shaping them into fists. Then he releases my hands and closes his robe. He gets up.

"But your hands can do the trick," he says.

I nod again, not knowing what to say.

"You think you want to do this?" he asks.

"I'd like to try it and see if I can do it," I say.

He tells me that there's a building in Midtown where he has two rooms reserved and explains how it works.

"By the way," he says, "I really like you, so just a word of caution . . . don't tell people your life story when you meet them the first time. You might scare them off. And in this business, it's not about your story. It's about the story people want to tell you."

Ma hums as she works in the kitchen, her hair tied up in a bun like one of those middle-aged women we've seen at church. Her demeanor is caused by Baldie's presence. I never saw her smile like this when she was with Papa. Is this the real Ma? Fragrant, sloppy, and reeking of this carefree abandon? It feels almost obscene.

"You're too happy," I say, my chest tight, drinking instant coffee. I'm flipping through the glossy magazines she brought back from the hospital break room.

"Shouldn't I be?" she asks as she scoops ground meat onto parboiled cabbage leaves before rolling them like an egg roll.

She enjoys being somebody's girlfriend.

"I deserve some happiness after everything I've been through," she says, putting the rolled cabbage leaves into a pot.

"Don't worry, Ma. I understand," I say, knowing this dish she's making is for Radu. After his shift, they'll go to his place in Bay Ridge. She'll spend the night there.

Ma beams at me and says, "You've always been a good girl."

"Filipino?" the man asks.

I nod. I don't tell him I'm mixed. It doesn't matter anyway. He is here because of what he wants. He is not much taller than me, and I am short. This makes me feel safe.

"I know my Asians," he says.

I say nothing and try to smile. What do you say to someone who tells you they know who you are?

He asks me for a name. I give him one. Something that sounds exotic. Something French. He gives me his name. I can tell it's made-up. A mask he wears even though he is completely naked before me. He wears only a pair of rimless glasses and a diamond and silver stud in his left ear. I look at the earring instead of his body. I commit its shape to memory—how it shines dully in the dim light. He says his name again. This time, a little louder. It doesn't have the strength of decades rolling off his tongue. I look down. Finally. Then there it is—his flesh. It already hangs on him. Tired of him, perhaps. Even his tattoos look worn-out, their ink fading into his skin, swallowed by his age and lifestyle.

"How old are you?" he asks.

"Does it matter?" I ask, and he laughs.

He lies down on what looks like an examination table in a health clinic. The paper underneath him crackles. The sound of waves from the noise machine hums. I massage him. First, his chest, then my hands move down, down, down. I exhale.

This is it.

I look away, then close my eyes. I begin to touch his flaccidness. I imagine that I am somewhere else, but my imagination is not strong enough. I feel bile wanting to explode from my throat, but I keep it down. He begins to moan. His hands reach up. My hands keep moving. His hands reach the space next to my chest. His hands lower. He moans louder. I finally look down at him. He looks up.

"Can I touch you?" he asks.

"Sure," I say, dreading his hands on me. How could I refuse?

He reaches up again, squeezes my breasts. I let him. I don't like it; I keep my face blank. No pleasure, no pain. Just disgust. *I signed up for this*, I think.

He puts his clothes on. I can see he is surer of himself. He has a satisfied grin. He repeats the fake name I told him earlier. He lets the name sit on his tongue like hard candy he's savoring. It sounds empty in my ears.

"I'll ask for you again," he says.

"Sure thing," I say.

When he leaves, he gives me sixty dollars.

No tip, I say to myself, thinking about Chris and how he gave me an extra hundred on top of what he paid the agency. At that time, the humiliation I felt cleaning his soiled body seemed insurmountable. But this. What was anything worth? His cum in my hand?

I feel anger and shame bloom and boil inside me. Of course, I say nothing. Like usual. I don't know how this works. I pretend I do. Fake it till you make it.

The door closes behind him.

The noise machine keeps humming. I close my eyes and imagine

I am far away. From this place, from myself, from my body. But the sound only carries me so far. When I inhale, I smell the oil in my hands, his semen still on me.

I take a deep breath and almost choke. I need to get out of here.

I call Jin's place. A girl answers. One of Jin's girlfriends. She doesn't have to rub anyone else's dick but his.

I give the same line: "I can't do this."

She doesn't bother to say anything. There is just a click at the other end of the line. They never call me again. They will not run out of women.

I walk around Union Square, and I see one of the girls from his stable. It's the Russian girl, the one with the book. What was her name? I try to remember. Masha. She is blond. Tall. Shaped like a fifties Coca-Cola bottle. She is beautiful. What men want.

I wonder if her perfect figure has a history.

What makes Russian women and Filipina women alike?

A Filipino always knows someone who becomes a mail-order bride, or if they're still in the Philippines, they hitch themselves to anyone who looks like a foreigner. These mail-order brides know that if they want to get out, they must use their charms. They're pen pals first. They exchange pictures. If the brides-to-be can't get better foreign passports, they'll settle for a pensioner who'll stay in their country and lavish them with a lifestyle that they've only dreamed of.

They are everywhere. They are in nooks and crannies, in the cement, in the carpet, in the walls, in the roofs, and in the soil. If they are lucky, they make babies, and the babies are mestizos and mestizas with fair skin and tall noses. These sons and daughters grow, and some of them may think they own the world, and that the world owes them for their pretty faces. But if they're unlucky, then the hell they came from and live in only grows bigger.

—

Before I know it, Masha turns around. She sees me and begins walking toward me. I freeze. "Hey, you're the new girl," she says.

"I just quit."

"Maybe you just didn't give it a chance," she says, joking.

I laugh at that. What does she know? She is what men want. I can see women envy her.

"Let's get a tea at Starbucks," she says, pointing across the street.

—

Masha sips her plain green tea and takes out a container of hummus and a ziplock bag of baby carrots from her tote bag. "Do you like jewelry?" she asks.

I shake my head.

"You should like jewelry because you can sell it if you need to run away," she says. She tosses her yellow hair, which catches the light when she moves. My eyes travel down to her breasts and then to her waist. I imagine what men see when they look at her. My face grows hot. She notices me looking at her. She looks back at me, the corners of her mouth moving. I notice how green her eyes are and how thick the lashes are.

"Your English is so good," she says.

"Yours too," I say, even though she has a strong accent.

She fingers the pendant, a white pearl with diamonds, sitting beneath her neck. She slowly traces the thin gold chain it hangs from.

"This is a Tiffany," she says.

"What's that?" I ask, feeling stupid. I should know this since Ma has been getting gifts from Radu and she does nothing but talk about the brands.

"Everyone knows Tiffany."

"I don't."

"You have a lot to learn," she says, but her eyes are fixed on someone else. I follow her gaze. She is watching a young girl wearing a T-shirt and pajama pants, and even though her hair is in a ponytail, it looks uncombed.

Masha says that in Europe, no one dares to go out looking like they've just tumbled out of bed.

"She probably goes to one of the schools here. NYU maybe. They have a dorm there," Masha says, waving her hand. "This place has so many children."

"What makes them children?"

"You can tell a lot about a person by how they dress," she says. She lifts her hands and looks outside. There is a mix of people from all walks of life: middle-aged men and women in suits and office clothes; young college students with backpacks and rumpled hair; men and women with mismatched outfits that look like they were bought from flea markets and thrift stores; a homeless person sitting on the pavement with layers of dirty clothing.

"That's a textbook case of judging a book by its cover," I say.

"Don't take this the wrong way," she says. "But don't be naive. We cannot survive this world without making judgments."

Perhaps she has a point. Anything coming out of her mouth seems true. I watch her move as she speaks. So refined and dainty.

"How are you so . . . ?" I ask, unsure of how to describe her.

"So . . . ?"

"Beautiful," I say, feeling dumb.

Masha's smile turns wider. Something in her seems to glow. She's even more beautiful than before. How is this possible?

"It's because I know who I am."

"What do you mean?"

"You have to know where you're from because that's how you

know where you're going. That's how you know. I'm going to tell you a strange story my mother liked to tell me when I was a little girl growing up in Novgorod." Her voice changes a little. "Where I'm from, it's a place with many names. You heard of Saint Petersburg in Russia? It was Petrograd, then Leningrad, and now it's Saint Petersburg. The name is different. But do you think the place ever changed? It's still the same place. It's people who give him meaning and tell him he's different."

"Why do you call the city 'him'?" I ask.

"In my language, city is masculine."

"That sounds strange."

"Language is strange," she says.

She tells me about her mother's city. When it was Leningrad, there was a famine for three years. There was a blockade. It was in the 1940s. No one came in and no one left. The Leningraders were trapped in the city, forced to be self-sufficient, eating what they had. First, they ate their normal food. They thought the siege would end soon. Then they began rationing their supplies. Everyone lost weight, but so what. They were still alive. Then they ate pigeons, cats, and dogs. They were thin and bony, but so what. They were still alive. Then they ate the leather clothes and belts they had by boiling down the hides into a kind of soup. The soup was shitty, but so what. They were still alive. Then when everything ran out, some people began to die. Before their bodies stiffened, their neighbors came to hack off an arm or two. They needed to eat. What's an arm or two when they were desperate and the cries of their children and the growling in their stomachs kept them up at night. It was an evil thing to steal your neighbor's dead flesh, but so what. They were still alive.

Masha is still eating her baby carrots with hummus. She tells me the story like she's reciting a childhood poem.

"That's where I came from," she says, finally. "I always remember this story. It keeps me going, knowing that my mother went through that when she was a little girl. Why don't you drink this?"

She hands me a small glass bottle filled with amber liquid. I drink. The alcohol goes down hard. I cough. My head feels light. I drink some more: to forget, to feel, to live.

"Do you drink often?" I ask.

"Only when I can't handle things," she says.

She looks at her hands and her right index finger traces the ring on her middle finger. It's a plain gold band. She is also wearing two silver bracelets with three small charms on each.

"Tiffany?" I ask.

She nods and lifts her hands to show me a bracelet.

"I like these," she says, fingering a small key and then a red heart charm.

"Pretty."

"They mean a lot to me. Gifts for myself," she says.

Maybe it's because she is paying attention to me, but I feel her beauty in a way that overwhelms me, and I just want to touch her skin. Or maybe it's the alcohol.

"Sometimes you need something to make yourself bigger inside because you feel so small," I say, beginning to see why people turn to alcohol when they're feeling too much from the crush of life. Like Papa. I take another sip and start coughing.

"Slow down," she says, and touches my arm. "You're going to lose yourself like that."

But maybe that's what I want: to let my thoughts permeate the air, to let out the blood that runs in circles in my body, to be free.

"Have you been to Fifth Avenue?" she asks.

"There's a Fifth Avenue in my neighborhood," I tell her. She laughs at me, but I don't take it personally.

"Everyone has a Fifth Avenue in their neighborhood, but there is only one Fifth Avenue in the world," she says, laughing.

We take the subway to Times Square and walk toward Fifth Avenue. We pass by St. Patrick's Cathedral, and I realize that I have never been inside. Masha crosses herself three times.

"Why cross yourself?"

"It's a habit," she says.

"Can we go inside?" I ask.

"Why not?"

The cathedral feels so solid, like it was built to withstand time. There is so much space. We sit at the back pew and people-watch. A couple walks by, a dark-haired woman wearing a long floral maxi dress and a man with a chiseled face. They look like tourists from Europe, impeccable and rich.

"Probably Russian," Masha says.

"How can you tell?" I ask.

"You just can."

I understand. Everyone has their own radar. Yan says he has gaydar, that he can even pick out the straight-looking ones.

Masha talks about her fantasy of marrying a celebrity, someone rich and famous. Like an American movie star. She says the biggest problems women have after marrying rich are how to decorate their homes, or that their husbands cheat on them.

"Wouldn't you care if your husband cheated on you?" I ask.

"Why should I? As long as everything legal is in my name, it's OK. I can find love anytime. But money is hard. You've seen what not having it can do? My father drank because we had no money."

I can't help but notice how good she smells, whereas I smell like Irish Spring.

"I used to date an American from Texas. He said Russian women like to take a shower with their perfumes. That he could smell them a mile away," Masha says. She takes a small, clear vial from her bag. She opens it and dabs a little on her wrist and rubs her wrist behind her ears.

"Cheap perfumes are the worst," she says.

She likes Chanel, but other name brands will do. She doesn't mind Guerlain or Dior. I look at her blankly. I don't know any of these brands except maybe Guerlain. Radu gave Ma something like that.

"I don't know those brands," I say.

"You don't? We have to change that!"

She takes me to Sephora several blocks away. We spray ourselves with tester bottles. She asks the salesgirl for a sample. The salesgirl eyes us with an expression that tells me she's not pleased by this request. "I'm sorry, but we don't do samples anymore."

"That's impossible. I got samples before."

"New policy," the salesgirl says.

Masha shrugs and we spray more white strips of paper to get a whiff of the different smells. I start sneezing.

"Your nose is sensitive," Masha says. "This is how I used to do it in the beginning . . . now I get it from people who want me."

She begins talking about etiquette and grooming. How she used to shave her pubic hair but now does Brazilian waxing. Beautifying. I've never heard anyone talking about these things. I wonder if Ma does it too.

"Who teaches you to be a woman?" I ask.

"You're so funny," she says. "You learn from everyone. Your mother, your grandmother, your sisters . . . every other woman. We are animals. We teach our young to be exactly like us. That's why it's so important for children to learn."

What did Ma teach me about being a woman? She wasn't even there when I bled the first time. I couldn't ask her over the phone, and we never talked about what it meant.

"How do you know so much?" I ask her.

"I'm thirty. The older you get, the more you know. You get hurt. You survive. You do what you have to do."

"Don't you want all this to end?"

"Of course. I can't keep doing this forever." She takes a pen from her handbag and scrawls her number on a piece of paper and tells me to call her, giving me a kiss on the cheek.

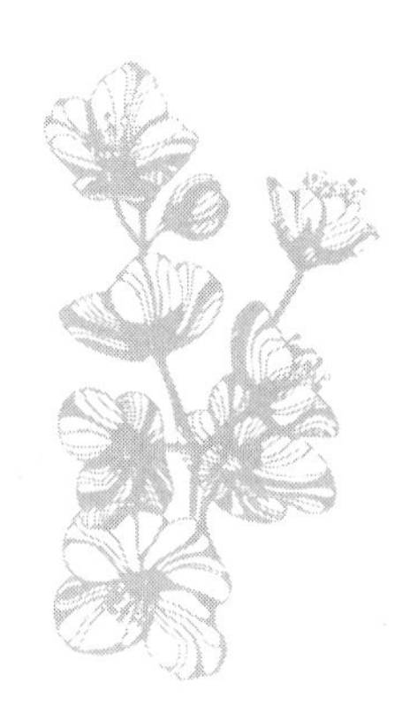

Brooklyn College. I can't believe it!

Even though it's already fall, the weather still feels like summer.

But it's like spring to me. A new beginning. Like I'm really doing it. Twenty-two years old and I'm here. I finally feel like a real American college student going to my beautiful American campus with a manicured green lawn and a clock tower in the center.

My English 1012 class is taught by Lorie Schwartz, a brown-haired white woman in her late twenties and a doctoral student at the Grad Center studying women and gender studies with a specialty in race and gender performance. I don't really know what that means. It's not something I have ever heard of. In the Philippines, we had basic subject matters that were permutations of the three R's—reading, writing, and arithmetic—as taught by the Thomasites, a group of six hundred Americans who had graduated from universities across the United States and arrived in Manila in 1901. Our subjects were home economics, math, English, history, Tagalog, music, and physical education.

Today's class is dedicated to unpacking a Judith Butler essay called "Performative Acts and Gender Constitution: An Essay in Phenomenology and Feminist Theory." I thought I was the only one who didn't understand most of it, but I wasn't going to admit it. One of the few lines I really understood was Butler quoting another philosopher named Simone de Beauvoir, who said, "one is not born, but rather becomes a woman."

In the Philippines, we would listen to the teacher's lectures and regurgitate all the material back on tests, verbatim. Here, you're expected to participate and provide your own answers to essay prompts.

Lorie opens the class by asking everyone if any of us understood the essay. We all look at each other with wary expressions. Most of us are freshmen or sophomores, transfer students, but a few are also older, coming back to finish their degrees. The oldest student is Magdalena, Maggie for short, a Puerto Rican lady who said that she has three kids, the oldest a freshman, also at Brooklyn College but not in this class. She's in her forties and let everyone know that she had opinions. On the first day of class, she told everyone, "I'm a mom, I went through shit, and I got opinions." We all look at Maggie expectantly. Even Lorie looks at her.

"Look, I don't get this at all and I'm not stupid. Why does anyone need to write like they don't want anyone to understand?" Maggie asks.

The room explodes in sound and movement, releasing our collective breaths and creating a storm of chatter. Everyone begins raising their hands and chiming in that they also couldn't fathom what the text was.

Lorie turns on the projector screen and shows us slides, quotes that she took from a *New York Times* article about academia and bad writing.

> [Bad writing] raises questions about the purpose of scholarship. What is the goal of literary and cultural criticism?
>
> Who should the nation's educated elite be talking to?
>
> Are scholars increasingly making themselves irrelevant?

Then in another slide, Lorie shows us a sentence taken from one of Butler's essays, which won first place in *Philosophy and Literature*'s 1999's Bad Writing Contest:

> "The insights into the contingent possibility of structure inaugurate a renewed conception of hegemony."

Lorie points out that the *New York Times* article quotes a law and ethics professor who said that it was hard to figure out what the essays mean. "Do these ideas help you with life? Like Maggie here . . . would it help her as a single mom raising three kids?"

Maggie nods in agreement. The rest of the class listens with rapt attention, hearing their thoughts translated into words, but in a way that makes sense.

"Don't you feel better?" Lorie asks.

Everyone nods.

"Now that you're not intimidated, you can tackle this essay."

It's a lightbulb moment for the class.

"Don't judge yourself before you read, but don't judge what you're reading either. Everything comes from somewhere. That's the law of nature. Nothing is created or destroyed, just transformed. You can help yourself by knowing the context of what you're reading. Don't be afraid to figure it out."

At Jim's duplex, Yan and I are staring at Bowie's shed skin, which is stretched out on a mirror and covered with a geode-colored resin that mimics the vastness of deep space. The resulting image is distorted in some areas, clear in the rest.

"He just had this made. It came today," Yan says. "He wanted you to see it. I don't know why Jim always asks about you. He wants to know why you're not staying at his place anymore."

"I transferred to Brooklyn College. Didn't seem to make sense to be here," I say, not mentioning what I overheard. If there was one thing I learned in the Philippines, it's don't overstay your welcome. People don't have to tell you to leave in the first place when you're visiting. They'll tell you to stay, but you should really go. It's an unspoken rule.

"I'd be jealous if you were a boy, but I know he fucks women sometimes for the hell of it, so maybe I should be worried," Yan says.

"Are you jealous?"

"No, just being moody."

"Why?"

"He's always comparing you and me. I feel like he's my dad," Yan says, and then, in falsetto, does a crude imitation of Jim. "Why aren't you more curious about the world? Why don't you read something else other than this trash?"

Yan's habits began changing when he moved in with Jim. It wasn't just the romance novels. He started to watch anime only when Jim wasn't around. His clothes are different, more expensive, brand name. He stopped using Victoria's Secret. The scent he favors now is muskier, with some floral notes.

"Maybe he just feels sorry for me," I say, reminding Yan that he was the one who told Jim about my life.

"Yeah, me and my big mouth."

Jim arrives as Yan and I are playing *Call of Duty* on his Xbox. He said that he needed a point-and-shoot game where he could feel like he was in control.

"That again?" Jim asks, glancing at us and then going to check on Bowie. Satisfied, he comes back and hovers.

"Yes, daddy, this again," Yan says, petulant, without looking at Jim.

Jim nods at me, takes a glass, and pours himself a drink from a Johnnie Walker bottle. He drinks the first shot and then pours himself another. Then he goes over to the sofa and puts the glass against his temple.

Yan pauses his game and looks at Jim. He stands up and walks over, giving him a deep kiss on the mouth, his left hand snaking and loosening Jim's belt and stroking his dick. I look away, horrified and thrilled at the indecency of something so intimate. My parents didn't even hold hands when they were still together.

"Hard day at work?" Yan coos.

Jim laughs and nips at Yan's ear. "We have a guest," Jim says, pulling back a little, but Yan holds on to him.

"It's OK, she's family," Yan retorts.

"Naughty, naughty."

Yan releases Jim and looks back at me, then gives Jim another kiss. Confusion spreads through me like wildfire. What in the world is Yan doing?

"What's this about? A show of power?" Jim asks.

"I think Yan just wants to make sure that I know whose man you are," I say, perturbed.

Jim laughs, disentangles himself from Yan, and fixes his belt. He takes the glass from the table and drains it. He is still laughing as he says, "I needed that."

—

"I used Bowie's discarded skin and had this mirror custom-made," Jim says, pointing at his creation.

"Calling it a mirror is like calling a chicken an eagle that can't fly. How is it a mirror if you can't even see your reflection in it?" Yan says.

"It's not a normal mirror. You're not supposed to look at your reflection on the surface. The key is you should look at yourself in a different way."

Jim says that the practice is called drishti meditation. Instead of being closed, the eyes are left open to focus softly on a certain point. He learned it from a lecture he attended at the Rubin Museum a few years back when he was in his Buddhism phase, trying out the Vajrayana, Hinayana, and Mahayana schools of thought.

"We're going to try meditating with this for twenty minutes," Jim says. He sets up the mirror in the middle of the room and takes some pillows from a closet for us to sit on. He lights a candle and places it in front of the mirror. Then he pulls the shades down and turns off the lights.

Jim shows us the proper form of sitting on the cushion. Our spines must be straight, and we must make sure that our shoulders don't slouch. Satisfied that we now know what to do, Jim sets the timer.

It's quiet in the room except for our breathing. In the darkness, I watch the candle flame flicker. My eyes rest on our distorted images. I don't recognize any of us and I fixate on a point in the distortion. My mind wanders from image to image of Ma and Papa fighting to Zeus giving me a small pill to holding a stranger's dick that somehow turns into an albino snake. Before I know it, the timer rings.

"What did you see?" Jim asks.

"Nothing," I say.

"This is stupid," Yan chimes.

Everything changes with one phone call.

Mr. Park's voice is shrill. I have never heard him like this before. His words are garbled, and I ask him to slow down because I don't understand what he is saying.

"Your father," he breathes into the earpiece. "There's been an accident."

He is crying and attempting to explain that Papa is in the hospital and decisions have to be made. His words echo in my ear. It strikes me that when men cry, the sky has fallen and the world has cracked.

"Where's your mother?" Mr. Park asks.

That's a good question and there's only one answer: she is with her new man.

—

Papa was found, face down, on the pavement a block away from the deli where he goes to buy lottery tickets, near the building where he works. His head was bashed with a brick. They said Papa was lucky. He is lucky to be alive. He could have died instantly. So I am told.

No one knows who did it.

The perpetrator hasn't been caught.

No witnesses in broad daylight.

Not even cameras.

—

By the time I get to the hospital, Papa is already in the surgical intensive care unit. He's a trauma patient with a severe brain injury. All the machines around him beep and ring in an eerie harmony. His breath is shallow and jagged, his eyes are closed, and he has a black eye and cuts on his face.

Leaves outside fall, called to the ground to kiss the earth.
    The cold comes and the days get longer.
    Winter sets in, the time for breath to sleep.

Papa is moved from unit to unit in the hospital. Most recently, he's been placed in a room on the surgical floor where he is put by the window. His roommate is a Mexican guy who has been there for over a year. I find out from the Filipino nurse aides that he is undocumented. He got into a fight over something at work. He threw a punch and then the other guy threw a punch. He fell and hit his head. Because of his legal status, he didn't qualify for Medicaid, so the hospital is responsible for his care and they've been trying to get rid of him. Maybe return him to Mexico where he can be a ward of the state. He is already a vegetable, and his family doesn't want him moved anywhere. They are all here. Maybe they are all undocumented. The brother talks to me one day and says he already met Ma. I forget his name even though I try my hardest to recall, but what I do remember is his hair under a trucker hat. It's dried up like a desiccated coconut—oily, with white flakes. I want to ask him, *Have you bathed and have you eaten?* but that might be too rude and too forward. It disturbs me until I look at a mirror and realize the condition of my hair is similar. I wish I could remember his name.

Mar, a middle-aged Filipino nurse aide, tells me that Papa sometimes moves involuntarily. She says that she speaks to him in

Tagalog because sometimes hearing something familiar might help a patient.

"Thank you po," I say, adding the honorific.

She complains to me about the Mexican patient. "Just look at him," she says while preparing the finger-stick machine in the hallway, her eyes sharp and narrow, "just a waste." She talks about how his care is costing taxpayers money.

Benny, the other aide, shakes his head. "We have to work, and that family just sits there while we pay taxes and Uncle Sam takes everything to give it to them."

Every time I see them, their mouths say the same phrases, the same exhausted anger. They remind me of a conversation my auntie Violetta had with Ma on the phone when she asked how Junior was doing in California. Ma put her on speaker, as she was chopping vegetables in the kitchen to make a stew. "Those who don't work, don't eat." Ma agreed with her, going on a tirade about how a lot of people just take advantage of the system and how hardworking people like them give so much of themselves to their work and they should get all the rewards.

They must think Papa is a burden too. He doesn't have all his papers approved yet. Ma hasn't divorced Papa yet because she wanted him to get his green card first, believing this a kindness she could do for him after they had been together for so long. "So he can't throw it in my face that I didn't help him," Ma said.

—

Ma calls Auntie Violetta to tell her the news: Papa has a traumatic brain injury, a head fracture that caused brain bleeding and lacerations to the face. I can hear Auntie Violetta over the phone say, "Oh my God," and asking for the details of what happened. Ma starts crying and her voice cracks. He was found by the garbage bins near his job. Someone passing by saw him and his bloody beat-up face on the concrete. Auntie Violetta asks Ma what she is going to do now that Papa's condition is like this. "I don't know," she says. But I know her mind is already turning. He doesn't have health insurance without her, but if she stays married to him her co-pays will keep skyrocketing.

—

Ma calls Junior. I call Junior. Junior can't come home. He doesn't want to. An almost-fifteen-year-old boy-man. He says that as soon as he turns eighteen, he will sign up to go to the military, and that now he is preparing for the rigors of basic training. "Gym rat activities," he says. He wants to be based in Japan because all he loves is Japanese culture. "Life is better with anime," he told me last time I talked to him a few months back. Ma screams at him. Doesn't he want to see his dying father? Junior screams, saying that he has no family. That his father and mother both abandoned him. He hangs up. Ma cries.

"He'll come around," I say, watching her body shake with sobs as she says what a bad mother she is. I understand Junior and cannot blame him.

I go back to the intensive care floor and look at Papa, listening to the rhythm of beeping machines. I turn to him and think, *I promise I'll be a good girl. Then you'll get better.*

After two months, Papa wakes up from his coma.

At first, I think I am dreaming. His eyes flutter open as I stare into his face, using the meditation Jim taught. In the last month, I would sit in a chair at the foot of his hospital bed for long periods of time staring at him, thinking that I could find something in his face.

"You're awake!" I exclaim.

I immediately alert the nurse. A flurry of activity. Some celebration. A miracle! Even Tita Cynthia comes with her novenas and church ladies, prayer warriors invoking all the saints and the Trinity to aid Papa.

—

Papa calls Ma different names. Norma. Nida. Natalie. Even Osmeña, the name of the Philippine president when he was born. He calls me Lisa and my heart cracks every time he does. But it is worse when he looks at me and says he doesn't know me at all. This cracking grows deeper in me until it is a chasm.

I show him a picture of Junior. Papa touches his temples, struggling to remember. He shakes his head. His voice is low. But he remembers his son. He says his name. Junior. Then he points to himself. Senior. At least there is someone he remembers.

The doctors say he shouldn't drink or eat anything by mouth.

That he could choke. They ask Ma about his nutrition. "He can still eat but not in the same way that you or we can," they say. She agrees to get the PEG tube installed.

What does it mean to be human if we can no longer do things associated with being one?

The smell of bodies disintegrating hangs in the air.

The smell of industrial cleaning products to cover the odor.

The most violent thing I've ever smelled is the smell of a hospital.

I receive an e-mail from Lorie saying she is concerned that I've missed many classes, and that I'm falling behind.

I ignore the message.

"How are you holding up?" Yan asks.

I shake my head, unable to answer. He holds my hand and pats it. We watch Papa try to breathe; his air passage is blocked by phlegm. He lifts his head slightly from the side of the bed railing and spits on the floor. Ma apologizes to the staff, who are people she has worked with before. She tells the other nurses and nurse aides to put chuck pads on the floor to catch the phlegm.

We sit on two visitor chairs at the foot of Papa's bed. Yan is telling me the story about his father again. He worked as a deliveryman for a Chinese takeout place in East Flatbush. One day, he took a delivery to a building, and someone hit him. He woke up in the hospital with no memory of the event after being in a coma for a week.

"He was lucky," Yan says.

"I think it was my fault."

"What's your fault?"

"That this happened."

"How do you figure that?"

"I feel like I've been bad, and this is karmic retribution."

Yan doesn't agree or disagree with me. He simply says, "Who knows."

He and I both know from Jim's lectures that in Buddhism nothing happens in a vacuum. If it's not because of something we did in this lifetime, it's something from a previous one. But who is to say what karma is? Is it instantaneous or does it percolate through lifetimes?

We watch Papa breathe.

Papa cannot stay awake. He falls asleep every hour. CAT scans show the blood in his brain growing one day and shrinking the next. Moving from the left side to the right. "With his advanced age we don't recommend surgery," the doctors say.

I want to cry out: *Just let him sleep.*

Ma cries in the beginning, feeling guilty that her elderly husband is now the way he is. Perhaps it was her fault. But what can she do? Life is sometimes harsh and cruel. "I'm only human," she says to one of the Filipino nurses, who makes cooing noises as they both change Papa's soiled linens. *Even though you*

Even though you
are with someone else

The way they say the words to Ma makes her feel better.

no

one *can*

blame

you

The nurse, Nona, a woman from the country Georgia, says Ma is young and beautiful, that she still has her life ahead of her, that she has done all that she can under these unfortunate circumstances. Ma doesn't tell her about Baldie, that she is already living freely. It would extinguish the tragedy of her story.

I am surprised the Filipino nurses haven't gossiped about Ma to Nona.

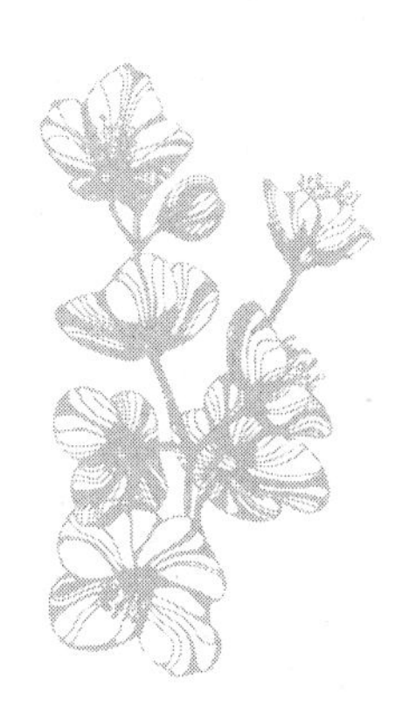

The next week, the divorce papers are signed. Ma sighs in relief, her face clears, and the corners of her mouth lift. The weight of a thousand sunsets disappears. She can now shape her own destiny. Ma belongs to Ma. No, Mel belongs to Mel. Both knowable and unknowable.

The hot water in Ma's foam cup has cooled down; the lipstick stain on the edge becomes deeper with every sip. The loud beeping of machines punctuates the silence after her words.

What is she still doing here, holding vigil? The guilt must be eating her alive. She brought us here. She brought him here and now he's barely conscious.

"You're lucky I'm not like Girly or Juliet."

Ma tells me about her friends from the old days. She rarely talks about her friends, because they were from a life she doesn't want to be reminded of. Juliet was one of the girls who told her about being a go-go dancer in Olongapo. Foreign tourists and American soldiers paid more than the local men who were trying to run away from their wives for the weekend, pretending that they had work that took them away from the barrios or cities in which they lived. "With a foreigner, you have a shot at getting a passport," Juliet told Ma. Juliet's plan was to make a foreigner fall in love with her so she could leave the hovel she came from and maybe help her six brothers and sisters finish their schooling. Juliet ended up marrying a sailor from Virginia. Within weeks of their meeting, Juliet was pregnant with the sailor's child, and the sailor married her. She left the nursing program and became a mother.

Girly, on the other hand, finished her nursing degree and ended up in California. She couldn't pass her board exams to become a full-fledged nurse, so she started working as a nurse aide. After a few years, she became a nursing technician, drawing blood on a medical-surgical floor in the hospital, turning deadweight patients from side to side and cleaning up their shit. She does almost everything a registered nurse would do except document their charts and call doctors to push their medication orders on their patients.

"Girly doesn't want her kids here. She could have petitioned for them to come. She's been here longer than me. She said she's suffered enough. I told her she should take her kids."

I want to scream at her and say she thinks bringing us here makes her a saint, but I don't. What would be the use?

"Do you know how almost impossible it is to be a nurse where I came from? Coming from what I did? So many try, but they fail. Juliet never finished. She's in some other navy town now in Virginia. She has four kids already, each with a different father. She could've been independent, but she chose to 'fall in love.' Love can't feed you."

"But is it really falling in love if she's on her fourth husband?"

"Third."

"Third, whatever. Same thing."

"I could have left your father a long time ago. But who would have brought you and your brother here?"

I wondered why, if she was already planning a new life without Papa, she didn't leave him in the Philippines. Junior and I could have traveled to America without him.

"We're not children. We could've flown by ourselves."

Ma's lips curl and she laughs a little. She shoots me a look and shakes her head. "Both of you were too sheltered. How could I let you fly on your own when you'd never even traveled by yourself to Manila?"

Ma goes on about how some bumpkins would travel to Manila

looking for work and suddenly find themselves disgraced and fallen women. Or worse. Everyone has heard of girls being kidnapped, drugged, and sold, never to be seen again. Even little boys disappeared.

"I didn't know what I wanted until I saw you all at the airport, but by then it was already done," Ma says, tracing the lipstick mark on her foam cup. "You have to understand. I don't really love your father. Maybe once when I thought he could get me out. But when I found out that it was just his family that was rich and not him, that he may have lied to me, I felt trapped. I already had you. What is love anyway? I'm grateful, yes, but shouldn't there be more than gratitude?" She is far away, looking into the distance. "It was a complicated time."

The complication was her being pregnant with me. She could have met a military man she liked who could get kickbacks or be somebody's political stooge, or a foreign student studying medicine at one of the universities. Maybe she did meet them.

"Weren't there other men? You could have gone with any of them."

"There were. Some didn't care that I had you, but I cared. Men say things to get you to go with them. Once you go with them, you realize it's a lie. How was I going to trust a man when I had a baby to think about?"

I'm too stunned to say anything.

"When I got pregnant with you, Juliet said I should get rid of you."

For some reason, this doesn't surprise me. But to hear it said out loud makes my ears burn.

"Why didn't you?"

Ma looks at the fourteen-karat-gold ring Baldie gave her their first Christmas together. She had wanted an engagement ring, but he gave her a gold ring with a turquoise inlay. Ma wasn't too thrilled, but she liked that he gave her real gold even if it was only fourteen karats.

"I couldn't go through with it," Ma says.

I imagine Ma at my age, pregnant by a man she wasn't in love with and her best friend telling her to get rid of the unwanted child. But of course Papa married her. He thought it was charity. He was also probably in love with her, and he let himself be driven crazy.

I almost didn't exist, yet here I am.

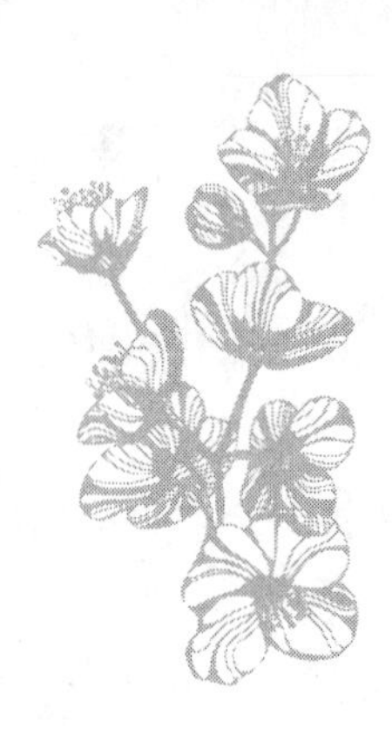

"Your face has changed," Masha says, noting the dark circles under my eyes. It's a face that cares too much, she tells me, and then says women are young and then, suddenly, one day we are already old.

"Botox might be the answer," she jokes.

It's been months since I last saw her.

I tell her about Papa. His body is here, but his mind is far away. This weighs down everything, including my face. Masha clasps my hand and makes a sound. Then she embraces me, saying some words in Russian, soft and comforting.

"Today I want you to think of something else," Masha says, telling me to say no more because words fail in times like these. She takes my hand again and hails a yellow cab.

—

Masha takes me to Tiffany's on Fifth Avenue. "Act like you belong here," she says. I'm not sure what she means, so I stick my chest out and swivel my hips. "What are you doing?" she asks. My body deflates at her attention.

"How do I look like I belong, then?" I ask.

"I don't know . . . you just have to feel it," she says, looking briefly at her reflection in her compact mirror.

I follow her around and watch how confident she is. She tells the salesperson she wants to look at a necklace and a ring. The salesperson, an older woman with white hair in a bun, turns to me and asks me if she can help.

"I'm good, thanks," I say.

"No, no . . . sorry, my friend is very shy," Masha says, insisting that I try on some of the bracelets similar to hers.

"I don't have money for this," I whisper in her ear.

"Shhh . . . it's OK," she says, and she takes out a credit card. "It's what this is for."

"I'm confused."

"Just try things on," Masha says.

I try on a rose gold bracelet and a platinum necklace but feel they are too delicate for me. The designs that fit me are more geometric and more expensive.

"I don't think I should try on anything else," I say, looking at the price tag of one piece shown to me by the thin-lipped woman.

"You're too worried over price," Masha says as she clasps the necklace around my neck. The thin-lipped woman makes a small sound that Masha ignores, and the small hairs on the back of my neck rise.

"You need to buy things with names on them. Real names," she whispers in my ear. Something with a name is like taking a chance. "These will last forever." She moves away and straightens her hair. Her breath is still on the nape of my neck, and I shiver.

I tell her that I've never really paid attention to these things, that I have a bad sense of fashion. Masha laughs and says it's OK, that I remind her of herself when she didn't know anything.

"Don't worry, I'm not insulting you," she says. "This is your armor and you're going hunting."

"For what?" I ask.

"Your destiny, of course," she says.

She tells the salesperson she will be taking two items. She buys a brooch and a pendant with a simple silver chain. She pulls one of the boxes from the robin's-egg blue Tiffany's bag and gives it to me.

"A gift," she says.

"What for?" I ask, my voice cracking.

"It's like giving a gift to my younger self," she says.

I open the box. It's the pendant with embossed print that says:

PLEASE RETURN TO

TIFFANY & CO.

NEW YORK

925

She invites me to her place. She lives in a fifth-floor apartment in a neighborhood called Kips Bay, on Twenty-Eighth Street and Second Avenue.

"Do you have a boyfriend?" I ask her, looking around the apartment, noting the tasteful decorations, a bit of modern and a bit of traditional, with a lot of wood, ceramics, and little details that scream money.

"Of course," she says.

"Does he know you do the kind of work you do?" I ask, then feel terrible that I am prying. "I'm sorry, I know this is none of my business. You don't have to answer."

"He knows," she says slowly, taking off her shoes and putting on slippers with pink bow ties. "He knows because he was one of my old clients. This is actually an apartment in his name where he stays when he isn't living on the Upper West Side with his family. He said he would divorce his wife and their two adopted children, but I told him not to. I want my freedom. Anyway, that's how people are when they're together. They get bored. This way, with this arrangement, there is no boredom. Then they return to you," she says.

She talks about the boyfriend she had in Russia. "Handsome, but stupid. Men always talk big. Show off their muscles, their guns, their money. But he didn't have money. At all. You cannot survive without money in this world."

"What happened to him?" I ask.

"Jail. We weren't married yet, so I left and came here," Masha says as she prepares tea. She offers me butter biscuits from a blue tin.

I tell her more about Papa, and how the last time I saw him, we were in a Vietnamese restaurant with Mr. Park. "He told me he was in love with a girl my age. A girl he met on Facebook." I tell her how angry I felt. I blamed myself when he was later found unconscious with a head fracture.

"Men can't stand being alone," Masha says.

"And what about women?" I ask her.

"We manage."

I think about how Ma dealt with loneliness. She worked all the time. She worked so much she forgot she had children.

"So Robert . . . he's married. I didn't ask him to leave his family. I'm not heartless," Masha says.

"Do you love him?" I ask her.

"Love has nothing to do with it."

"Is he old?" I ask.

"Twice my age," she says. "What would I do with a man that age if he didn't have anything to offer me?"

I tell her about Ma and Papa's age difference, and how it ended with Papa pulling a knife and then leaving. Ma and her new boyfriend. Papa in the hospital and Ma divorcing him so the state wouldn't garnish her wages.

"I'm not surprised. She's doing what she has to do."

On Masha's face, I see Ma's and other girls' faces. They all do what they have to. The faces shift, age, transform.

"You're daydreaming again," Masha says, trying to catch my attention.

"Sorry," I say.

"What are you thinking about?"

I don't want to tell her that I want to nuzzle my nose in her neck and sniff her. Instead, I talk about the country where I came from.

"In the Philippines, we didn't have lights every other day, so you learn to live without them. The rich people have generators. We also didn't have running water . . . so we used these huge drums to collect rainwater. Then we would boil it and use it to bathe."

"You want to know how I ended up here?"

I nod.

Masha's ex-boyfriend, before going to jail, had asked her to do a job to help him out of a loan. That job turned out to be a night with the loan shark. They even wanted her to shoot porn, so she did. Somewhere on the Internet there are videos of her twenty-year-old self, performing deeds she barely tolerated. She got a student visa to come to the United States when she was twenty-three by pawning the gold jewelry she inherited from her grandmother. The only jobs available to her paid meager salaries for waiting tables in Upstate New York or answering the phones or cleaning hotel rooms in the Poconos. She cleaned for six months, biking ten miles each way from her shared apartment to the hotel. She slept with one of the guests, a man jilted by his fiancée for a rich man she met while on vacation in Miami. Masha made the man feel like he still had something to live for and he ended up taking her back to New York. He threw her out of his apartment after a drunken rage when his ex-fiancée contacted him and flaunted her new life. Not too long after that, she saw a

Village Voice ad and started working for Jin. Soon she had regular clients including Robert.

—

"You need to relax," she says.

She leans toward me and touches my face. Her finger traces the contours of my cheeks, and my mouth goes dry. "You remind me of me when I was younger, but you also remind me of my childhood friend from Uzbekistan," she says.

"How so?"

"Just how you look—" Then she asks me, "Have you ever tried getting massaged yourself? By one of the girls?"

I shake my head.

"I think you should experience it once."

She instructs me to shower and to go to the bedroom when I'm done. My heart is pounding. I don't know what to expect, but I comply. When I reach the bedroom, she is wearing a robe. She tells me to take off the towel I have wrapped around me.

"Lie on your stomach," she says.

She puts a towel on me and begins to run her hands over my body with lotion. I feel a thrill at her touch, and she kneads my back, then slowly massages the rest of me. Her warm hands. I close my eyes, and all I know in the darkness is the sensation of her fingers on my skin, and my entire body throbbing.

"Turn over on your back," she says.

I push myself with my hands, and I feel her breath behind me. I turn around and let the towel slide from me.

Our eyes meet, and I can't help but breathe hard. I can feel heat rising everywhere, and she begins touching my breasts. I close my eyes. There is only the feeling that I am chasing inside me.

"You see how you're eating out of my hand? Remember this

feeling. That's what you want to do. To make yourself indispensable. That's how you get them," she says, and proceeds to kiss me on the lips.

I kiss her back, my lips touching her softness, and we feel ourselves swallowed by heat.

I thought it was only old men who tether their dreams to young women. That they are the only ones who hunger for that youth because it reminds them of a glorious past before their skin sagged and the smell of death rose from their bones. But no. It's also women. Older women who have seen more, and lived more, who will take you, and then turn on you.

I receive another e-mail from Lorie.

> Dear Queenie,
>
> I'm not sure what's going on, but I hope that you're OK. I know you were often quiet in class, but I enjoyed reading your response papers and I think you've got a lot to contribute. I'm concerned that you're not doing well. Are you all right?
>
> It's past midterms, and the semester is more than halfway done. I would hate to see you not pass this class. Please let me know what I can do to assist you.
>
> Best,
> Lorie

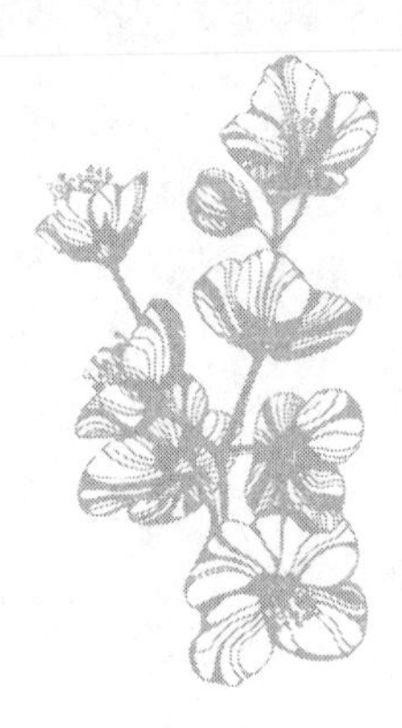

I respond:

> Dear Lorie,
>
> Thank you for the e-mail and for asking if I am OK. I really appreciate that. I'm sorry I missed so many classes and homework assignments. There's a lot happening right now. My father is in the hospital. He was found unconscious with a head fracture in the street. We don't know what happened to him.
>
> I'll try my best to make up my work.
>
> Thank you for understanding.
>
> Best,
> Queenie

Within the hour, Lorie responds:

> Queenie! I'm so sorry to hear about your father! We can talk about what to do with your classwork. I know you're going through more important things right now. I'll work with you. I want you to pass the class, but I also want you to do what is best for you and your family. Let me know how I can help.
>
> Warmly,
> Lorie

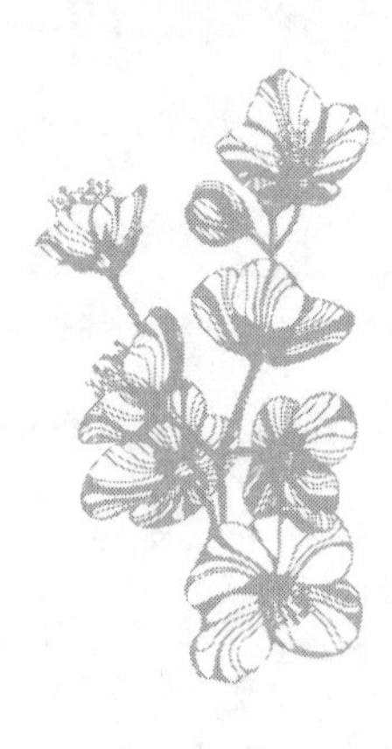

"I need to see you again," I tell Masha.

"You can always come here," she says.

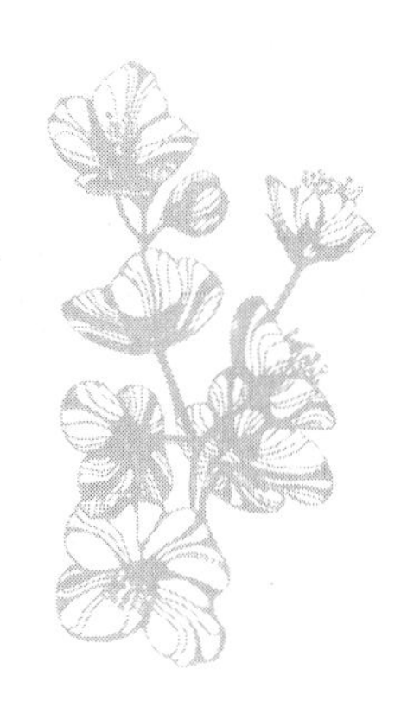

"Can I kiss you?" I ask Masha.

"You don't have to ask," she says.

"Lunch was lovely. Let's do it again," I tell Masha.

"Next week," she says.

I listen absently to a pair of parakeets shrieking in Masha's hallway. I didn't notice them the first time I came over because Masha had a blanket over their cage so that they would sleep.

"Sorry, they are making such noise today."

"I didn't know you were a bird person."

"I wouldn't have gotten them even if I wanted to. They're a birthday present from Robert."

"So you haven't had them that long."

"No. I'm still getting used to them."

She gets up from the bed, long-limbed, her blond tresses trailing behind her like a cape as she begins talking to her birds in Russian, calling them Master and Margarita. When I asked her about the names the night before, she laughed and said that it was the name of a famous Russian novel. Masha said that everyone was expected to read the classics when she went to school: Pushkin, Dostoyevsky, Bulgakov, Lermontov. "But no one knows them here." Masha said that it was strange how something so profound and presumed in her world was alien and meaningless here—how people don't even know geography.

"Do you know where Djibouti is?" she asks, and I shake my head no. "That's what I mean. How can a nation not know about the world it exists in?"

Masha opens the cage, and the birds fly out. One perches on a windowsill while the other one flies around the room, still shrieking, looking for a place to land. Finally, it settles on one of Masha's jewelry racks.

"Did you sleep well?" she asks.

"No, I was thinking about my paper that's due for one of my classes."

"You'll do it later and everything will be fine."

"I want to stop going. It feels pointless," I say, looking up at the ceiling.

"Continue, even if life's a mess. It's hard to go back once you stop. It could take years," Masha says. "I'm in school again, but it took time. I told you what happened with my boyfriend. He used me."

I nod.

Masha quiets the birds down, speaking softly in her native tongue.

"When does Robert come to see you?" I ask.

"Sometimes the middle of the day during the week. Sometimes he'll tell his wife he has a conference to go to and then he's here for three days. It all depends."

"How do you know he's not coming to see you today?"

"He hasn't texted. He usually texts or calls me."

"Do you think his wife suspects?"

"Poor thing. Probably not. She's too wrapped up in her condition. Robert said that she changed after she kept miscarrying. Now she can't have children. She's at that age. Anyway, she has their adopted kids to keep her busy. He didn't want to adopt. She did."

"What's her name?"

"Gina."

It scares me how this woman named Gina has both a body and a husband that betrayed her. And now there are others who know the intimate details of her life and her suffering.

Masha says Gina begged him to do things and then cut him down when he didn't measure up. She blamed him for losing all the children they could have had. He couldn't handle the begging and then the blaming, and so he would give in even if he didn't want to. He even agreed to adopting two little girls from China. He was sometimes disgusted with himself, feeling less manly as the years went by. Until he met Masha, who made him feel like a man because she let him take the lead.

It scares me how fickle people are, reminding me of what Jim told me the previous week when we talked about Papa: "Humans, as a rule, crave certainty, but we forget that there is one thing that's certain: that there is no certainty." I told him that he sounded like a fortune cookie. But he was right. People make vows and sign contracts because everyone knows people change their minds. A man and woman could be married twenty years and that is how long their forever lasts before it crumbles. The vows in their mouths—once uttered in the sacred space of the Almighty with those around bearing witness—turn to ash.

Masha prepares a simple breakfast of herbal tea, sliced apples, and some cheese for me. She only drinks the tea.

"Aren't you eating?"

"Later," she says.

I fix a bite and raise it to her mouth. My heart beats fast. Our eyes lock. Without her breaking our gaze, her lips take the apple and cheese from my fingers. I watch her chew. She watches me watch her. After a moment, she swallows and then takes my fingers into her mouth, sucking on them. She leads me to the bedroom, lies down, and puts the apple and cheese on her soft white belly. I am standing over her, a tree.

"Eat," she says.

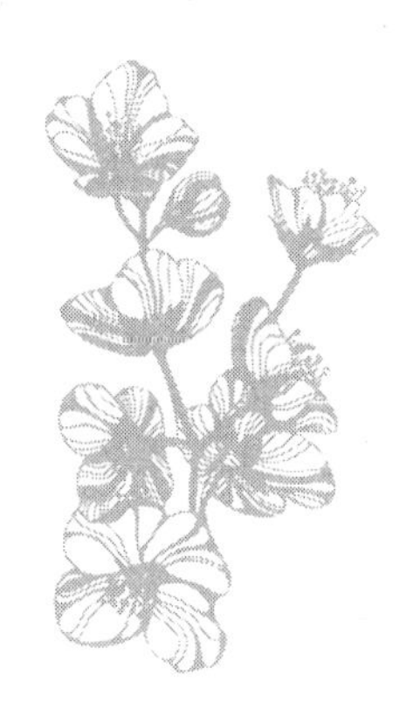

Her scent mixes with the smell of balsam and cedar from a candle burning next to us. We both look at the ceiling, stroking each other's skin as the shadows around us dance, the daylight hidden by the impenetrable dark curtains.

"So, what is this?" I ask, tentative, wondering how to label what we are and what we are becoming.

Masha turns so that she is looking into my eyes, but her mouth is close to my breast. She starts licking and sucking the nipple, her other hand snaking down. Then, just as suddenly, she stops.

"We don't need to have a name for this. Just enjoy it."

"I still like guys," I say. Then, as an afterthought: "I think."

She laughs and says, "Don't worry. I like men too."

When Masha was a child, her grandmother told her fairy tales that were different from the stories of war and hunger that her mother shared. Her favorite one was the story of Vasilisa the Wise, which was about a beautiful young woman cursed by the Koschei for disobeying him. He created a frog skin that she had to wear; otherwise she would die. By day, she turned into a frog. By night, when no one could see her, she turned back into a princess. She lived like this for three years. The curse would be lifted only if someone could look past her frog form and love her for herself. One day, she found an arrow that belonged to a handsome prince named Ivan. He was dismayed when he saw that the arrow he shot landed by her. The prince told Vasilisa that his father had ordered him and his two brothers to shoot an arrow and to marry the woman nearest to where the arrow landed. Ivan's brothers married a noblewoman and a merchant's daughter and they both laughed at him for bringing a frog bride home. The king asked for the would-be daughters-in-law to perform household tasks, and Vasilisa performed them the best. The last task was to perform a dance in front of the king and his court. Of course, Vasilisa danced the best. But before the end of the night, Ivan found the frog skin in her room and set it ablaze thinking that he would finally be rid of his frog bride.

"Then what happened?" I ask.

"Vasilisa needed to wear the frog skin one last night, but Ivan either couldn't wait or didn't know about how she would stop being a frog, so he burned the frog skin."

"Bad timing on his part."

"Either that or he's stupid. But he realized his mistake, so Ivan went to look for her and consulted with the Baba Yaga, who told him how to rescue her."

"Did he rescue her?" I ask.

"Yes, he always rescues her. But my babushka would always change the tasks Baba Yaga gave to him," Masha says.

"What kind of tasks?"

"Killing a dragon, cleaning a cave with no broom . . . that kind of thing."

"Why is she called 'the Wise'? Seems to me that prince is the one doing everything."

"Wisdom is mysterious. Vasilisa is full of mystery."

"Is that what you really think?"

Masha sits up and looks at the palms of her hands and then traces the small hairs on the nape of my neck with her fingertips. "It's to teach us that women have restrictions. We disobey, we're punished. We learn to live with our punishments. When we do see escape, we cling to the hope of escape until the end. Sometimes, there is no Ivan to rescue us, and we must live with that."

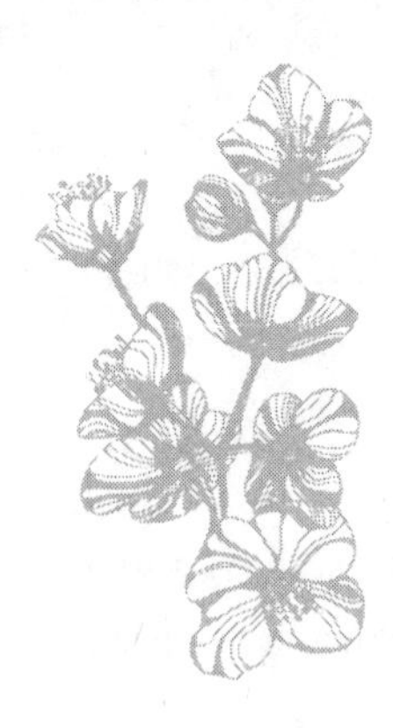

It's the end of Papa's hospital stay. There's nothing more that can be done for him. Not medically anyway. He needs to be transferred somewhere else. The doctors say he is stable. He is awake but asleep at the same time. Or he seems to be asleep. He cannot clothe or feed himself. He shits and pees in diapers. He doesn't have the strength to stand. Even though his eyes are open, they are empty. Maybe his soul has already left his body.

"There are no improvements at this time," the doctor says. "We can't keep him here any longer."

But we see Papa being taken to physical therapy. We're even there with him some days and work with the physical therapists to get him to make his body remember to move. We tell him to kick, and he kicks. We tell him to throw the ball, and he throws. He is improving.

Until he's not.

He can barely keep his eyes open.

The latest MRI shows the blood clot in his brain growing on one side.

"Why don't you do surgery?" Ma asks.

The doctor shakes his head. "He's already old. His body might not be able to handle it."

"Why is he falling asleep?" I ask.

"He's in between states. Somnolent maybe. But he is also showing signs of obtundation. But I wouldn't be surprised if he was stuporous."

"What does that mean?"

The doctor explains that there are levels of consciousness. Papa was, at one point, comatose. No stimuli could wake him. But now, he could fall into one of the other categories. *Somnolent* means that the patient is sleepy. *Obtunded* means the patient has decreased alertness and psychomotor responses. *Stuporous* means the patient has little or no spontaneous activity.

"We've been giving him Provigil and Cymbalta."

"Aren't those Parkinson's medications?" Ma asked.

The doctor explains that Provigil is to keep Papa less drowsy, and Cymbalta is for a dopamine boost because of Papa's flat affect.

"Is he a vegetable?" I ask.

"No, he's alert, but confused."

I breathe a sigh of relief.

Papa is moved to another place, this time a rehab facility that specializes in traumatic brain injuries.

"It's a nursing home," Ma says. "It may take a few years, but that's where people go to die."

I work as a security guard at a hotel near Times Square for a New Year's Eve shift, a job I got from Mercedes, whom I kept in touch with even after leaving BMCC. It's a part-time gig, something to do in between classes. It reminds me that there is a real world outside of school and the pursuit of a degree.

Being a security guard seemed easy enough. All I needed was to attend a licensing workshop. Today I am paired with one of the regular guards. Rick. He reminds me of a bear—big, burly, mustached, with a slight belly. He tells me he wonders what I'm doing in a uniform.

"What do you mean?" I ask him.

"You're too pretty to be a security guard," he says.

"I bet you say that to every female security guard," I say.

"Only to the cute ones."

We are posted by the escalators. The boss figured I should stand with a male security guard since I am a girl. We watch people entering and exiting.

"Where you from?" he asks.

"Philippines," I say.

"Yeah, I could tell," he says.

"Why do you have to ask if you could tell?"

"I didn't want to assume," he says.

Then he tells me that he once had a Filipina girlfriend, but that her family only wanted money. She broke up with him because he worked as a security guard, and she could not face her family with someone of such standing.

"Maybe you should try nursing," I say.

"That's what she said! Is that what all Filipinos say?" He recounts how not only her mother said that but her aunties too. Even the men in her family worked as nurse aides in the hospitals or nursing homes where their wives worked.

"It's a sure path to stability, so yeah."

"So you're taking that too?"

"Nope," I say.

"What are you studying, then?" he asks.

"Literature."

"What are you going to do with that?" he asks.

"I'm going to make a lot of money with it," I say, and smile.

After a while, when he tires of asking me questions, he says he hopes I'm not stuck-up like the other girls he knows, and then he tries to ask me out. I tell him I would but that I'm already with someone, then he gets bored and says he wants to play a game called "Who is the escort?" My ears prick and I turn toward him.

I wait, but he says nothing more. We people-watch in silence.

"That's one," Rick says a few minutes later.

I look at the man he's pointing at. He looks distinguished. Tall, with salt-and-pepper hair. Perhaps a businessman. A very lonely businessman.

"He's going to a room, and there's going to be an escort," he says.

"How do you know?" I ask.

"I been working here five years. I know a thing or two at this point. You'll see."

We watch the man head to the bar. He sits down and orders a

drink. He talks to the bartender, a man cleaning highball glasses with a washcloth. Both men laugh.

"He's going to meet someone there. Just you watch," Rick says.

Ten minutes later, a young woman with brown hair and milky skin sits next to the man. She is wearing jeans, a tube top, and a jean jacket, and she is carrying a small purse. I can tell it's a designer bag. Masha taught me well.

The girl is talking to the man, already touching him. She is between twenty and thirty. The man looks at her from head to toe. He buys her a drink.

"This is just the prelims. In about five minutes, they're going to leave and go to his room."

Just as Rick says, the man and the woman get up after five minutes and head toward the elevators. As soon as the doors close, Rick turns to me and grins. "Bam!"

He says that in about an hour the woman will come down on her own, her hair will be damp, and she will leave.

"How do you know all this?" I ask.

He smiles like a schoolboy about to show a trick. "You watch."

Just as Rick says, the same woman reappears in an hour, and her hair is damp. She walks out with hurried steps while looking at her watch.

"Girl's in a hurry for her next appointment," Rick says.

"I really want to know how you know," I say.

Rick studies me and looks around before saying, "Fine. I'll tell you. You know that guy? The suit? Around here, we call him Casanova. He comes here every few weeks. Same deal. Sits at the bar, a gorgeous woman comes to sit next to him, and then they go up to a suite. All the boys and me wondered who this guy was, getting all these foxes, so we all started pooling our info. A few weeks and we got the rundown. One of the boys even talked to one of the girls, and he got her to talk. You know, they even take credit cards! They use this blue plastic card reader. Can you imagine that?"

"Wow," I say.

"Isn't that something?" he asks, and gives me a wink.

"It really is," I say.

I see the men who look at me in the same way they look at other girls they've seen in the Philippine Islands or in places like Pattaya, Phuket, Phnom Penh. They expect me to say *Me so horny, me love you long time,* just like that girl from that Kubrick film *Full Metal Jacket.* When I don't, they get upset.

The dreams and fantasies are different, yet they're all the same.

Nightmares underneath.

A knife in the neck and their words saying *how pretty.*

I am on the D train at West 4th Street station.

The train doors open, and an older Chinese woman carries three large bags of empty plastic bottles and soda cans. She's carrying two of them with a long pole slung across her thin, bony shoulders, and she lugs the third bag with her hands. They are so massive, they overwhelm her. She looks tired too, a bone weariness in the droop in her eyes, and the constant shifting of weight from foot to foot. Her shoes are worn from all the walking she's doing. She smells like her cans. Rancid. People try not to sit next to her and scrunch their noses. I catch her eye and wave at her. I motion for her to sit down beside me. She nods, puts her bags down, and walks toward me to sit.

"Thank you," she says in an accented English. I nod at her and see liver spots on her face, the discoloration from too much sun. She has crow's-feet, and the skin around her mouth is sunken. She rotates her wrists, and I notice how large the joints of her fingers are, as though the bones in them had to have grown larger to indicate the passage of a hard life. She slowly opens her hands. They remind me of Ms. Beatriz's hands. Arthritic. Aged.

She is someone's daughter.

She is someone's mother.

She was a girl, then a woman, now a crone.

I stand, and she sits. The woman sitting next to me goes to another section of the train car, away from the offending odor.

On my right, two men are standing, both well-dressed, one darker-skinned and the other lighter-skinned. They're in their own world.

The lighter-skinned man asks, "Are those shoes Hush Puppies?"

The darker-skinned man looks up from his phone. "Yes, they are," he says.

It begins there. They ask each other questions about shoes, the kinds they like, the details of the cut, and the material. In ten minutes, they learn about each other's tastes and exchange phone numbers before the darker-skinned man gets off at Pacific Street in Brooklyn. So efficient.

From my book bag, I take out the Moleskine notebook Yan gave me for my twenty-third birthday. This is where I write my observations. I sprayed it with Masha's perfume when I was at her place last week. A whiff of Guerlain. I smell it and remember her scent. Where she likes to put the perfume. On the nape of her neck and a dab in the hollow of her breasts.

I open the notebook to a blank page, and I write about the two men and their shoes. My writing is a little uneven from the motion of the train, and I let the pen zigzag whenever the train abruptly stops in between stations.

I'm surprised to see Junior and Ma together at the long-term-care facility.

"You're here," I say, unable to hide my surprise and delight. I run toward him, almost tripping over the duffel bags by his feet.

"I just got in," Junior says.

We hug each other for a long time. He smells faintly of sweat, deodorant, and hair gel. I look up at him. He's grown several inches since I last saw him. His face is covered with an awkward mix of craters, stubble, and pimples.

When we all sit down again, Ma can't help but talk. Her excited voice rises so much we have to remind her that we're in a medical facility and that we should let people rest. Ma waves us off, saying, "People in places like this like life, they need it . . . a little noise doesn't hurt."

Maybe she's right. Most of the people here have complex medical needs and no family to take care of them.

Junior came earlier in the afternoon and spent time alone with Papa, then called Ma to pick him up, so she's here, visiting with her two boxes of Entenmann's chocolate chip cookies for the staff taking care of Papa. She said that at the hospital where she works, the staff would pay extra attention to the patients whose families brought them pizza, cakes, and pastries. They appreciated when the families understood how hard they worked caring for their loved ones. Turning deadweight patients from side to side to prevent bedsores is backbreaking work, and the smell is constant: pee, shit, phlegm, blood, vomit. "We deserve a cookie at least," Ma would say.

Everything appears normal and we might even seem like a happy family to anyone looking. Papa would seem like the progenitor of this brood—Ma the oldest, Junior the youngest, and me, the middle child. Papa has aged. His fragile body has become even more fragile. The distance between him and Ma more palpable. He looks even older than Lolo Manching, still alive in the Philippines, still asking Ma for money when he needs it.

Junior decided to come to New York for a week because Uncle Roland told him to start going to therapy. The therapist suggested Junior come visit Papa, that he should make amends "before," as she said, "it's too late."

"You should come back with us," Ma says. "Radu is waiting outside."

I shake my head. "I'll catch up with you later."

I sit next to Papa and hold his hand.

I play the Carpenters' "Top of the World" on my Discman and put my headphones up to his ear. I wonder if Karen Carpenter's voice will make Papa remember how he used to listen to their songs nonstop while he played solitaire, humming along out of tune. I watch him to see if he reacts to the music. His eyes flicker and his hands move a little. The doctors and the nurses keep telling me that all these movements are involuntary. His body is not his own anymore.

I tell Papa that I am going to Brooklyn College now. That they call it "the poor man's Harvard." That I transferred out of BMCC. That I'm an English major because I like reading. I ask him whether he likes that Junior is here. I tell him that he probably still wants to join the navy and get stationed in Japan, where anime and his Nintendo video games came from, and because he wants to travel the world.

I tell Papa about Yan and Jim and Zeus and Ma and Radu and Masha.

I whisper secrets piled up over the years into his ear, things I would never dare say to anyone else.

I put my hand on his stomach and lift the hospital gown a little. His PEG tube is still there. The liquid nutrition, as the nurses like to call it, goes into his stomach directly. Even Ms. B didn't have to go through this. He has drool coming out of his mouth, and sometimes when there's too much phlegm, they have to suction him. The smell is terrible, always.

Mr. Park told me that the worst part for him was when he'd visit Papa and they'd be in the middle of changing him. "Watching him like this is painful," Mr. Park said. The stink of human waste is meant to be private, and when things have gotten to the point where it no longer is, human dignity is lost. Only the people around can help maintain this dignity. "Like with my wife," he said one time while he was sweeping lint and dust from the floor, the industrial washing machines whirring behind him. I didn't want to ask him more because I could see he had already traveled back to the time when his wife was still alive. But I know what Mr. Park means. I've helped the nurses and the nurse aides clean up. Even though Papa's mind is no longer there, his body still performs its duties like a machine. Pissing, shitting, farting.

I close my eyes and tell him it is snowing outside and that he doesn't have to shovel snow anymore. The first year he had to, he wore the wrong clothes. Nothing waterproof. The snow shovel was like a regular shovel and the packed ice like regular dirt, he thought. Then he slipped and fell on his back. "I'm lucky I didn't hit my head," he said.

I try to remember the stories he told me so I can tell them back to him, imagining a long chain of related stories that lead up to now, where he is lying in this state of suspended living. Is he still alive? Is he dead?

Unlike Ma, he never liked fairy tales. He preferred folklore and ghost stories. He said they come from real people in real times. The woman who loved too much. The soldier who was killed while guarding the gold. The child who died too young. The man who slept too much.

—

I look at the window ledge where I've placed a small blue globe. Papa told me once he wanted to travel the world, so I brought him this as a reminder that, somehow, the world is still within his reach if only he would wake up. I put a three-section mirror behind the blue globe, so that if he ever opens his eyes, he will see a sliver of the infinite reflections of the universe. He would see the waves and lapping of seas and oceans. The daybreaks and nightfalls. The multitudes of beings in the world.

I take the small globe and put it on his bed and guide his finger to spin it slowly. "We are here," I say. With every movement of our fingers, we are flying. His fingers quiver and his eyes flutter. Then he shifts his weight a little and goes back to sleep and all I can do is watch until visiting hours are over.

ACKNOWLEDGMENTS

First, all glory to the Almighty, who has seen to it that I thrive whether I want to or not.

Second, my heartfelt gratitude to the congregation of people who have helped me realize my potential as a writer and for bringing this work to fruition:

To my agents, Amanda Orozco and Laura Cameron, whose belief in me and my work gave me the confidence to continue drafting this story even when it was still in its roughest form.

To my editor and literary doula, Pilar Garcia-Brown, and her assistant, Ella Kurki, as well as the Dutton team—thank you for taking me into the Dutton family and for making this book shine.

To my writing mentors and prose teachers over the years: Kiese Laymon, Jessica Hagedorn, Lynn Steger Strong, Porochista Khakpour, Alejandro Varela, K-Ming Chang, Mila Jaroniec, Zeyn Joukhadar, Helen Phillips, Kyle Lucia Wu, Garth Greenwell, Maria Alejandra Barrios, Janice Lee, Danielle Lazarin, Rob Spillman, Emma Brodie, and Cleyvis Natera—thank you for imparting what you know of writing and the writing life, as well as for your generosity in sharing your time and resources.

To Mac Wellman and Erin Courtney—I learned from you what playwriting can be.

To Kimberley Phillips-Boehm—you made it possible for me to get my MFA in playwriting.

To the Catapult novel-generator group (Jillian Eugenios, Kristina Francisco, Jeanette Hannaford, Jared Elms, Angela Workoff, Kristin Vukovic, Annabelle Larsen, especially Claudia Cravens and Alex Zafiris)—thank you for reading the early rough drafts of parts of this novel. I hope it wasn't too painful!

To my circle of artist friends that is comprised of prose writers; poets; and playwrights, performers, and directors—Achiro Olwoch, aureleo sans, jj peña, Jenzo DuQue-French, Stephanie Wong-Ken, Yvette DeChavez, Jami Nakamura Lin, Mio Borromeo, Anes Ahmed, Connie Pertuza, Di Jayawickrema, Asha Thanki, Victor Yang, the Duende Collective, Eri Nox, Arika Larsen, Kate Kremer, Lisa Clair, April Ranger, Lyndsey Bourne, Michael Shayan, Naz Hassan, Deepa Purohit, Martha Southgate, Raquel Almazan, Monet Hurst-Mendoza, Ray Yamanouchi, Andrew Rincon, Yilong Liu, Wesley Straton, Fred Yu, Mike Vicencio, Monica Sok, Arturo Vidich, Malik Crumpler, Amina Henry, Hidetaka Ishii, Sachi Lovatt, Aya Ogawa, Gaven Trinidad, Amanda Andrei, Ariel Estrada, Anna Strasser, Stephen Gracia, Nathan Alan Davies, Nehassaiu DeGannes, Lynette Freedman, Dustin Chinn, Kimille Howard, Dennis Allen II, Charisse Tubianosa, Nick Jones, Matt Elzweig, Julia Cho, Melissa Llanes Brownlee, Jenelle Chu. Thank you all for making the writing and artistic journey less lonely (and a special mention to Fred Yu and Arturo Vidich for reading an earlier draft of the novel; Kate Kremer, Lisa Clair, Sachi Lovatt, Lynette Freedman, Aya Ogawa, Di J, and Anna Strasser for talking me through the birthing and mama journey; and to Dustin Chinn for reaching out when my father passed and sharing your parents' stories with me).

To Meredith Talusan and the Fairest community, with special

mention to Anne Godenham—thank you for your generosity in sharing writing resources.

To Megha Majumdar—thank you for reading the first rough draft of the novel and being so generous with your comments.

To Alexa Stark—thank you for your time reading the manuscript and for giving me such honest feedback.

To Ann Garvin—thank you for reading an early draft and for persuading me to start submitting.

To Evelyn Guzman and the BC Scholarship Office team—thank you for all the insider knowledge of how a university system works! Plus, you are the university's unsung heroes!

To Tennessee Jones—thank you for the editorial input on an earlier draft.

To Yahdon Israel—thank you for making me believe that my novel is a future classic and that I belong with Hall of Famers and, most important, for gifting me the novel's title.

To Lara Stapleton—thank you for your time talking about BMCC and your experiences in the CUNY system as a lecturer.

To Gary Chen and especially to Danielle Peterford—thank you for your help in looking through my contract.

To the Rinkydinks, especially Akash Jairam, Dany Mendoza, Phil Ruan, Anita Chan and Alvin Khaled, Stanley and Noel Zheng, Raphael Quiroz, Mandy Li, and Krishnan Chandra—thank you for providing laughs and company especially during the pandemic.

To my colleagues at Brooklyn College / CUNY: Diana Pan, Jocelyn Wills, Soniya Munshi, Rosamond King, Joseph Entin, Ken Gould, and Jeanne Theoharis—thank you for making Asian American Studies a priority and for helping me with the Asian American Studies Project. Even though I was an adjunct lecturer, you made me feel valued.

To the members of the Asian American Studies Project from 2021 to 2023: Annie Ho, Joshua Leonard, Bridge Squitire, Amanda Lopez, Niara Johnson, Rhema Mills, Jason Richter, Bridget Robshaw, Xiaoen Liang, Jean Chen, and Cynthia Leung—thank you for your involvement and for helping me heal.

To my four-step meeting group, especially Aurin Squire, Rebecca Vinacour, Cynthia Hanson, Deborah Yarchun, Tea Ho, Ryan Stanisz, Tanya Everett, Will Blomker, Erik Potempa, Rebecca Ozer, and Susan Lerner—thank you for creating the space to learn and practice the four steps.

To Nina Cornyetz—thank you for introducing me to poststructuralism.

To Ping Chong Company, especially Ping, Bruce, and Sara—thank you for bringing me into the "Undesirable Elements" family. It was truly life-changing.

To my late uncle Tony and auntie Cora—thank you for your generosity and for giving our family a place to stay when we needed a roof over our heads.

To the twins Ron and Bob Galluccio and the New Sun community—thank you for being the family that I needed growing up.

To my bestie and artistic partner, Eugene Ma—may we do more meaningful theater and eat good food!

To my closest and bestest friends over the years: Lena Tam, Ley Gil Wu, Andi Zhao Seymour, Oudom Inthisone, Tushna Gamadia and Stephen Murkoff, Cory Blaiss, and Blanka Dmoszynska—thank you for the years of friendship and emotional support.

To my primos Jennifer Nadal and Sahil Pabby—thank you for being part of the family and for your constant support as well as all the baby tips.

To my mom, Merlita Cariño—I may not be a nurse, but I hope you're still proud of me.

To my siblings, Leah Sy, Manuel "Jay-R" Sy, and Michael Sy—thank you for being supportive. You are the best set of siblings anyone could ask for.

To Sasha—I am grateful to you for introducing me to an East I only had an inkling about and for being a partner. You are my rock; thank you for always pushing me to be the best I can be.

To Baby A, you have brought so much love and inspiration to mamatchka already.

To my brilliant friend Kimarlee Nguyen—I still think about you every day.

Lastly, to my father, Manuel Gan Sy—your memory is already a blessing.

ABOUT THE AUTHOR

CHERRY LOU SY is a writer and playwright originally from the Philippines and currently based in Brooklyn, New York. She has received fellowships and residencies from VONA, Tin House, and elsewhere. *Love Can't Feed You* is her debut novel.